PRAISE FOR
THE NOVELS OF ERIN KNIGHTLEY

THE PRELUDE TO A KISS SERIES

The Baron Next Door

"A delightfully fun novel filled with music, laughter, and plenty of sizzle." —Night Owl Reviews

"Sexy, humorous, and tender—a delight."
—*RT Book Reviews*

"If you enjoy sweet romances . . . with plenty of humor, sass, and romance, *The Baron Next Door* is the one for you." —Romance Junkies

"Supremely gratifying." —*Publishers Weekly*

"A tender love story with a few twists and turns . . . a fun and charming tale that will have you smiling."
—My Book Addiction Reviews

THE SEALED WITH A KISS SERIES

Flirting with Fortune

"An emotional and refreshingly original Regency tale."
—*Kirkus Reviews*

"Charming, sensitive, and compassionate, this tale is Knightley at her best." —*RT Book Reviews*

"A wonderful story of two real people . . . a fun summer read." —Romance Reader Girl

continued . . .

A Taste for Scandal

"Very sweet and heartening....The characters are likable and well written; the plot is delightful and . . . sigh worthy."
—Smexy Books

"As satisfyingly sweet as one of the heroine's cakes, Knightley's delightful and charming romance is both tender and adorable." —*RT Book Reviews*

"With endearing characters, eloquent writing, and a spoonful of charm, you've got the perfect recipe for a perfect read!" —Under the Covers

More Than a Stranger

"This sweet treat of a romance will entrance you with its delicious humor, dollop of suspense, and delectable characters. It'll make your mouth water!"
—Sabrina Jeffries, *New York Times* bestselling author of *When the Rogue Returns*

"More than a romance—it's a witty and engaging love story that had me turning pages well into the night just so I could find out what would happen next . . . a truly captivating tale."
—Lydia Dare, author of *Wolfishly Yours*

Also by Erin Knightley

The Prelude to a Kiss Series
The Baron Next Door

The Sealed with a Kiss Series
More Than a Stranger
Miss Mistletoe (Penguin digital special)
A Taste for Scandal
Flirting with Fortune

ERIN KNIGHTLEY

The Earl I Adore

A PRELUDE TO A KISS NOVEL

A SIGNET ECLIPSE BOOK

SIGNET ECLIPSE
Published by the Penguin Group
Penguin Group (USA) LLC, 375 Hudson Street,
New York, New York 10014

USA | Canada | UK | Ireland | Australia | New Zealand | India | South Africa | China
penguin.com
A Penguin Random House Company

First published by Signet Eclipse, an imprint of New American Library,
a division of Penguin Group (USA) LLC

First Printing, January 2015

Copyright © Erin Rieber, 2015

SIGNET ECLIPSE and logo are trademarks of Penguin Group (USA) LLC.

ISBN 978-0-451-46679-2

Printed in the United States of America
10 9 8 7 6 5 4 3 2 1

*To my father, Mark, who gave me nothing
but wonderful childhood memories.
I'm so lucky to have a dad like you!*

*And to Kirk, even though you'll only sing
when you think no one is around.
I wonder when you'll learn that there is no sweeter
sound to me than the voice of the man I adore.*

Acknowledgments

My heartfelt thanks to Louisa Cornell for her opera expertise, and to Anna Lee Huber for her knowledge of the oboe. Also to my lovely and talented plotting partners, including Anna, Heather Snow, and Hanna Martine. You ladies each brought something wonderful to the table!

To my editor, Kerry Donovan, and my agent, Deidre Knight, I'm so grateful to have both of you on my side!

Less conventionally, I would also like to give a shout-out to YouTube. Where else could I watch dozens of opera performances—often at two in the morning—without ever having to leave my home? I may adore the Regency era, but it's modern conveniences like this that let me know I was born at exactly the right time!

Chapter One

Sophie Wembley had always prided herself on being able to find the bright side of any situation. When she was compelled to play the oboe when all the other girls were learning violin or pianoforte, she'd chosen to embrace her mother's belief that the more unique the instrument, the more memorable the musician.

When she'd discovered how embarrassingly modest her dowry would be, she'd brushed off any pangs of disappointment. At least she could be sure that no self-respecting fortune hunter would ever consider her prey. Any man wishing to marry her would do so because of his regard for her, not her money.

Finding the silver lining today, however, was proving somewhat more elusive. But then again, hearing the words "Your sister has eloped" did tend to drown out all other thoughts in one's head.

Without the least twinge of guilt, she reached for yet another shortbread biscuit. It was her fourth of the morning, but with news of the elopement sending her mother into such a dither, Sophie's indulgence was the least of their worries. Taking full advantage of her mother's distraction, Sophie bit into the crisp treat, savoring the buttery goodness. It was absolutely divine. So good, it *almost* made up for the minor issue of Penelope ruining the family's good name by running off to Gretna Green with the estate manager's son.

Sophie sighed deeply, still unable to believe her sister could have done such a thing. If the missive hadn't been written in Papa's own hand, Sophie could have easily believed the whole thing was a cruel joke.

One look at her mother confirmed that this was no laughing matter.

"What could she possibly have been thinking, Sophie?" Her mother paced past the sofa table for perhaps the hundredth time, her hands red from hours of wringing them. Tearstains marked the pale skin of her cheeks, though thankfully the tears themselves had finally abated. "Does she hate us so very much? Does she think herself above the lot of us?"

Swoosh. Her emerald skirts billowed out behind her as she turned for another circuit of the tidy drawing room. "The *ton* will have a field day with this. I'll never be able to show my face in polite society again. And you — " she said, shaking her head with the quick, jerky movements of one who had consumed entirely too much tea for one morning. "You and Pippa will never find husbands now. Thank God Sarah is safely wed."

Sarah's marriage last month was the only reason Sophie had been allowed to travel to the two-month-long first annual Summer Serenade in Somerset. So far, the music festival had been everything she had hoped it would be, filled with musicians and music lovers from the world over, and with so many events and activities, there had yet to be a dull day in the whole first month. It was absolute heaven.

Her mother had claimed the trip was a special treat, a

chance for Sophie to relax after such a whirlwind spring, but Sophie knew better. The festival had drawn many an eligible bachelor, and where there was an unmarried gentleman, there was opportunity for matchmaking.

Or at least there had been.

She took another bite, willing the tastiness of the biscuit to overwhelm the dreadfulness of the morning. Numbness had settled deep in her chest. In a few weeks' time, when news of the elopement got out, she'd be a pariah. All the things that she had taken for granted these two years since her debut—the grand balls, the lavish dinners, the friendly waves during rides at Hyde Park—all of it would be gone.

Taking a deep breath, Sophie fought back against the fear that threatened to dislodge the numbness. This wasn't the end of the world. They'd figure something out—hopefully *before* life as she knew it ceased to exist. Hadn't she spent the last two years wishing that Mama would stop pushing so hard for her to make a match? She almost laughed. *Be careful what you wish for.*

Setting down the uneaten portion of shortbread, she wrapped her icy hands around her still-warm teacup. "At least we have a bit of time before the news becomes known. We might even be able to make it to the end of the festival! Since there is nothing we can do to change what Penelope has done—though hopefully Papa will come up with something—I say we make the most of the time we have." She offered up a helpless little grin. "Why walk the plank when we can waltz it instead?"

Her mother blinked once, twice, then not at all, staring at her as though she'd quite lost her mind. Perhaps she had. Why else would she suggest they carry on as though their family hadn't just been shaken by what was sure to be the scandal of the summer? It was fanciful thinking, born of desperation.

At a loss, Sophie stuffed the rest of the biscuit in her mouth and flopped back against the sofa. What were they going to do? They'd undoubtedly be packing for home before the day was out. For the first time, a spark of anger pushed past the shock at hearing of her sister's impetuousness. Why did Penelope have to do something like this *now*, just when things were going so well? This had been the best summer of Sophie's life so far, and she wasn't ready to give it up yet.

Blast it all, she wished she could turn to her friends in Bath now for their advice. May would know exactly what to do. She was bold and fearless and unswayed by such insignificant trifles as scandal and rumor. And Charity would know exactly what to say to calm the emotions building in Sophie's heart like steam in a teapot.

But Charity was away for a funeral until next week and May's aunt had decreed that Sundays were strictly for worship and reflection, so Sophie was well and truly on her own until tomorrow at the earliest.

"You are right."

Sophie looked up, startled by the pronouncement. "I am?" she said around a mouthful of biscuit. It was not a sentiment she was used to hearing from her mother, particularly when Sophie herself wasn't sure if she was making a good point or simply sounding delusional.

Nodding with impressive confidence, Mama swept her skirts aside and sat for the first time since receiving Papa's letter. "Indeed you are. I imagine we'll have two, perhaps three, weeks before the gossips catch wind of the scandal. That is more than enough time, if one is committed."

She leaned forward and poured herself yet another

cup of tea as though the entire issue had suddenly been resolved. Sophie eyed her mother suspiciously. Was this what hysteria looked like? Calm, rational words said with overbright eyes and the nervous tapping of one's foot? Should she ring for a footman just in case Mama suffered a fit of vapors from the stress of it all?

Brushing the crumbs from her lap, Sophie tried to work out what exactly her mother meant. After a minute, she finally gave up and asked, "Committed to what, exactly?"

Mama held up her index finger as she took a long sip of her tea. Soft morning sunlight filtered through the pretty white sheers on the windows overlooking the street, lending a much cheerier atmosphere to the room than the subject warranted.

"We must carry on as we have been. Parties, recitals, dances—we shall attend as many events as possible for the next two weeks."

So, if they weren't going home after all . . . then they were merely postponing the inevitable. "To what end? Do we pretend that all is well, laugh, dance, eat, and be merry until the moment someone points in our direction and brands us outcasts? No, thank you."

There was no mistaking the determination tightening her mother's mouth. "No, my little magpie. *I* shall laugh, dance, eat, and be merry. *You* shall laugh, dance, eat, and catch yourself a husband."

Choking on her shock, Sophie fumbled for her tea, nearly knocking it over before getting a proper grip and downing the contents of the cup. "You can't possibly be serious!" she gasped. "If I haven't caught a suitor's attention in two years, what on earth makes you think I could catch one in two weeks?"

Her mind spun. It was absurd in the extreme. She

wanted a husband she could adore, and who could adore her in return. She was even mad enough to hope for a love match, despite what the *ton* thought of such a thing. Finding such a man took time and, well, more *time.* She put a hand over her suddenly rioting stomach, heartily wishing she had stopped at biscuit number three.

Mama's eyes changed in an instant, narrowing on Sophie with utter seriousness and disconcerting intensity. "You haven't a choice, my dear. I don't care how you go about it, I don't care whom you choose, but by the end of a fortnight, you *will* be betrothed." She stood, smoothed her skirts, and smiled. "Now, if you will excuse me, I need to write to your father. Be ready in an hour, if you please. The husband hunt begins today. I do hope you have someone in mind."

Sophie watched in openmouthed shock as her mother swept out of the room, a vision of efficient determination. For a moment she couldn't breathe, couldn't even think. Had she really led her mother down this absurd path with one ill-considered remark? She couldn't possibly be expected to woo a man in a fortnight. She wasn't beautiful, or alluring, or the least bit captivating. Though she normally talked entirely too much, she hadn't even been able to say two words to the man she'd—

She sat bolt upright, her heart nearly leaping from her chest. *To the man she'd secretly admired for the past two years.* Actually, *admired* was much too tame a word. *Desired* was more apt. A *tendre* to end all *tendres.*

She pressed her icy fingers to her mouth, her pulse pounding wildly in her ears. He was here in Somerset to attend the summer festival. Coward that she was, she'd yet to speak to him. It was simply too intimidating, especially after how she'd gotten tongue-tied the last time she'd talked to him in London.

Drawing in a long, deep breath, she dropped her hands to her belly. Desperate times called for desperate measures. Her mother would be forcing her hand over the next few weeks, so . . .

It was time to woo the earl.

Chapter Two

"Julia! What on earth are you doing here?" John Fairfax, Earl of Evansleigh—otherwise known as Evan to all but his mother—gaped in surprise at the road-dusted apparition of his sister standing in the doorway of the townhouse's study. "Is something the matter with Mother? The estate?"

"No, no, nothing like that," she said, her tone casual in a way that belied the fact that she had traveled more than sixty miles from Ledbury to Bath without so much as a hint of her intent for doing so. Smiling breezily, she tugged off her gloves, sending motes of dust into the shaft of early-afternoon sunlight streaming through the window. "It simply occurred to me that the festival wasn't any kind of bloated London event, filled with the sorts of people I'm meant to avoid. This is a music festival, and is therefore perfectly suited to my interests and tastes."

She said it as one states one's mild preference for a particular fruit. Evan blinked a few times, then ran a hand over his hair. "Perfectly suited . . . Julia, are you mad? You can't go traipsing across the country alone without a single word as to your intentions."

As heads of families went, he was hardly strict or censorious when it came to his sister, but this little stunt showed unbelievably poor judgment. She lived a fairly sheltered life, but she was ignorant of neither propriety nor common sense when it came to safety. Or so he had thought.

"What, are we afraid of highwaymen and scurrilous knaves who may or may not accost a lady's carriage?" Her lighthearted laughter brought a scowl to his face.

"That, or worse."

She waved her hand, the dangling gloves swinging with the movement. "Oh, Evan, don't be so dramatic. And I wasn't alone—I had my maid, a footman, the coachmen, and a groom along to keep me safe. I daresay I was better protected than you on your own journey." One burnished-gold eyebrow rose in challenge.

"That's different and you know it. You're a single female—"

"Who is five-and-twenty and quite capable of taking care of herself, thank you."

It was Evan's turn to raise a brow. "That remains to be seen," he said, though without much heat to his tone. Where had this boldness come from? For years his sister had always been one to follow her own drum, but never before had that drum led her so far from home. Something must have happened for her to leave the haven of their estate and travel here without preamble.

He blew out a breath and regarded her for a moment, his fists resting on his hips. There was no use arguing at the moment. Might as well wait until she'd settled in and cleaned up. "Well, you are here now. Why don't you tidy up and join me in the drawing room in half an hour?"

"Perfect," she said, her smile wholly angelic. She thought she'd gotten her way, but he wasn't through with her yet.

She turned, revealing a lurking Higgins in the corridor behind her. "See? I told you he wouldn't mind the interruption. Now, do be so kind as to show me to my room."

The servant shot Evan a look, half indignant, half in search of his approval. Poor man. Here was his chance to prove himself a proper butler and Julia had bullied her way past him like a stampeding steer. "The suite adjacent to mine is fine, Higgins. And arrange for refreshments to be sent to the drawing room in half an hour, if you will."

"As you wish, my lord." He bowed and started to back out of the room.

"Oh, and Higgins?"

The man paused, his dense black eyebrows raised in question. "My lord?"

"When it comes to my sister, you needn't ever worry that I'll be bothered. Julia is and always shall be my first priority."

No matter how grown-up she got, his protectiveness toward her would never waver. It'd been the two of them against the world since their father's death a dozen years ago. Yes, their mother was alive, but she'd been distant their whole lives, even before the old earl had met an early grave.

Higgins's expression relaxed. "Very good, my lord."

Precisely twenty-eight minutes later, Julia glided into the salon, as fresh as a spring daisy. Her dark honey-colored hair was brushed and neatly coiled at the base of her neck, her face and hands scrubbed clean, and a crisp white gown draped her slender frame. "Oh, good. I was hoping you'd have biscuits." She immediately lifted one from the tray Cook had sent up and popped it in her mouth.

Evan sipped his coffee as he waited for her to take a seat. It was brewed exactly right—strong and bitter—despite the fact that the kitchen staff acted as though it constituted treason every time he requested it. When his sister had settled onto the opposing chair and prepared a cup of tea, he finally spoke. "Let's have it, then. What has you showing up on my doorstep like a thief in the night?"

Her hazel eyes, exactly the same hue as their mother's, narrowed in obvious displeasure. "A thief doesn't use the front door and isn't greeted—warmly, I may add—by the butler."

"Stop avoiding the question." He tilted his head and added, "And, for the record, I sincerely doubt Higgins's reception was at all warm."

She gave a dismissive little shrug before lifting the cup to her lips. "I'm not avoiding it. I'm merely pointing out that I am not exactly stealing through the night by visiting." She took a small sip before continuing. "You've only yourself to blame, I'm afraid. Your last letter made Bath sound so very delightful. The festival is not a society event, so to speak, so I saw no harm in coming."

"Unannounced." He set his cup down and pinned her with his most authoritative look. She'd hardly left the county for a decade, for God's sake. He wasn't about to let her act as though this wasn't a highly unusual circumstance.

"Well, I could have sent the groom ahead of me, but it wouldn't be fair to have the man rush ahead when apparently there are highwaymen and knaves on the loose." She gave him an arch look before taking another dainty sip of her tea.

"Julia," he said, his patience wearing thin, "if you truly wanted to come to the festival, you need only have asked and I would have made the arrangements." He leaned forward, watching her carefully. "What happened to compel you to do such a foolhardy thing as to dash across the country on a whim?"

Something flickered in her eyes, but she looked away before he could decipher it. She set her cup down and plucked an invisible piece of lint from her gown. "You're reading far too much into the decision. I knew the festival would last only another month, and I didn't wish to waste another two weeks corresponding back and forth with the details of planning a trip that I am perfectly capable of doing myself."

Right, so he looked as though he was born yesterday. He didn't know what she was trying to keep from him, but she obviously had no plans to share the reason for her journey with him just yet. Fine, he could be patient. They were far too close for her to ever keep anything from him for long. Lord knew she was the only true confidante he had, and vice versa.

Changing tactics, he purposely relaxed his posture and settled back against the stiff padding of the sofa. "Very well, what's done is done. And now that you are here, what are your plans?"

She eyed him suspiciously for a moment, as though trying to determine if he was really giving up that easily. "I'm not sure," she said slowly. "I'd hoped you wouldn't mind escorting me to your existing engagements until I've had a chance to look over the festival itinerary. After all, I can't imagine I'd know anyone else in town."

"No, I suppose not. Very well, you may accompany me starting tomorrow. I'm sure you'll wish to rest for the remainder of today." It was a good idea to keep her close. Until he knew what kind of breeze she was raising, it was best not to leave her to her own devices.

"Oh, but I'm feeling most refreshed, and I'm much too excited to laze about my chambers tonight." She scooted forward in her chair, eager to prove her claim. "Please, can we do something this evening? What did you originally have planned?"

"I don't think it wise. I was planning to attend a ball this evening at the Assembly Rooms. It's open to the public, and as a result can be quite tiresome. Tomorrow is soon enough."

A bit of the forced enthusiasm dropped away, and she looked him straight in the eye. "Evan, I need distraction. It's why I'm here. I've been stuffed away in Ledbury my whole life, and I need to live for a change. Please don't make me languish for another moment."

God's teeth, where had *that* come from? He looked at her, aghast, trying to understand what was going on here. She had never expressed any interest in having a Season or participating in the social whirl of the *ton*.

He cleared his throat, at a loss as to what to say. There was a hint of desperation clouding her eyes. All teasing and lightheartedness had fallen away, and what he saw in her expression reflected a part of him that he strove to keep at bay. Was that what this was all about? Was she feeling as suffocated by fate and circumstances as he sometimes did?

After a moment, with nothing but the sounds of the busy city and the steady tick of the tall clock in the corner filling the warm air between them, he finally nodded.

"Very well. We can dine at seven, and depart at eight. Have you something appropriate to wear?"

Her relief was palpable as she exhaled a pent-up breath. Regaining her composure, she lifted her chin, pretending to be insulted. "Yes, of course. A woman doesn't travel cross-country without a proper ball gown in tow. I'll be ready at seven."

She stood and brushed her hands down her skirts. "Thank you, Evan." Her voice was determinedly steady, but he knew her well enough to hear past the dam holding her emotions in check. She was relieved, and pleased, and probably a thousand other different things.

He nodded once and offered her a wry smile. "You say that now, but we'll see what tune you're singing after a week of the organized chaos that is Bath's Summer Serenade in Somerset festival."

Her laugh was free of the weight that had only moments ago been evident. "I could use a little chaos in my life right about now."

She bussed a kiss to his cheek before slipping from the room. No matter what front she presented, something was still bothering her. She hadn't come on a whim; of that he was certain. He wished he could take pleasure in the reunion with his only sibling, but this was so very unlike her. He sighed and reached for his coffee. Whatever she was looking for by coming to Bath, he sure as hell hoped he could help her find it.

"I'm doomed, May. *Doomed.* There's simply no way I'll ever be able to accomplish something like this in a fortnight. I don't even know if I could accomplish it in a fort*year.*"

Mei-li Bradford set down her glass of lemonade and shot Sophie a grin that was somehow reproachful and sympathetic at the same time. Sophie had shown up on May's doorstep a little after eleven—entirely too early for a civilized visit, but she couldn't wait another moment before talking to her friend. She needed help, and of everyone she knew, May was by far the most worldly.

"Don't be silly, Sophie. Someone of your loveliness could accomplish this in a fort*hour*, were she so inclined. You merely need to decide that it will happen, and go about making it so."

A warm breeze ruffled the leaves of the potted lemon trees that surrounded the little seating area set up on May's aunt's terrace. It was blessedly private despite being located in the heart of Bath. The house was Lady Stanwix's permanent residence, so the gardens were lush and beautifully tended, creating a living screen from any prying eyes.

Thank goodness. Sophie needed an oasis right about then.

Blowing out a hopeless breath, she wilted against the cushions of her chair. "Easily said when one has the look of a blond goddess," she said with a wink. "We lesser mortals have to be more realistic. Not that I think everything is easy for you, just that I imagine them to be *easier*, although I am quite sure it wasn't exactly a walk in the park to move halfway around the globe on your father's whim." Sophie cringed and threw an apologetic look to her friend. "Don't mind me. If you thought me loquacious when happy, that's nothing compared to when I'm upset."

"Deep breaths, my dear." May demonstrated, her long, graceful hands lifting as she filled her lungs, then sweeping back down as she exhaled. "And remember, you are beautiful, sweet, and in possession of some very enviable curves. Any man would be lucky to call you his wife."

Sophie raised her eyebrows in disbelief. "Surely you must be joking. I'm short, plump, and overly talkative—hardly the stuff of men's matrimonial dreams. If it were, I doubt I'd have made it through two Seasons without a single proposal."

"Did you *want* a proposal?"

Sophie paused, toying with the silky fringe of her shawl as she considered the question. Her entire first Season had been such an overwhelming experience, she'd simply wanted to soak it all in. The dancing, the fashion, the music—it was all so glorious. And then there were the less than glorious parts: being looked down upon for her family's modest funds, feeling the sting of the *ton*'s sometimes viperous tongues, nearly falling down the stairs at her first ball. Choosing a husband in the whirlwind had seemed ludicrous.

And then she had met Lord Evansleigh.

A fresh swell of nerves assaulted her stomach and she sat up straight again. "Yes and no, I suppose. It seemed mad to meet a man, dance with him and see a play or two together, and suddenly decide that he would be the perfect person to face across the breakfast table for the rest of my life. It seemed even more so when I met a man who made my pulse race, and I could hardly put together a coherent sentence in front of him. If I couldn't inquire about his feelings on the weather, how on earth was I to inquire about our suitability in marriage?"

May stared at her in utter disbelief, one golden eyebrow raised in an impressively high arch. "You, at a loss for words? Impossible."

"It's true!" Sophie leaned forward earnestly. Suddenly it seemed very important that May know exactly how doomed Sophie was thanks to her mother's ultimatum. "Whenever I see him, my brain seems to go utterly blank, like a sheet of parchment left out in the rain, leached of all its former content."

May's other eyebrow joined the first. "Oh, there's a specific 'him'? Well, this just got infinitely more interesting. Do tell, my friend."

Heat promptly flooded Sophie's cheeks. If May was to help, it was best that she know everything. "You've met him, actually."

"Lord Evansleigh, I presume?"

Sophie gasped. "You knew?"

May broke out in a wide grin, delight shimmering in her brilliant blue eyes. "I knew you said you embarrassed yourself in front of him the last time you spoke, but that didn't quite explain your desperation not to speak with him at the opening ball. I suspected you might have had a bit of a *tendre*."

If ever there was an understatement, that was it. "It's worse than that," Sophie said, burying her face in her hands. "Honestly, I fear I could love the man if given half the chance."

"Excellent," May replied briskly, not a trace of sarcasm or amusement in her voice. "I should hate to participate in marrying you off to someone you were only mildly fond of."

Sophie peered up from her hands and offered a weak smile. May winked and continued. "Furthermore, he's handsome, wealthy, and best of all, available. I'd say he's perfect for you."

Leave it to May to make it all sound so easy. Sighing, Sophie nodded. "I have come to that exact conclusion ever since Mama issued her ultimatum, but there are so many problems, I scarcely know where to start. I mean, I've only seen him a handful of times since arriving in Bath, and when I have seen him, I've ducked away like a proper coward because if I were to speak to him, I would only say something asinine like last time, when I inquired after the health of his deceased father."

"Deep breaths, remember?" May smiled, then gathered her celadon silk skirts and scooted over to sit beside

Sophie. She wrapped a reassuring hand around Sophie's elbow and said, "I can help you with the first part if you can take care of the second."

Grasping onto the less scary part of her response, Sophie gave an indelicate snort. "My dear May, you know fewer people in the *ton* than I do—how can you help get me in the same room as the man?"

Her friend's confidence didn't waver. "I've spent my life in the company of very clever and somewhat less than scrupulous sailors and tradesmen. You may know the way of the *ton*, but *I* know the way of the world."

Oh dear. Sophie bit her lip, not entirely sure whether to be grateful or worried. Perhaps both were in order. "I don't know. What if I make a cake of myself in front of him again?"

"What have you to lose if you do?"

What had she to lose? She counted them out on her fingers. "My reputation, my pride, my heart, and my chance at a happy life, to start."

May's smile was oddly smug, as though Sophie had said the exact thing she was waiting for. "In that case, I suggest you take a deep breath, look him in the eye, and show him *exactly* what he's been missing these past two Seasons."

With her heart pounding at the mere prospect, Sophie nodded. She could do this. She could walk up to him, smile, and behave like a normal person. She could talk to him, woo him, and convince him to marry her in two weeks. A slightly hysterical giggle threatened to escape from her tight throat, but she valiantly held it back. "Absolutely."

Tilting her head to the side, May regarded her silently for a moment. "Sophie," she said, her voice gentle, "you don't have to do this if you don't wish to. There are worse things in life than not marrying."

Sophie closed her eyes and exhaled a long breath.

Looking back at her friend, she said, "It's not as easy as that. I may be the granddaughter of a viscount, but the truth is my family has very limited means. My parents cannot afford to support me indefinitely. I suspect the only reason my father agreed to the expense of this trip was in order to position me in front of potential suitors who enjoy the one thing I have a talent for."

Smiling so as to blunt the stark truth, she shrugged. "Besides, I want half a dozen children, and a messy home to call my own, and, well, *romance.*"

May reached out and grasped both Sophie's hands in her own. "Then, my darling, you shall have it. We will fight together to make it so."

"Well, then," Sophie said, blinking against the unexpected prick of tears. She gave a little laugh and squeezed her friend's fingers. "I am very glad to have you at my side. We'd best prepare, for the battle begins tonight."

Chapter Three

"Lud, Evansleigh, you've been holding out on us." The unmistakable baritone of Lord Derington's voice rumbled over the high-pitched notes of the lively quadrille.

Evan glanced to his left and nodded in greeting, though he made no effort to hide his grimace. "Not at all. I'm quite certain I've mentioned my sister before."

Crossing his muscled arms over his barrel chest, Dering cut his eyes to the dance floor. "Yes, but not a word as to her beauty."

Evan followed the other man's dark gaze to where Julia and her partner, the young vicar, Mr. Thomas Wright, danced in time with the music. The golden-brown curls around her face bounced with each step she took, highlighting her rosy cheeks and framing her smile. Her *overbright* smile, as far as Evan was concerned.

"Not that I blame you," Dering added, flicking his gaze back to Evan. "No doubt you'd have suitors lining your drive when word got out. In fact, I'll be interested to see what kind of traffic your drawing room sustains tomorrow."

Evan scowled, his jaw clenching at the thought. "None.

Julia is not in the market for a husband." Even as he spoke the words, she laughed and said something to Wright, her eyes dancing with delight that was visible from half a room away. The scene could very well be titled "Gaiety at the Dance Hall."

"Hm. Are you sure she knows that?"

"She knows," he replied tersely. Perhaps he should have turned her around and marched her back to Ledbury when he had the chance. He bit the inside of his cheek. Not that he'd ever *had* the chance. She'd been so determined, he doubted anything he would have done could have compelled her to leave.

The question was, what had happened to distress her so much? And why was she here now, laughing and dancing like some sort of freshly presented debutante?

"It begs the question, you know," Dering murmured, his voice a dull rumble.

Evan did know. He didn't even have to ask what his friend meant. "She's of sufficient fortune and family to make her own decisions, and she decided to pursue spinsterhood. Brilliant idea, in my opinion." It was an explanation they had decided on together, and he always had it at the ready.

"Perhaps she is simply waiting on the right man to turn her head. Sounds like a challenge to me."

Pointedly turning away from the dance floor, Evan looked up at his towering companion. "Don't you need a drink?"

Dering shook his head. "No, actually. I've a dance card to sign when this set is over." He winked, a rakish grin turning up one corner of his mouth.

Damn it. Evan liked the man, but he wasn't above thrashing him should Dering get the idea in his head that Julia was fair game. Gritting his teeth, Evan nodded. He'd rather not make too big a concern out of it, lest he pique the viscount's interest any more. "Suit yourself."

Dering chuckled. "To think I imagined you an easygoing type of fellow."

He was—when his "friends" weren't eyeing his sister as though she were some sort of dessert. "Do you have a sister, Dering?"

"You know I don't."

"Then shut the hell up."

Considering the hundreds of people crammed into the Assembly Rooms, it shouldn't have been so easy to spot Lord Evansleigh, but Sophie had seen him almost the moment she arrived. He stood on the perimeter of the dance floor, ridiculously handsome as usual, his attention riveted on the gliding dancers.

Given the likelihood of his attendance—Evan seemed to enjoy the dances as much as she did—his presence should have been a forgone conclusion, yet she still breathed a long sigh of relief. Operation Woo the Earl had begun.

Sophie stepped a few feet to the left, out of the way of the steady flow of traffic pushing into the cavernous Ballroom. The air was warm and humid, yet every last candle on the five monstrous chandeliers was blazing, surely two hundred of them if there was one. She stood on her tiptoes and tried to keep the earl in her line of sight, madly fluttering her fan all the while.

Step One—being in the same room with the man—could officially be considered accomplished. Step Two—having him fall in love with her—and Step Three—accepting his proposal—were surely right around the corner now. She bit her lip against a slightly deranged laugh. This was hopeless.

Already the butterflies had taken flight in her belly, and he wasn't even within speaking distance. Did the earl have to fill out his jacket quite so well? Really, if he could have a bit of a humpback, or a face full of spots, perhaps, then maybe she wouldn't feel quite so thoroughly out of her league.

No such luck. He was perfect, with gorgeous shining mahogany hair just long enough to tie back in a dashing tail, and a jaw that was surely the envy of statues everywhere. Lord Derington stood at his side, but instead of dwarfing the earl, the comparison actually served only to make Dering seem oafish and Evan just right.

She dropped down from her toes and sighed. Oh, why had she eaten supper tonight? She should have known her stomach would be rioting at the prospect of actually going over and talking to the man. Putting a hand to her middle, Sophie started edging back to the door.

She couldn't do this. The sort of bravery such things required was beyond little mousy her. She would simply have to return home, learn a trade, and be self-sufficient for the rest of her life. Or perhaps there was a great need for oboists that she hadn't known about, but for which she would be perfect. Or even better, she and her youngest sister, Pippa, could join forces, triumphing in the underserved niche of oboe and viola duettists.

"Where do you think you are going?"

Fiddlesticks. Sophie smiled guiltily and met May's stern expression. "Nowhere. Why?"

"I know a retreat when I see one, Sophie Wembley, and I shan't let you get away with it." She stood tall and straight, as effective a barrier as a silk-draped stone wall.

"I was afraid of that." Wrinkling her nose, Sophie sent her friend a rueful glance. "Where is Charity when she's needed? She would understand the deep and abiding need to flee."

"She'll be back soon enough. In the meantime, you have me." Despite her firm tone, May's aquamarine eyes were soft. Looping her arm around Sophie's elbow, she pulled her close. "You deserve a future, my dear. And the clock is ticking before news of the scandal breaks. This is not the time to turn tail and run. Now, chin up, breasts out, and go forth and enchant your man."

"May!" Sophie exclaimed, sending furtive looks in all directions to make sure no one had heard the outrageous comment. Horrified laughter bubbled up from deep within her, eclipsing the nervousness. "You can't say things like that in public. You'll get us thrown out. Though at this point, I'm not sure that's a bad thing. On second thought, can you say it again, only a little louder this time?" She fluttered her eyelashes, only half teasing. Still, May's reminder of why Sophie was here was exactly what she needed.

Now was the time to be bold. Or, at the very least, to *attempt* to be bold.

Without answering, May started forward, pulling Sophie along with her through the crush. Given May's height and the striking jade-and-cream silk gown she wore, there was certainly no blending in with the crowd. People naturally gave way to her, which meant that they were proceeding much more rapidly than Sophie was prepared for. Her heart pounded jarringly in her chest, so loudly that she was sure others could hear it above the din of the packed Ballroom. Ahead, she could see Dering's wide shoulders, a beacon in the rushing tide of revelers sweeping by on the dance floor.

As they approached, she caught better glimpses of

Evan. Sophie smiled vaguely to those she brushed past, all the while keeping her gaze firmly on the earl. His attention, in turn, seemed captivated by the dancers, his eyes tracking their movements with the dedication of a theatergoer at a particularly well-done play. How strange that he should be standing to the side instead of dancing. She had presumed he loved to dance just as much as she did, and she rarely saw him without a partner.

Tonight he looked . . . dour. Stern, even.

"May," Sophie said, tugging against her friend's momentum. "Wait."

She paused, lifting an eyebrow. "Yes?"

The music ended then, and a swell of conversation rushed to fill the void. Sophie rose on her toes so she could speak close to her friend's ear. "I don't think this is a good time. He looks almost cross, and I certainly don't want to approach him when he is in a bad mood, because, really, if one wants to make the best impression, shouldn't one approach one when one's positive reception may be most assured?"

She was babbling, but this suddenly felt all wrong. She fumbled with her forgotten fan, desperate to cool her overheated face. Snapping it open, she swished it back and forth so rapidly that her carefully coiffed curls lifted from her temples.

May pursed her lips, probably attempting to decipher Sophie's rush of words, then gave a decisive shake of her head. "I won't let your nerves get the best of you simply because he's—" She stopped abruptly, her eyes narrowing in the direction of where the earl had stood. "Oh, Lud, where did *she* come from?"

Sophie followed her friend's gaze, then nearly cursed right there in the middle of the Ballroom. *Miss Har-*

mon. Sophie's nose wrinkled in displeasure and not a little jealousy. The woman was a menace. Or a plague. Yes, a plague was more like it. She was beautiful—as well she knew—and a talented pianoforte player, but she was the type of individual who preyed on other people's weaknesses so that she might feel better about herself. At least that's what Sophie assumed her motive was; it could just be that she reveled in making others look bad.

Marianne was the youngest daughter of Lord Wexley, and when she and Sophie had debuted together two years ago, someone had confused the names, accidentally calling Marianne Miss Wembley. Gasping in overdramatic horror, she had proceeded to verbally berate the man for daring to confuse her dignified family with the lowly Wembleys. Sophie had been only a few feet from them, too shocked to do anything other than back away and escape to the ladies' retiring room.

Sophie had since learned how better to stand up for herself, but she still disliked the woman. And now here she was, resting her gloved fingers on the arm of the one man Sophie longed for above all others, leaning toward him as though she needed his warmth to survive.

"Go, now," May urged, giving her a nudge. "Don't let her get her claws into him."

Nodding, Sophie squared her shoulders, pulled herself up to her full height—all five feet two inches of it—and started on her way. With every step, the butterflies in her stomach fluttered a little faster, until she was sure she would lift from the ground and be carried away. But she stayed the course. Somewhere between Step One—being in the same room with Evan—and Step Two—having him fall in love with her—she probably needed to actually be within speaking distance of him.

Of course Marianne would look absolutely beautiful tonight, with her golden hair piled in gorgeous twists and curls atop her head, and her bronze and ivory gown making her skin fairly glow in the candlelight. No doubt her eyes would be luminescent as well, since bronzes and golds always complemented their amber hue.

Meanwhile, though Sophie had felt quite confident in her minty green dress and remarkably tamed curls when she had arrived, she had the sinking feeling she would look like an overripe pear by comparison.

She slowed, now only a few yards away. Perhaps she should wait until Miss Harmon moved on. Yes, that was best. No use offering herself up for an unflattering comparison, one that she knew from experience the woman would have no qualms about pointing out. Even though deep down Sophie knew she was grasping for a reason to turn around and release the tension building within her like a teakettle with a clogged spout, she still desperately wished she could take the coward's way out and retreat.

Steeling herself, she marched forward. She could do this. She was good enough, pretty enough, talented enough, and intelligent enough to not only speak to Evan, but stand up to the comparison with Marianne. Now she was six feet away, five feet, four . . .

At the last second, she spun on her heel, doing an about-face. She couldn't do it—she just couldn't. All at once the tension vibrating through her body eased. She exhaled a pent-up breath, relief and dismay sagging her shoulders.

"Miss Wembley!"

Sophie froze. Oh God, that was Evan's voice. That was Evan's delectable voice, and he was saying *her* name. With her heart lodged firmly in her throat, she swiveled on the balls of her feet to face him. Or rather, to face his chest, which just happened to be at her eye level. It was a very nice chest, one that she would be quite happy to stare at, especially if it meant not having to meet his gaze. Gathering every bit of nerve she had in the world, she forced herself to look up into his gorgeous pale blue eyes. "Yes?" she squeaked.

"There you are," he said, smiling as though they'd been intimates for years. He stepped forward and held out his hand to her, his long fingers holding steady only a foot away so there was no mistaking that she really was the person he wished to address. "I believe this is our dance."

Their *dance*? Of their own volition, her hands covered her heart. *Me?* She had meant to say the word, but no sound had escaped when she opened her mouth.

He nodded, the movement small but unmistakably in the affirmative. His hand stayed right where it was, beckoning her to slip her fingers into his. The very thought sent shivers cascading down her back. With his smile still firmly in place, he tilted his head and said, "Shall we?"

Evan gritted his teeth even as he smiled, willing the girl to agree to his ruse. God's teeth, but he'd do anything to escape the clutches of that blasted Miss Harmon. She was about as subtle as a stampeding bull when it came to her interest in him, and he'd be damned if he would be wrangled into dancing with her after she had just subtly insulted both his sister and his friend in the space of a single sentence.

Of course, if he had given two seconds of thought to his choice of coconspirators, he would have never dragged poor Miss Wembley into it. She looked exactly like a startled mouse who'd been caught in the corner by a hungry cat. "Erm," she said, something akin to panic swimming in her wide, dark-brown eyes. Her gaze dropped to his hand, considering it as one might a loaded pistol.

His conscience pinged, but it was too late to withdraw the offer. If she wished to correct him, then so be it, but he was committed to the ruse until then. It probably would have been better just to have given the Harmon chit the cut directly when he had the chance, no matter how distasteful such an action would have been.

Plunging ahead, he lowered his brows in a look of contrition. "You must forgive me for losing track of time," he said, his voice sincerely apologetic. Her eyes darted up to meet his, and he locked gazes with her, trying to convince her that he was not setting her up in some sort of trick. "I must have gotten carried away with my conversation with Miss Harmon, but I would never miss our dance, I assure you."

For two interminable seconds, she didn't move or say a word. Then, finally, she slipped her small hand into his. "Yes, course. *Of* course," she corrected, then blushed and looked away.

"Why, Miss Wembley," Miss Harmon said, her voice holding a flat note of disingenuousness. "How *lovely* to see you." Turning back to Evan, she added, "Do mind your toes, my lord. Sadly, Miss Wembley's excellent sense of rhythm when she plays her oboe doesn't always translate to the dance floor."

Evan stiffened. Christ, he hadn't expected her to lash out at the girl. "You must be thinking of someone else. I can assure you, Miss Wembley is an accomplished dancer." His words were sharp as he sent her a cutting glance. Dismissing her without another word, he turned to his innocent accomplice. "Shall we?"

She darted a shocked glance from Miss Harmon's direction before meeting his eyes once more. This time, a hint of a smile curled her lips as she drew a breath and nodded.

It didn't matter that the music had not yet even started for the next set, or that his sister had been waylaid by Dering and was nodding as he gestured at her dance card. Offering his partner a subtle wink, Evan grasped her hand more tightly and pulled her toward the very center of the dance floor. After what she'd done for him, he was keen to make this the best dance he could.

"It's all right, my lord. You needn't dance with me to prove a point."

He ignored her softly spoken words and tugged her into the waltzing position as the conductor tapped his baton to signal the start. "You're absolutely right," he said, holding her firmly in place, one arm at her back and the other at her elbow. "What a relief to be able to dance with you for the pure pleasure of it."

Her mouth dropped open half an inch or so as she drew another swift breath. But then the music started, and he swooped into motion, swinging her along across the rapidly filling dance floor. Here he felt comfortable. He was an excellent dancer, and was at ease moving in time to the music. His partners' skills never much mattered; he had a way of leading them that never failed to lend grace to even the most awkward of dancers.

But, much to his surprise, Miss Wembley wasn't awkward. Not in the least. Once the dance was really under way, her eyes lost that anxious gleam and instead reflected true pleasure in their coffee-colored depths. She moved beautifully, in fact, and he couldn't help but return the genuine smile that graced her lips at last.

"Thank you," he said, leaning a bit closer. He caught a hint of her light scent, a sort of lemony rose fragrance. "You are an absolute gem."

"Am I?" One raven brow lifted with a hint of playfulness. "And here I thought I was a means to an end."

Chapter Four

There now—that was a completely normal and intelligent response. Sophie relaxed a little more. She could almost feel her wits returning, albeit slower than she'd like. It was pure heaven, dancing in his arms. She was giddy and light-headed and happier than she'd been in days.

They'd danced only once before, last season during the Harlestons' annual ball. She hadn't been able to say a word to him that time, so tonight she was already heaps better off than she'd been back then.

"A brilliant means to an end," he replied, his pale blue eyes daring her to deny it. "Not only did I escape the dragon, I gained a wonderful dance partner. I only regret that you were a little singed in the exchange."

She pressed her lips together against the giddy laughter that threatened to escape. *Dragon?* Oh heavens, she couldn't wait to share that with May and Charity. "No harm done," she assured him.

They swept along among the other couples for a few measures, moving quite well with each other. Perhaps she really could do this. Perhaps she could actually be a normal human being around him, and show him that she could be fun and exciting and graceful and—

Sophie's body suddenly jerked as her foot caught in the fabric of her skirts. She gave a little squeak of alarm, knowing in a flash what was about to happen. One second she was floating in Evan's arms, and the next she was stumbling backward like an overloaded packhorse on ice, tangling with the man of her dreams as he vainly tried to stop the inevitable.

It was too late. Arms flailing, Sophie tumbled to the floor, hitting the unforgiving wood surface square on her bottom. The impact knocked the air from her lungs, eliciting a squawk not unlike that of a dying goose. Her legs flew up in the air as she fell backward, and before she knew it, she was looking up at the gigantic chandelier above her, tears of pain and mortification blurring the candlelight into one big fiery ball.

The music abruptly ceased, and the soft swoosh of several hundred heads turning to gawk was immediately followed by the low roar of excited whispers, snaking out in all directions at the speed of wildfire.

Dear Lord, this can't be happening! But the throbbing of both her backside and her right ankle told her all too clearly that the embarrassment was real. She could have died, right there on the scuffed floor of the Assembly Rooms Ballroom.

The blurry form of Lord Evansleigh appeared in her teary gaze as he dropped to his knee beside her and grasped her hand. "Miss Wembley, are you injured?"

Her nightmare was complete. She shook her head, unable to actually speak. If she so much as opened her mouth, she was sure she'd either embarrass herself further or burst into tears. Actually, one was not necessarily exclusive of the other.

May emerged out of the crowd, her normally golden complexion pale with concern. "Oh, Sophie, you poor thing. Here, let us help you up."

Yes, good—a plan. May could help her up, walk her outside, and accompany her to the banks of the Thames, where Sophie could happily toss herself in. She nodded, her movements feeling jerky, and May grabbed one elbow while the earl supported the other. Together they lifted, and Sophie was halfway off the floor when she put weight on her own feet. Sharp, burning agony shot through her right ankle, and she cried out, eliciting gasps from those around them.

Evan's jaw clenched and he quickly lowered her back down. "What is it? Your leg? Ankle? Knee?"

Oh good Lord, was he actually enumerating her body parts in public? Her face flamed even hotter, if it were possible. Unable to bring herself to answer the question, she settled for simply nodding.

May shared a concerned glance with the earl. "We must get her away from here," she said, her voice low but insistent. Sophie nodded again, this time more urgently. Yes, away from this disaster of an evening. The sooner, the better. She gritted her teeth against the pulsing pain that radiated from her ankle. All she really wanted was to be hied away to somewhere private where she could have a proper breakdown, but at this point she'd settle for just being off the dance floor.

"Agreed," Evan said curtly. Without so much as a word of warning, he hooked an arm beneath her skirts at her knees, and used his other to support her back. With one smooth motion, he lifted her from the floor and straightened to his full height. "Beg pardon, please. Coming through."

Closing her eyes, Sophie leaned her head against his shoulder. Yes, she was fully aware that closing one's eyes did not make one invisible, but it did save her from having to see the expressions of those around them. It was best not to know exactly what they were all thinking.

It also had the unexpected benefit of heightening her sensitivity to him. She could feel the bulge of his biceps and the taut muscles of his chest. The scent of his shaving soap teased her nose, a fragrance that was musky and crisp and put her in mind of a winter forest.

"My *dear* Miss Wembley, whatever has happened to you?"

Sophie's eyes popped open as Evan slowed to a stop only feet from the Ballroom exit. Marianne stood directly in his way, her perfect features arranged in a perfectly correct mask of concern. A complete fiction, of course. Her delight at Sophie's distress was plain as day in her glittering gaze. People surrounded them on all sides, no doubt keenly interested to know the answer to Marianne's question.

"An injured ankle, I fear," Evan responded. "If you'll be so kind as to step aside so we may pass."

"Yes, of course," she said, though she made no move to comply. "Poor Miss Wembley. You do try so hard. What a shame that gracefulness always seems to elude you." She spoke with a sort of loud whisper that somehow seemed to carry twice as effectively as a raised voice might have. With a patently false sympathetic smile, she glided out of their way. There was more than one person smirking behind her.

The dreadful, spiteful, hateful, awful, self-important she-devil. Mercifully, Evan started forward again, not bothering to waste his breath responding to such drivel.

At least that's what Sophie hoped he was thinking. He may very well have been silently agreeing with Marianne, but was simply too tactful to verbalize his agreement.

As they strode through the doorway, the orchestra finally began to play again and she closed her eyes in relief. Well, if nothing else, this evening was good for something: Sophie now knew for a fact that it wasn't possible to die of embarrassment. If it were, she'd be well on her way to the pearly gates by now.

Now that it was less crowded, May made her way around them and gestured to the small bench outside the ladies' retiring room. "Here, I think this should do. It will allow you to elevate your feet."

As easily as he might have set down a feather-filled pillow, Evan lowered Sophie to the seat. Even through the all-consuming fog of humiliation, she mourned the loss of his warmth and scent as he straightened.

That was *not* how she'd pictured her first time wrapped in a man's arms. Or being swept off her feet, for that matter. Although, technically speaking, she'd swept *herself* off her feet, so perhaps there was still hope for calling it a first when a man actually did the honors.

"I cannot apologize enough, Miss Wembley," Evan said, tucking a lock of hair that had fallen forward over his forehead behind his ears. Between his hair, bunched waistcoat, and crushed cravat, he looked quite a bit the worse for wear, thanks to her. "Can I send for a doctor?"

The handful of people around them all openly stared, their curious gazes bouncing back and forth between them. They needn't fear. Sophie was confident that they and everyone else in the city would know every detail of her disgrace by the end of the night.

Honestly, though, it was just an annoyance. The only person she really cared about knowing had been right there for the entire debacle. Fresh heat singed her cheeks. No doubt she'd be first in his mind when he thought of graceful, elegant women who might serve as future candidates for Countess of Evansleigh.

Doing her best to ignore the throbbing in her foot, Sophie shook her head. "No, please. I'd rather go rest at home." She glanced helplessly toward May, imploring her to do something to help her escape.

Thankfully, her friend took the hint. "If you're safe and sound for the moment, I'll just go find your mother." She turned and pushed her way toward the Tea Room, where Mama had been headed the last time they had seen her.

Normally her mother was the consummate chaperone—entirely too nosy to let Sophie out of her sight for long. But with both their hopes pinned on Sophie's making a match, Mama must have decided it was best for her to be scarce this evening. She hadn't said as much, but Sophie suspected she was hoping prospective gentlemen would be more free with their affections without a chaperone hovering about.

Sophie absolutely dreaded her mother's reaction, but it was definitely preferable to having the earl stuck there minding her. Already awkwardness had settled over them. She shifted uncomfortably on the hard seat of the bench, wishing fervently that she could do something about the pain hammering away in her foot.

"Evan, there you are." A pretty young woman slipped between a pair of spectators, her brow furrowed in concern. "Dear me, are you quite all right? I tried to reach you in the Ballroom, but the gawkers were thick as bread pudding—impossible to wade through."

The woman went straight to the earl's side and laid a hand on the sleeve of his jacket. Sophie sat up straighter, indignation overriding any pain. Not that she had a right to be indignant, but still. Where had this woman come from?

She didn't look familiar in the least. After two Seasons with an overzealous matchmaking mama, Sophie would have sworn she was aware of any female in the *ton* whom her mother might construe as competition for her daughters.

With her striking greenish brown eyes and clearly superior taste in fashion—or at least excellent taste in choosing a modiste with good fashion sense—the interloper would certainly qualify as a threat.

Her threat level increased dramatically when the earl placed his hand over hers and gave it a reassuring pat. "I'm fine. Miss Wembley wasn't so fortunate, I'm afraid." He glanced back toward Sophie. "Speaking of whom, Julia, please allow me to present—"

"Oh, my goodness, Sophie!" Mama's cry cut off the rest of the introduction, much to Sophie's consternation. Just what she needed—*more* attention being drawn to them. "A thousand thanks, my lord. Miss Bradford told me how you rescued my dear daughter. However could we repay you?"

He offered a polite smile and shook his head. "Consider it amends for not preventing the mishap in the first place. Shall I order your carriage to be brought round?"

"Oh, no, we haven't one. If you could be so good as to have a hackney hailed, we would be most grateful."

Evan glanced down, catching Sophie's gaze. Lacking the funds for a carriage was one thing she refused to feel embarrassed about. He gave her a wink so subtle that she almost doubted it happened at all. Turning his attention back to her mother, he said, "I won't hear of it, Mrs. Wembley. I'll have my carriage brought 'round posthaste and instruct my driver to take you home."

Obvious pleasure lit Mama's face, but she demurred. "Oh no, my lord, we couldn't possibly."

"You haven't a choice, I'm afraid." He tugged on the hem of his jacket, straightening out the wrinkles he'd sustained. "I proved a terrible dance partner, but I am quite determined to be a proper gentleman. Besides, what good is my carriage to me while I am here? Better to use it than leave my driver twiddling his thumbs for the whole of the evening."

If he was aiming to impress her mother, he succeeded handsomely. Her eyes shining with delight, she pressed her hands to her generous bosom. "You are much too kind, my lord."

It was a good thing that Mama had the wits to thank him, because Sophie couldn't have spoken if she'd wanted to. He was ordering his own carriage to deliver her home? Despite what he claimed, the fall was entirely her own fault, and they both knew it. The fact that he was willing to show such kindness—well, it certainly did give one hope.

Emerging from the ashes of mortification, the butterflies slowly fluttered back to life. If absolutely nothing else could be said for the evening, at least Lord Evansleigh was unlikely to forget her anytime soon.

*   *   *

"Of all the years I pictured you in the ballrooms of London, not once did I imagine you dropping your partner on her arse."

"Language," Evan admonished his sister sternly. Sighing, he leaned back into the plush gray velvet squabs, which seemed to hold the lingering scent of lemon and roses. "And she tripped on her skirts somehow." It had happened hours ago, but he still felt terrible about the debacle on the dance floor. He sincerely hoped she hadn't broken anything. He didn't think she had, but he couldn't be sure.

"Oh sure, blame the injured party," she said, her teeth flashing white in the carriage's dim interior.

Impertinent female. How was it that she actually seemed more invigorated than when they had left the house? He, on the other hand, was thoroughly exhausted from a night spent trying to keep watch over her like an anxious old woman. At this point, he was in no mood for teasing. "I can assign no blame to Miss Wembley. You, on the other hand, have some explaining to do."

"I? What have I done?"

As though she didn't know. Scowling, he said, "It is one thing to enjoy a dance. It is quite another to flirt and laugh with the abandon of a fresh-from-the-schoolroom debutante. Or worse, a widow."

She drew back, her eyes narrowing. "I beg your pardon? What exactly are you implying?"

He clenched his jaw. He wasn't handling this well. Still, his point was valid, and he had every right to make it. It was his duty, really. "Julia, you are a shiny new plaything to those members of the *ton* who were present this evening. They will be eager to observe you, evaluate you, *judge* you. I want you to have a care as to how you present yourself."

For a few seconds she just stared at him, her expression mutinous. "And you think I am somehow flaunting myself? Inviting notice?"

He rubbed his tongue back and forth over his teeth as he tried to find the words he wanted. "You've invited notice just by being here. I simply wish for you to have a care as to how you are seen."

She shook her head, averting her frustrated gaze to the ceiling. "Yes, I know. I should have stayed shut away in Ledbury like the pariah I am. God forbid a man get the wrong impression because I smile at him. God forbid I have a spot of fun." She pressed her lips together and met his eyes. "Meanwhile, you've been doing heaven knows what in London all these years."

Where the hell had that come from? "I've been fulfilling my duties. Trips to London are a requirement for a sitting member of parliament."

She crossed her arms over her chest. "Yes, I'm aware. But all these years, I never pictured you dancing the night away with woman after available woman. I imagined your club, a coffeehouse, card games, and musicales, but certainly not waltzing as though it is your duty to do so."

That stung. He already felt guilty that he had left her behind again and again to go to London. Yes, it was part of the requirements of his title, but it was also an escape. It was a sanctioned reason to leave his mother for a while, to climb out from under the darkness that she'd lived under for as long as he could remember. In theory, Julia could have come with him, but they had decided long ago that the risk was too great. After all, while a man was free to attend any event he wanted with no ulterior motives being assigned to his actions, an unmarried woman's sole purpose could only be to find a husband.

Rubbing a hand over the stubble at his chin, he sighed. "There is nothing wrong with a little dancing, Jules."

A smug grin emerged from her scowl. "My point exactly. You've had years of harmless fun. I don't see how you can begrudge me the chance to do the same."

God's teeth, but the woman needed a keeper. There was no telling what she was imagining when she spoke of harmless fun. She may have lost her rational sense of late, but he had no intention of letting good judgment fall by the wayside. Though he hadn't a clue where to even begin, by Jove he planned to have a proper chaperone for her by the end of the week. "I haven't sent you home yet, have I?" he said gruffly. "But let me be clear: If you engage in behavior that I feel is inappropriate, I'll escort you back to Ledbury myself. Understood?"

"You do realize that I am past the age of majority, yes?"

"I do. And do you realize that you're staying in my rental, riding in my carriage, and eating my food?"

Her bravado faded to something much more brittle. "Every day of my life."

Damn it all. She knew exactly how to gut him. He leaned forward, resting his elbows on his knees and looking his sister square in the eye. "We're still a team, Jules. I'm not against you. I'm trying to do the right thing here."

Some inscrutable expression dashed across her face, but was gone before he could properly analyze it. "I know. But you need to realize that I'm not going against you in anything. Can't you just trust me?"

Trust her? What an ironic question. She was the only person in the world he *did* trust.

"Yes, of course," he murmured before leaning back against the squabs again. He may trust Julia, but he sure as hell didn't trust the men around her. The sooner he found someone to look after her, the better.

Chapter Five

Contrary to what one might expect, there were benefits to being relegated to the sofa for the day with an injured ankle. Yes, Sophie was missing out on an uncomfortably large portion of her allotted husband-hunting time, and yes, her poor ankle, though not broken, did hurt like the devil, but at least she had an ironclad excuse for why she couldn't go out and face the general public today.

Thank God.

That being said, she was bored to death. May had already stopped by for a few hours that morning. In her typical no-nonsense way, she had acknowledged that while the incident was indeed the talk of the night, Sophie had at least succeeded in capturing the earl's attention for much longer than originally hoped. Somehow, that point didn't make her feel at all better about the situation.

Since May's departure, Sophie had received a letter from Charity, read said letter—hooray, she was coming back within the week!—and responded with a lengthy one of her own. She'd also read a collection of poems, practiced on her oboe, and endured her mother's constant fretting with the patience of Job. Very well, with somewhat *less* patience than Job, but certainly with enough to earn her sainthood.

Even now, Mama paced back and forth across the room, her feet following nearly the same path as they had when she'd discovered the elopement. "Perhaps you should write him a note. Expressing your gratitude, alluding to the hope of seeing him again soon, et cetera, et cetera."

Sophie caught herself before rolling her eyes. "I'm not going to write him a note. I'd rather not remind him of the Incident. Best to simply start anew the next time I see him." It was reaching to imagine that he would forget the whole thing, but one could hope.

"Well, you must do something. You cannot just sit here and expect him to come to you."

A light scratch on the door announced their maid's presence. "Pardon me, ma'am, miss. A Lord Evansleigh has come to call."

Mama's gasp was only slightly louder than Sophie's. He was here? *Now?* Sophie started to scramble to a sitting position before a white-hot bolt of pain reminded her of her injury. Gritting her teeth, she sat back and sent a desperate look to her mother. "I can't see him now, not like this!"

Her hair must look an absolute fright. Curls and humidity never did seem to get along. It was likely frizzy, and her gown was wrinkled, and—

"Don't be ridiculous," Mama said, interrupting Sophie's runaway thoughts. Turning back to Lynette, she flapped her hands. "Go! By all means, show him in. And order tea. And biscuits. And perhaps some cordial just in case. Quickly now, what are you waiting for?"

As the servant scurried off to collect the earl, Mama

rushed to Sophie's side, excitement brightening her plump cheeks to a blotchy pink. "You can and you will see the man. From what I've heard, the earl never calls on *anyone*."

She leaned down and fussed with the fringe around Sophie's face before shaking her head. "Oh, those curls are hopeless. They've already turned to cotton and you've not even stepped foot outside. Here," she said, unpinning her mobcap and yanking it down over Sophie's head. "That will have to do. Hurry, pinch your cheeks and sit up straight. On second thought, recline a bit. There, that's better."

Oh heavens, Sophie could only imagine what she looked like now. A mobcap? Why not throw a shawl over her shoulders and add spectacles for good measure? Just what she needed, Evan seeing her at her worst directly on the heels of last night's debacle. She didn't even attempt to pinch her cheeks—Lord knew, they'd be red enough on their own.

Footsteps reached the squeaky spot on the landing, sending Mama hurrying to her chair. She grabbed a handful of yarn and her knitting needles seconds before Lynette showed the earl in.

Sophie's breath caught in her throat when he entered the sitting room. Had she ever seen him in daylight before? No, she would have remembered the effect it had on those crystalline eyes of his. It was like sunshine through a stained-glass window.

As her mother greeted him, Sophie sat looking up at him in awed silence, her tongue too tied to say a word. He looked handsome and completely composed. In other words, her exact opposite in almost every way. He wore buff-colored breeches that hugged his legs like a second skin. His boots were polished, free of so much as a speck of dirt. Even his hair seemed to be showing off, each strand exactly in place. How in the world had this man come to be in her drawing room, completely of his own free will?

In unison, Mama and Evan turned and looked at her, as though expecting her to say something. Oh drat, what had she missed? In order to properly ogle him, she'd completely ignored whatever they had been saying.

Swallowing against what felt like a lump of wool lodged in her throat, she smiled. "How good of you to visit, my lord." The floppy edge of her mother's cap drooped across her eyes, and she tried to blow it away as inconspicuously as possible.

"It is my pleasure, Miss Wembley. I do hope you are feeling better today."

How was it possible to want someone to stay and feel so desperate for them to go at the same time? "Yes. Much. Thank you." For heaven's sake, could she sound like any more of an idiot?

He nodded, blessedly ignoring the stilted nature of her response. "Though still off your feet, I see. Nothing broken, I hope?"

"The doctor said I merely turned it. Hardly worth all the fuss." Oh drat, had that sounded ungrateful? She rushed to clarify. "Not that I'm not terribly appreciative for all you did for me. I am. Thank you."

"Think nothing of it. A damsel in distress, and all that." He smiled a perfectly disarming smile, which of course only served to make her more nervous.

"Rescued quite handily. Thank you. Again." She gritted her teeth in an effort to keep from grimacing. For the love of biscuits, *stop saying thank you*!

Mama cleared her throat and smiled. "Well, then. I

think I'll go check on the refreshments." She rounded her eyes briefly in Sophie's direction before heading for the door.

Sophie stared after her in absolute horror. She was leaving them? *Alone?* Good heavens, such a thing simply was not done! Evan stood silent for a moment, likely contemplating making a dash for freedom. After a pause, he gave a little shrug—did he know such a thing highlighted his deliciously broad shoulders?—and took a seat in the chair closest to her. "It is a shame that you should be bedridden on such a lovely day. Or sofa-ridden, as the case may be."

She was alone with the earl. Completely, utterly, sinfully alone . . . and they were talking about the *weather*?

Suppressing a sigh, she nodded, which had the unfortunate effect of making the cap slip a bit farther down her head. "Indeed," she murmured, lifting her hand as casually as possible to tug the blasted thing back. In all her daydreams of being alone with the man, she had never once been wearing her mother's cap, while being laid up on the sofa like some sort of invalid.

Well, she had hoped for more time with the earl, hadn't she? She sunk down into the sofa another inch. Next time she'd have to remember to be more specific about what she wished for.

It was all Evan could do not to crack a smile. What on earth was she doing wearing that dreadful thing on her head in the first place? Clearly it was driving her mad. He had the most absurd desire to walk right over to her and yank the damn thing off her head. Perhaps throw it out the window for good measure.

It was almost worth it just to see what she would do. With her mother gone, however, he wasn't inclined to move a muscle. He was still shocked that she had left the two of them alone. Did she think Miss Wembley's injury superseded society's rules? Or was she really that clueless? Or perhaps underhanded. Hard to say which, from what little he knew of the woman.

This was what he got for breaking his own rule.

He did *not* call on unmarried females. Or married females, for that matter. Since he had no intention of wooing a wife, he had no need whatsoever to engage in such a tedious task. He also didn't want anyone to get the wrong impression about his interests. Miss Wembley, however, deserved an exception to his normal behavior.

If Evan had not pressed her into dancing as he had, she would never have tripped and fallen, and thereby would have been spared the pain and embarrassment of such an ignoble event. She wouldn't have been forced to endure Miss Harmon's waspish tongue, or the unrepentant stares of a ballroom full of curious people. Most of all, the poor girl would not have injured herself, making a visit like this necessary.

At least she looked well this morning—ugly cap aside. Her cheery yellow gown complemented her pale complexion, which, together with her rosy cheeks, made her look the very picture of good health. The afternoon sunlight filtered past the gauzy white sheers covering the front windows. The effect was much more complimentary to her dark eyes than the candlelight had been last night. Today, their rich color reminded him of shimmery chocolate-colored silk.

He needed to get to the point. Scooting forward a bit on his chair, he said plainly, "Miss Wembley, I want you to know how much I regret dragging you into service yesterday. In my attempts to avoid a scene, I somehow managed to cause a much worse one."

Her small nose crinkled as she shook her head. "No, please. I am the only one to blame for my own clumsiness."

The movement of her head further dislodged the doily, making it slide an inch toward her right ear. He did his best to ignore it, focusing instead on those pretty eyes. "You never would have been dancing if I hadn't dragged you out there."

"I *like* to dance," she said, her voice quiet but firm. Sighing, she sat up a little straighter, gestured to the thing on her head and said, "Would you mind?"

"Be my guest."

Plucking the cap off, she tossed in on the sofa table. "My apologies if my unruly hair offends, but I couldn't take another moment of that thing on my head."

Her hair was indeed unruly. Dark brown, almost black curls sprang up as if freed from bondage. Instead of the coiffed, pinned style he had seen her wear, it was all piled rather unceremoniously on top of her head. He smiled. "Nonconformity is a good thing, in my opinion." He also liked that she seemed to be loosening up with him, if only a little. That was probably the longest sentence she had ever spoken to him.

The smile she gave him was nearly worth the whole visit—wide and wholly without censure. For the first time since he'd known her she actually looked at ease. "Tell that to my mother," she replied, a hint of dry humor lightening her tone.

Dimples creased her cheeks for a moment before vanishing. His gaze flicked to her mouth, a feature he had never paid much attention to. In that moment, with her face relaxed and her full lips curved in a sweet smile, he was surprised at just how inviting her mouth was. "I'd be happy to. Though unless I'm much mistaken, she does subscribe to at least some amount of nonconformity."

Both brows lifted. "My mother? What would cause you to think so?"

"I've been to one of your concerts. I know exactly how unusual your family's choice of instruments is. And the word is your younger sister, who comes out next year, I believe, is accomplished in the recorder. Bassoon, oboe, recorder—all bold choices."

Instead of laughter or agreement, her eyes clouded and her brows fell. It was like watching shutters slam shut or a candle blown out. Damn it all, he hadn't meant for her to take offense. "Bold, but excellent choices," he clarified. "You in particular have a great talent for your oboe."

Mrs. Wembley chose that moment to come bustling back in. A maid followed behind her, her arms laden with an overlarge tea tray. The older woman clapped her hands together lightly. "There we are, now. I hope you like your tea hot, my lord." Her eyes landed on the mobcap on the table, and she shifted her narrowed gaze to her daughter.

"Yes, the hotter the better," Evan said, wanting to deflect her scrutiny. It didn't matter that not only did he not want tea, but it was much too warm to wish for especially hot refreshments of any kind.

"Excellent. Now, did I hear you say you are an admirer of Sophie's playing?" She sent him a coy smile before attending to the business of pouring. "How do you take it?"

"Just as it is, please. As for the talents of your daughter, yes, I think she is quite skilled." He accepted the cup of undoctored tea and looked at Miss Wembley. "I was late to your trio's recital last month, but I heard so much about it, I wish I had seen it."

She looked down, those lovely lips curving upward into a pleased grin. "Thank you. It was a wonderful experience. I hope we can play together again soon."

Mrs. Wembley set the teapot down with a thump. "I know! Sophie, why don't you play your part for Lord Evansleigh? We could have a miniature concert, right here in the drawing room."

Eyes wide, Miss Wembley shook her head. "No, Mama, please." It was a real plea, not the feeble protest of one looking to elicit more praise.

"Don't be shy, my dear. Play for your guest."

The older woman's demand was just that. It was said with a smile, but the steel in her voice brooked no argument. Miss Wembley looked as though she'd as soon sink into the floorboards as be forced to play for him right then. Once again, he had managed to get her wrangled into something she'd rather avoid.

"*Sophie,*" her mother nearly hissed this time, "you mustn't keep his lordship waiting."

"Never fear, madam; I may have missed this most recent concert, but I certainly have had the pleasure of hearing her play. Miss Wembley is very talented."

The girl blushed, clearly pleased, but her mother wasn't so easily deterred. "How lovely for you to say so. Just wait until you hear her play solo." She gave her daughter another insistent look. She had the tenacity of a seasoned matchmaking mama.

"Speaking of solo," Evan interjected quickly, wanting to spare the girl from having to either give in or further refuse, "it occurs to me, Miss Wembley, that I never completed the introduction with my sister yesterday. Julia has only just arrived, and is in need of a friend or two, I should think." Friends who were of the *female* persuasion.

Now that he said it, he realized it was true. Miss Wembley might even be a good influence on his sister. She at least would never pick up and travel halfway across the country on a whim. And who knew? Perhaps if Julia had a few female friends in town, she'd be less inclined to spend time with the young bucks dangling after her.

Warming to the idea, he smiled encouragingly. "When you are recovered, I'm certain Julia would be grateful were you to call on her."

Mother and daughter exchanged a quick glance before turning to him in unison. Mrs. Wembley beamed at him, obviously delighted by his suggestion. "What a wonderful idea! Sophie has always been my little magpie. I'm certain she and your sister shall become fast friends."

At that, he wondered whether she was already planning the wedding, or merely the betrothal announcement. And what was this magpie nonsense about? Miss Wembley was about as talkative as his horse. Thankfully, she didn't seem at all as ambitious as her mother. She did seem to appreciate his suggestion, however.

"Thank you, my lord. I'd be honored." Dimples bracketed either side of her mouth as she offered him a small but sweet smile.

"Excellent. Shall I have a carriage sent 'round on Thursday or Friday, perhaps?"

"No!" Mrs. Wembley flushed and cleared her throat. "That is, I'm sure she'll be on her feet before the day is out. How about tomorrow afternoon?"

Evan had to work not to show his irritation. While he was more than happy to have Miss Wembley visit tomorrow, her mother's anxiousness to push them back into

each other's company made him want to rescind the offer altogether. The only thing that kept him from doing
so was the look of mortification on Miss Wembley's face.

It was a look he knew and understood well. He, more
than anyone, knew that one could not be held account-
able for a parent's sins. *Shouldn't be,* he silently amended,
knowing full well how often people were.

"Very well," he said, dipping his head in consent. "If
you are feeling suitably improved by tomorrow, send a
missive and I'll dispatch my carriage to collect you."

He stood and straightened his jacket, more than ready
to conclude the visit. "I must be on my way. Thank you
for the refreshments."

"Oh, but you haven't finished your tea, my lord." Mrs.
Wembley gestured to the mostly full cup on the sofa table and fluttered her eyelashes hopefully. Evan gritted
his teeth. If she thought to keep him there, she could
think again. His patience at an end, he grabbed the cup,
lifted it to his lips, and downed the entire contents in
three long swallows. The tea had cooled in the past few
minutes, but was still hot enough to burn a path down his
throat. The flavor of the vile stuff was enough to make
him grimace, but he stoically refused to show it. Returning the empty cup to its saucer, he nodded briskly to his
gaping hostess. "Good day, Mrs. Wembley, Miss Wembley. I can show myself out."

With that, he turned and escaped from the room,
breathing a sigh of relief when he made it to the street.
He liked Miss Wembley well enough, but her mother
was another story altogether. He'd have to be careful not
to allow the woman to get her hopes up for something
that would never happen. He'd be damned if he would
ever find himself in the parson's noose.

Chapter Six

The earl's townhouse looked every bit as opulent as his carriage—and that was truly saying something. As they glided to a stop, Sophie gazed out the open window to the towering building rising from the hillside.

The stone was the same as the façade on her own rented townhouse, but the likeness stopped there. Here, the buttery yellow stone was carved into pillars and scrolls and all sorts of beautiful design elements. The windows were both wide and tall, undoubtedly reaching from floor to ceiling. Black wrought iron railings covered the lower half of the uppermost windows, in addition to lining the walkway to the front door.

She knew he didn't own the house, which begged the question, who exactly could afford to rent such a place? She stifled a nervous giggle. The answer, of course, was an earl.

The coach shook as the driver dismounted and came to open the door. Sophie drew a deep breath and smoothed an anxious hand down her skirts. Lord Evansleigh was giving her exactly the chance she needed, even after Mama had acted so appallingly obvious yesterday, and Sophie intended to make the most of it. Smooth curls, carefully chosen jewelry, her best afternoon gown—she was leaving nothing to chance.

Well, nothing except the very real possibility of not being able to get a proper sentence out in his company. She'd been able to relax a little yesterday, which actually allowed her to sound like a normal person in the earl's presence, but that was in her own drawing room, without the man's sister hearing their every word.

Lynette, who had sat quietly across from her for the whole of the ride, offered an encouraging smile. Sophie smiled back, grateful for the servant's small gesture of support. She could do this. Talking was what she did best, for heaven's sake. She just needed to get over the fact that the very sight of the earl set her stomach to knots.

Within minutes she was waiting in the beautifully appointed drawing room, trying for all she was worth to sit still. The soft greens and polished golds would have been calming were she anywhere else but the earl's private residence. Was it her imagination, or did the room smell like him? She breathed deeply, remembering the scent of him as he'd carried her through the Ballroom.

"Miss Wembley?"

Sophie glanced up as the woman from the ball who had been so familiar with Evan made her way to the seating area. She felt a little silly for her reaction that night now that she knew the woman was his sister. "Lady Julia, how do you do?" Sophie stood and offered an awkward little curtsy, favoring her right ankle.

Waving a dismissive hand, Lady Julia returned Sophie's smile with a somewhat brusque one of her own. "Do please sit down. I wouldn't want you overtaxing your ankle on my account."

"It's much improved, I assure you," Sophie replied, though she did accept the offer to sit. She waited as Lady

Julia settled onto the settee and smoothed out her skirts. Her gown, a lovely pin-striped white muslin day dress with perfectly puffed sleeves and braided satin piping, was easily worth more than Sophie's entire wardrobe combined. Her golden-brown hair, so much like her brother's in color and texture, was arranged in perfect little finger curls threaded with a ribbon that matched the piping of her dress.

Sophie sat up a little straighter, oddly self-conscious. She was quite used to socializing with those of superior wealth and status, but there was something about Lady Julia that was intimidating. Perhaps it was the fact that she was Evan's sister, but Sophie didn't think so. Was it fair to say she was standoffish when they hadn't even spent a minute in each other's company yet?

Stifling the urge to start talking—because heaven knew she wouldn't stop once she got going—she laced her fingers together and waited for her hostess to speak first.

Thankfully, Lady Julia didn't keep her waiting too long. "I must say, Miss Wembley," she said, folding her hands primly in her lap and leveling her gaze squarely on Sophie, "this is something of a first. Evan doesn't usually invite people to call, and he certainly doesn't do so on my behalf. I wonder what has him doing so now."

Good gracious, but that was blunt. Sophie blinked, at a loss as to how to answer such a question. "I'm sure I don't know," she hedged, suddenly wishing she had turned down the earl's offer to come today. For some reason, she had imagined his sister to be much like him: kind, genial, quick to put one at ease. Stupid assumption, really; of her own sisters, Pippa was the only one who was even remotely similar to Sophie.

Lady Julia tilted her head, inspecting Sophie as though she were an animal in an exhibit. "The way I see it, there are two possibilities. Either my brother has an interest in you personally, which I highly doubt, or he feels you would be some sort of appropriate chaperone for me, which is equally unlikely, given your age and unmarried status."

Ah, so apparently they were moving from blunt to rude. Good to know. "I can't purport to understand his lordship's decision. He asked, and I accepted. Nothing nefarious or underhanded about it, at least not from what I could tell." No wonder the earl thought his sister needed a friend. If this was her normal behavior, the woman probably didn't have any.

"I see," she said, in the way one does when one doesn't really see at all. "Well, I can assure you that I have no need—" She abruptly stopped talking as Evan strode into the room.

Thank God. Sophie didn't know how much more she could take of the interview. She never did waste her time with people who didn't wish for her company. Her mother did enough of that for the both of them.

Smiling toward her savior, Sophie watched as he made his way to the seating area. His long legs were encased in a pair of off-white breeches that contrasted with the navy blue of his jacket quite nicely. His cravat was simply tied and his hair was left unbound, skimming the tops of his shoulders. As always, the sight of him warmed her. "Ah, good, I see you've met."

Sophie nearly snorted, despite the fluttering nerves that seemed to get worse with every step closer he took. They'd met all right, though she wouldn't necessarily call that a good thing.

"Yes. Miss Wembley and I were just having a little chin-wag. *Lovely* girl," Julia said, not bothering to conceal her sarcasm.

Evan slowed in the process of taking his seat, looking to his sister with the sort of caution one shows a cat with its claws out. "I agree completely. What were you discussing?"

Even if Sophie had been her normal chatty self, she still wouldn't have touched that question. She watched Lady Julia with interest, curious to see what she would say. *Just pushing the limits of rudeness with Miss Wembley, dear brother. Would you pass the tea?*

Lifting her chin, Julia easily met her brother's gaze. "We were discussing the possible reasons you might have invited Miss Wembley to visit. Because, frankly, I can't imagine why."

At the very least, the woman was honest. In an odd way, Sophie could appreciate that in a person—even as, at that exact moment, she wanted to snap her fingers and magically disappear. Evan's jaw tightened to a hard line. Turning away from his sister, he peered at Sophie with those gorgeous, nearly hypnotic icy blue eyes. And icy was exactly the word for them at that moment.

"Please accept my most sincere apologies, Miss Wembley. You were invited because I consider you to be a friend."

"Really?" Lady Julia said, her voice rife with disbelief. "You seemed to hardly know her when we spoke of her on the way home from the ball."

"Julia," Evan barked, making both Sophie and the churlish sister jump, "that is quite enough. Miss Wembley, would you please excuse us for a moment?"

Her heart still pounding from the shock of his raised voice, Sophie nodded. She started to stand, but he put a hand to her wrist, brushing the fine hairs with his bare fingertips. Sucking in a sharp breath, she froze. Evan was touching her. On purpose. Skin to skin.

"Please, stay." His voice was much gentler this time, and against her will she met his gaze. "We'll be back in a moment."

Without another word, he stood, tugged his sister to her feet, and stalked from the room with her in tow. Sophie sat there, gaping after them long after they had disappeared from sight. What in the world had just happened?

Blowing out a breath, she looked down at the place where their skin had met. Gooseflesh covered her forearm. She rubbed her hand over her arm and shivered. No matter what happened when they returned, the whole visit was worth it for the handful of seconds his fingers had warmed her wrist. Yes, it had felt amazing, but more than that, it reiterated what she already knew.

She really, really wanted the earl. She couldn't let Lady Julia, Marianne, or even her own mother ruin her chances. Straightening her shoulders, Sophie made herself a promise. When Evan and his sister returned, she would swallow her nerves and show them both the person she really was. Evan had called her a friend, which was a step in the right direction. With any luck, he'd be calling her countess before the month was out.

If sororicide had been legal, Julia would have been in serious trouble.

Evan stormed up the stairs, propelling his sister along by her elbow. She must have sensed his fury, because she wisely refrained from speaking as he looked for a room far enough away that he could be sure Miss Wembley wouldn't hear their argument.

Deciding on his own bedchamber, he yanked open the door, pulled his sister inside, and slammed the door shut with enough force to rattle the walls. The heavy gray curtains were closed to keep the summer sun out, but there was enough light to easily make out the room's dark and imposing furniture.

Releasing his hold on her elbow, he wheeled around and glared at her, his nostrils flaring. "What in the name of God has gotten into you? How dare you insult that poor girl so disgracefully?"

She didn't have the decency—or the intelligence, if she knew what was good for her—to look contrite. She glared right back at him, her eyes as resentful as a reprimanded child's. "I don't need some sort of keeper, Evan."

"After that little stunt of yours, I beg to differ," he retorted. "Regardless, what the hell does that have to do with you behaving like an ill-bred harpy?" He was at a complete loss as to what was happening to his once kind sister. She had always been dry-witted and candid, but this was beyond the pale. Hurting an innocent person's feelings? It was as if he didn't know her at all.

Her hands went to her hips. "You said you trusted me, yet not even two days later, this 'friend' whom you hardly know shows up at the door." Her words were angry, her chest stained red above the white fabric of her gown.

He threw up his hands. "What are you talking about? She's younger than you are—how do you imagine she's here to be your keeper?"

His sister narrowed her eyes. "So you are saying you didn't intend for her to keep an eye on me?"

"What, am I running a bloody spy ring? She is a good person, very sweet and agreeable, and I thought she might be a good friend for you. Since when is it a capital offense to try to introduce you to prospective acquaintances?"

"Oh, so she's a friend for *me*, is she?" Julia gave a

disbelieving snort. "More likely you're the one interested in her. I'm beginning to wonder if you are as dedicated to our agreement as you purport to be."

"I'm not interested in her!" he roared, his anger boiling over. Where the hell was all this coming from? He'd never given her reason to doubt him. He dragged a hand through his hair, gritting his teeth as he tried to rein in his temper. "I may have hoped she'd be a positive influence on you, but I honestly also thought she could make your time here more enjoyable. Forgive me for making such an egregious error in judgment."

For the first time, she looked unsure. "You truly have no interest in her?"

"She's an acquaintance. Nothing more."

The air whooshed from Julia's lungs. "Oh. *Oh*," she said again, the truth of his words sinking in. She slowly wilted onto the crimson cushion of the bench at the foot of the bed. "My apologies, then. I was wrong to jump to conclusions."

"I'm not the one you need to apologize to," he replied, not bothering to filter out his annoyance. Why, for the love of God, did he keep subjecting Miss Wembley to such indignities, however unintentionally? He had thought it was a *nice* thing to introduce the two of them.

Julia looked up, regret darkening her eyes. "Yes." She drew a long breath before getting to her feet. "Will you come with me?"

"As if I'd leave her alone with you," he grumbled, though his anger had dissipated to worry. Julia wasn't herself, and he felt further than ever from being able to discover why. He didn't want to keep Miss Wembley waiting, but he intended to get to the bottom of Julia's uncharacteristic reticence. "I wish you'd tell me what has you acting so oddly."

She stood, her eyes unreadable in the dim light. "And I wish you would quit analyzing my every move. I'm away from home for the first time in my life, Evan. Of course I'm going to act a bit differently. Come now, we mustn't keep our guest waiting."

He sighed and rubbed a hand over the back of his neck. "Sooner or later, I will figure out what's bothering you."

"So you keep saying. I'd assure you that there is nothing to uncover, but I imagine my breath would be better spent apologizing to Miss Wembley." With a determined lift of her chin, she headed for the door.

Shaking his head, he followed after her. There'd be time to chew over the topic later.

They made their way back downstairs, both more subdued. He was not looking forward to the next few minutes. Dealing with offended women was never his strong suit—particularly when the offense was so well warranted. Affixing an apologetic smile on his stiff lips, he entered the drawing room. *What the devil?* He stopped and looked around, confusion creasing his brow.

The room was empty.

Chapter Seven

In hindsight, Sophie's decision to flee from the earl's house may have been a bit rash. Except, really, what choice had she had when the earl had declared, quite vehemently, that he had no interest in her? So vehemently, in fact, that the words had easily filtered through the drawing room ceiling from the room above it.

Yes, tears had burned at the back of her eyes, what with hearing such a sentiment from the man she fancied herself in love with—and was actively attempting to entice. So much for their supposed friendship soon blossoming into something more. And yes, the visit had already been going rather dismally, thanks to the man's sister.

However, perhaps she should have considered the fact that her ankle was still healing, and the earl's home was almost a mile from her own. Worse, she hadn't a single farthing on her person. Why would she? She was supposed to have been ferried by Lord Evansleigh's own coach for this little excursion.

Sighing, she trudged on, following the curving road down the hill toward the city center. At least the weather was cooperating. The clouds kept the sun at bay, and a cool breeze made the walk almost pleasant. Discounting the fact that her ankle was throbbing, of course. And that she wasn't entirely sure she knew the way home. And that she would die a lonely spinster because the man on whom she'd pinned her last hopes was most ardently and decidedly not interested in her.

"Miss Sophie?" Lynette's quiet voice penetrated Sophie's gloomy thoughts. She'd nearly forgotten the poor maid was with her.

Taking the opportunity to stop and lean against the wrought iron fence lining the pavement, Sophie raised an eyebrow. "Yes?"

"Do you think it might be prudent to go back? Perhaps the butler could send for a hackney." There was so much hope in the servant's green eyes, Sophie couldn't help but feel guilty.

The problem was, she didn't think her heart could take the further humiliation of returning for help. She wasn't an overly proud person, but everyone had their limits. She shook her head, even as she discreetly lifted her right foot to rest it. "I'm sorry, Lynette, but I cannot. As a rule, I pride myself on not imposing my presence where it is not wanted."

"Yes, Miss, but what if I went to the servants' entrance and asked? Surely that would work." Blowing an escaped lock of hair from her eyes, she added, "We needn't give your mother the vapors by showing up looking like shipwrecked vagrants."

She had a point. Sophie pursed her lips, glancing back up to the top of the street where the earl's house stood. Was it just her, or was the thing looking down its nose at her? Still, Lynette's idea did have merit. She started to say as much when a figure caught her attention. A man was rushing down the pavement, much faster than the other pedestrians. She squinted her eyes. No, it couldn't be. Could it? Her heart gave a little panicked leap. Was *Evan* actually coming after her?

The clothes were the same, and the hair was a dead giveaway. Yes, it was definitely the earl.

Sophie turned away, sucking in a bracing lungful of air. Why would he do such a thing? With her heart drumming away in her chest, she grabbed Lynette's arm and started down the hill. "Come along. We must be on our way."

"But, Miss Sophie," the servant protested, looking over her shoulder. "I think that's Lord Evansleigh!"

"Yes, I know," Sophie hissed, walking all the more quickly. Her ankle ached in fierce protest, but she would rather die than face the man just now. She leaned heavily on Lynette, eternally grateful that they were walking downhill.

"He'll help us, I'm sure of it," her maid persisted, glancing back again.

"Lynette, if you look back one more time, so help me I will . . . do . . . *something*," she finished lamely when nothing appropriately awful came to mind. How was one supposed to think properly when one was being chased by an exceedingly handsome and dreadfully unwanted peer of the realm?

"Miss Wembley?"

Oh, dear Lord. Sophie kept her eyes on the pavement and doggedly hobbled along, even as she realized there was no way for her to outrun him. Or outwalk him, as the case may be. Even if she was only delaying the inevitable, she didn't want to face him any sooner than she had to.

"Miss Wembley," he said again, this time much closer. "Miss Wembley, please. I know you can hear me." He was only slightly out of breath, while she was as winded as a racehorse.

Fine. She might as well get this over with. Coming to a stop at last, she paused to pant for a moment before turning to face him. "Did I forget something? Other than my dignity, of course."

He drew back, surprise clear in his raised brows and widened eyes. He recovered quickly, however, shaking his head and offering what she could just imagine was his official Look of Concern. "I cannot begin to express my regret for the way you were treated in my home. Please, allow me to escort you back to the house. My sister is anxious to apologize."

Yes, Sophie would just bet she was. She refrained from pointing out the significant difference between apologizing in earnest and apologizing under duress, a distinction anyone with three sisters and one long-suffering nursemaid would understand. The truth was, though Lady Julia had surprised Sophie with her clear dislike, the woman's reception had little to do with Sophie's escape.

What really galled her was that even though Evan had proclaimed his lack of interest in her not ten minutes earlier, her traitorous body still hummed at his nearness. The slightly uncivilized look of his windblown hair didn't help things, either. He looked like a dashing naval officer fresh from his ship. She gave herself a mental shake. No, she would *not* let her heart be waylaid by a beautiful head of hair, for heaven's sake.

Wrapping herself up in what was left of her pride, she lifted her chin. "Apology accepted. Now, if you will excuse us."

"Come now, she feels terrible. Allow her to make proper amends."

"Really, we must be on—"

"Please," he said, boldly interrupting her. He curled his lips into a gentle smile and added, "It would mean a lot to both of us."

Fresh embarrassment heated her cheeks. Why was he pushing the matter? A sense of misplaced obligation to her? Was he still feeling guilty for her stupid injury? Drawing herself up to her full, albeit short height, she said, "Lord Evansleigh, might I offer a suggestion?"

He paused, no doubt cautioned by her sudden change of demeanor. "Of course."

"In the future, I would recommend you hold your private conversations somewhere other than directly above the person you wish to discuss."

Damn it all, Miss Wembley had overheard them. Evan frantically sorted through the conversation in his mind, trying to remember exactly what was said.

But thinking clearly was hard when she was looking at him like that, like a kicked puppy attempting to be brave. Blowing out a breath, he stated the obvious. "You heard us."

She gave a single nod. "I heard *you*," she said, the emphasis unmistakable.

She heard him? What had he— Oh, Christ. She must have heard him lose his temper and make his position on her clear. He pressed his eyes closed for a moment before meeting her gaze. "It didn't mean what it sounded like. Please, let us return to the house and allow me to explain. I'll have my carriage at the ready, so you may leave at any time."

Though she couldn't see it, her maid was nodding vigorously just behind her. He couldn't believe Miss Wembley had been willing to walk home on her wounded

ankle just to get away from him. If that didn't make a
man feel as honorable as a speck of dust, he didn't know
what did. "Your mother entrusted your well-being to me.
At least allow me to return you to her in one piece." He
held out his elbow, silently urging her to join him.

She stared at it for a moment, then back up at his face.
With a great sigh, she nodded and laid her hand on his
arm. Thank God. At the very least he could be sure she
made it home alive. They trudged back up the hill in silence, with him setting a pace roughly on par with that of
a snail in deference to her limp.

The moment they reached the house, she released his
arm and solemnly followed him back into the drawing
room. Julia looked up from where she sat on the settee,
her smile cautious. Coming to her feet, she approached
their guest. "I'm so relieved my brother found you, Miss
Wembley. I am also relieved that we are female, as a duel
at dawn wouldn't be uncalled for, given the way I treated
you."

Miss Wembley smiled wanly. "I'm a terrible shot, so
it's just as well."

"Either way, do please accept my most ardent apology. Only Shakespeare could have written a greater
shrew." Julia shook her head ruefully, clearly contrite.

"Apology accepted," Miss Wembley replied, giving a
little dip of her head. Even so, her shoulders didn't relax
in the least as she stood stiffly at his side. "I really should
be getting back home, however. Mama will want us to
prepare for tonight's events."

Julia's eyes brightened with interest. "What is sched-
uled this week for the festival, anyway? My brother is
rather unforthcoming."

Miss Wembley swallowed, her gaze remaining steadfastly on his sister. "A night of Austrian composers this

evening, then tomorrow the Music Around the World series is offering an introduction to polka as well as a duet featuring two Italian opera singers. Oh, and on Friday afternoon, there's a lecture about the history of British composers."

"My, what excitement," Julia said, her tone as dry as parchment. "I'm quite the music lover, but a lecture isn't exactly my idea of an enjoyable afternoon. I would love to see the opera singers, however. Would you be willing to accompany me? Or us, rather," she amended, flicking a glance to Evan.

The smile slipped from Miss Wembley's lips. "Thank you, but—"

"Julia," Evan said, shamelessly interrupting Sophie's attempt to decline the offer. "It's my understanding that Miss Wembley is a great lover of all things musical. Why don't you play your harp for her before she leaves us?"

His sister blinked in surprise, obviously startled by the request. "I'm sure she doesn't wish—"

"Oh, but *I* wish," he ground out. "A little ambiance, if you please." He met her confused gaze with steel in his eyes. After how things had gone earlier, he was willing her not to balk.

Finally, she nodded. "Very well. Any requests?"

"Surprise us."

Nodding, she made her way to the other end of the room, where she'd insisted on keeping her harp. Apparently, the acoustics of this room were superior to those of the actual music room located down the corridor. Evan refrained from looking at Miss Wembley while his sister prepared to play. He didn't want to open the door to her expressing her desire to leave. When the first strains of heavenly music filled the room, he turned to her at last.

"Thank you, Miss Wembley, for giving me a chance to explain."

In Sophie's opinion, she hadn't so much given him a chance to explain as he had simply taken one. Still, she nodded, not wanting to come across as ungracious. The whole thing was embarrassing in the extreme, but it was best to deal with it now and be done with it.

He gestured toward the pair of mahogany chairs opposite the sofa, and they both took a seat. For a moment, she ignored the jumble of emotions that tangled like a knot of thread in her stomach and listened to the angelic music Lady Julia elicited from her harp. She wasn't a particularly disciplined player, but the music was still lovely, and it was blessedly calming.

Evan perched on the edge of his chair, positioning himself so that his feet were only a few inches away from hers on the floral Aubusson rug. "You have to understand, my sister and I are a little different from most siblings."

She tilted her head a bit to the side. This was not the apology she was expecting, but it succeeded in rousing her curiosity. "Oh?"

"When my father died, I was fifteen and Julia was twelve. Our mother . . . well, let us just say she didn't handle the loss very well. My sister and I leaned on each other for support, but at the same time, I was filling the roles of father, mother, and brother for her."

Sophie could hardly believe he was speaking with such frankness. It might have had something to do with the harp music lending his story an almost mythical quality, but she found herself leaning forward the tiniest bit.

"We've always looked out for each other, but sometimes my sister is less than amenable to my attempts to keep her natural enthusiasm within the bounds of propriety. When I invited you here, she assumed I was attempting to find someone to keep her in line."

How very odd . . . and terribly interesting. "I see," she said, though in all honesty, she wasn't sure she did. How did that assumption lead to Evan's declaration? That aside, Sophie was quite intrigued to know what sorts of activities Lady Julia wished not to have curtailed. Sophie could like a woman with a little rebellion in her.

Evan licked his lips before continuing, a move that drew her attention to his mouth. They were such nice lips—full but not plump, wide but not distractingly so. Actually, they were quite distracting. Very kissable. She caught herself and jerked her gaze back up to his. She could feel the heat rising in her cheeks, but there was nothing she could do to stop it.

"I'm afraid that when I explained that you were a friend, not a spy, she jumped to a conclusion that I felt the need to correct before her imagination ran away with her. I was angry with her at the time, and I'm sure my response was much more vehement than I intended. I hope you can overlook my thoughtless words, and accept my apology."

The floating notes of Lady Julia's song softened the mortification Sophie had felt when she'd originally heard his exclamation. If he had no care for her, then he certainly wouldn't go through such effort to comfort her, would he? In her experience, it was a rare man who apologized, and an even rarer one who actually attempted to explain himself.

The way she saw it, she had a choice. She could run away, lick her wounds and continue to be embarrassed by how things had progressed today, or she could ignore his comments and pay attention to how important it seemed to him that he set her mind at ease.

He claimed to think of her as a friend, and she believed him, despite what he had said. She bit her lip. There were worse places to start a courtship. "Of course, my lord. And thank you. You didn't need to say all that, but I do appreciate it."

"So we are friends again?"

The smile he gave her sent a silvery flash of attraction through her blood. She nodded, not trusting her voice.

"Does that mean I can stop playing?" Lady Julia called from the other side of the room, the words laced with dry humor.

Sophie had almost forgotten that they weren't alone. One would think that would be obvious, given the music the woman was playing, but it was easy to believe they were alone when lost in the crystalline depths of Evan's eyes.

Glancing toward his sister, he chuckled and shook his head. "Yes, brat. Though try to keep the eavesdropping to a minimum next time." He came to his feet and offered Sophie his hand. "Shall we collect you tomorrow before the duet?"

She slid her hand into his, trying not to betray the hitch in her breathing as she allowed him to help her to her feet. It had been an odd visit, but she was relieved to be back on good terms with the earl. With an uncharacteristically shy smile, she nodded. "I look forward to it."

Chapter Eight

"So Lord Evansleigh's declaration of disinterest was a *good* thing?"

Poor May. She looked quite lost after Sophie's retelling of the day's events. They were only halfway through the Night of Austrian Composers event at the Pump Room overlooking the Roman Baths, but Sophie simply couldn't wait until the end to share her rather harrowing experience. Since intermission was a half hour in length, Sophie had rushed to explain it all as they stood in the corner of the hall beneath the stern statue of Beau Nash, sipping their restorative yet disgusting cups of the famous waters of the Baths.

At least two hundred other concertgoers were packed into the space, but the resulting din only worked in their favor. Anyone wishing to overhear their conversation would have to be right on top of them. As it was, she and May had their heads together like the gossipers they were, assuming it was possible to gossip about oneself.

"Yes. Well, no." Sophie paused, pursing her lips. "Actually, it was somewhat of a good thing, liberally flavored with a healthy dose of humiliation and insult and, in the end, more or less worth the suffering." She took another sip of her drink, wrinkled her nose at the warm, bitter flavor, and quickly took a bite of her shortbread biscuit.

"In what way, exactly?" May asked, waving away a server who would have taken her nearly empty glass.

"Well, it secured me an invitation to join them for the operatic performance. Considering that he barely knew I existed four days ago, I count that as a success." Step One and a Half—having a conversation with the earl—may have come about in an unforeseen manner, but it *had* come about. Clearly Step Two—having him fall madly in love with her—was practically at hand. She gave a mental roll of her eyes at that particular thought.

Beside her, May flipped open her fan with a practiced hand and put it to use. Despite the pleasant evening outside, the room seemed to be getting warmer by the minute. The wisps of pale hair at her temples stirred in the manufactured breeze as she lifted an eyebrow. "Yes, but the real question is whether or not you wish to pursue the man at all."

"I did give quite a bit of thought to that," Sophie admitted. "But it speaks well of him that he would put so much effort into setting things right. I can't imagine my father ever doing so. Or my mother. Or most people, for that matter."

May dipped her head in a sort of doubtful agreement. "I suppose so. But wouldn't it be lovely if men weren't quite so adept at the art of putting one's foot in one's mouth?"

"Yes, quite." Sighing, Sophie finished off the rest of the biscuit, savoring the buttery sweetness. The earl's willingness to apologize wasn't all of it, of course. The truth remained that the very sight of him still made her stomach drop to her toes. The sound of his voice sent chills whispering down her neck, and the feel of his skin against hers was enough to make her weak in the knees. Truly, everything about him seemed custom made to send her heart racing.

The good news was, after he had chased her down on Camden Road, she had found it somewhat easier to form a complete sentence in his presence. That was progress, wasn't it?

"So what is your plan?" May asked, interrupting Sophie's wandering thoughts. "For your outing with him tomorrow, I mean."

"Do you mean, how do I make him fall deeply and irrevocably in love with me?" She winked, and May chuckled, amusement lighting up her blue eyes. They were a darker blue than Evan's, but still quite striking in the candlelight. "I'm working on that part. Perhaps you could lend me your captivating good looks for the evening? Or your confidence—that would work, too."

May rolled her eyes, clearly not impressed with Sophie's humor. "Very funny, but you are perfect exactly as you are. Besides, I think we need a plan that is a little more practical than that." She sounded as though she had something in mind.

"What sort of plan?"

"The kind that involves your dear friend May monopolizing dear sister Julia's attention, so that you may steal off with the earl and woo him properly. Perhaps you can show him how nicely your ankle is healing."

"May!" Sophie exclaimed, laughing at another of her outrageous suggestions.

"What? A little flash of leg has helped many a lovesick woman's cause, I imagine."

Shaking her head, Sophie said ruefully, "Perhaps if one has their heart set on becoming a mistress. I want to be his wife." She belatedly glanced around, making sure no one could overhear their conversation.

"I imagine it works for both. The difference is, a mistress lets him have what he wants, while a wife keeps him breathless for more."

Sophie covered her mouth, attempting to stifle her laughter. "You shall surely be the death of my innocent soul, Mei-li Bradford. It's little wonder your aunt wishes to keep her thumb on you."

"Oh, please. I can see for myself you like being scandalized," she replied, grinning wickedly.

"Did I hear someone say 'scandal'?"

Gasping, Sophie whirled to find Mr. Thomas Wright—a *vicar*, of all things—lifting a devilish blond brow as he approached. She had met him only in passing, but from what she knew of him, he was an easy, amicable fellow. Sophie started to respond, but May beat her to it.

"Hard to say. Were you eavesdropping?"

He put a hand to his heart, the very picture of innocence. "'Pon rep, I was not. There isn't an eave in sight," he added with a wink. "I do have remarkably good hearing, however, particularly when there is something involving two beautiful ladies and scandal."

May's fan paused as she gave him an arch look. "Does that come in handy when you are in the midst of your flock, kind vicar?"

"Not nearly as much as when I'm away from it."

May's laugh was clear and luminescent, rising above the buzz of the crowd. Several people turned to stare, including Lord Wexley. Sophie bit her lip at the censure she glimpsed in the viscount's eyes, but May didn't pay the least mind. "You, Mr. Wright, are clearly a devil in vicar's clothing."

"No, simply a *man* in vicar's clothing." He waggled his eyebrows, plainly teasing. "Now, to the true reason for my visit. I hear tell that you lovely ladies are two-thirds of a rather magnificent trio that I had the dreadful misfortune of missing."

Sophie grinned. "Well, if that is what you heard, then who are we to argue? And as a matter of fact, our trio shall be made whole again in a few days when Miss Effington returns."

"So I heard. Which is why I come to you, hat figuratively in hand, to beg you to lend your considerable talents to a small party I am hosting on Monday, before my father arrives and leaches all the fun from the place. Terribly short notice, I know, which is why I thought it prudent to remind you that we are practically family."

Both May's eyebrows shot up. "Family? How on earth do you figure?"

"Well, your Miss Effington shall shortly be my sister-in-law . . . in-law. Once removed." He rolled his fingers dismissively. "Something like that, anyhow."

Sophie couldn't help but chuckle. "Your logic sounds remarkably like my own. In a word: convoluted. However, I am never so happy as when I am performing with my fellow trio members, so I for one would be delighted to play. May?"

"Oh, I wouldn't miss it. Assuming Charity is in agreement, you may count us in, Mr. Wright. Heaven knows my aunt would never have me turn down an invitation issued directly from one of God's servants."

"Excellent," he replied, clapping his hands together in a prayerful position. "God bless, and all that." With a final bow, he turned and disappeared back into the crowd.

At that moment, the master of ceremonies stepped onto the conductor's podium and announced that the program would resume in five minutes. Sophie sighed and turned to May. "I suppose we should go back to our seats," she said, wishing they could spend the rest of the night planning a way to win the earl's heart.

May nodded as she snapped her fan closed, letting it dangle from the ribbon tied to her wrist. "What can I do to ensure that things go well tomorrow night?"

Shaking her head, Sophie said, "Illicit leg flashing aside, I do like your suggestion of monopolizing Lady Julia. Do you think you can talk Warden Stanwix into allowing you to attend the performance tomorrow?"

May gave a delicate little snort. "Don't worry about my aunt; I'll think of something. Anything I should know about Lady Julia, other than her sharp tongue?"

Sophie thought for a second. "She is a harp player. Also, she never had a London Season. Or *any* Season, as far as I can tell. She's spent the majority of her life at home in Ledbury, so this is all quite new to her."

"Sounds very much like a woman I can relate to," May replied with a wry shake of her head.

"Indeed. Let us hope you have better luck with her than I did." As for Lord Evansleigh . . . well, if things didn't go well tomorrow, there would be no hope of achieving Step Two. Therefore, Sophie intended to put everything she had into capturing Evan's interest. If that meant breaking a few rules of propriety, well, as Mama was wont to say, the ends absolutely justified the means.

Evan had one objective for the evening: to not wound, insult, aggrieve, or otherwise cause harm to poor Miss Wembley. One would think this would be an easy enough task, but their past encounters had disproven that theory.

He glanced at his sister, who was watching the city passing by as their open-topped landau wended its way down Camden Road. Much to his relief, she had been even-tempered since Miss Wembley's departure, but still . . . "Be nice," he admonished, admittedly out of nowhere from her perspective.

Startled, she cut her gaze to him, her lips twisting in a grimace. "Pot, I see you've met Kettle," she said, mimicking an introduction.

Touché. Still, he didn't relent. "You know what I mean. I intend to be on my best behavior tonight, and I expect the same from you."

"You needn't lecture me. I apologized, and I meant it." She shrugged, fingering the tassels of her little beaded reticule. "I rather think I might actually like the girl."

"Well, that is a relief," Evan replied, sarcasm tinting his words.

"I'm serious. I'm impressed with how well she handled things yesterday. If I had been in her shoes, I don't know if I would have reacted half so well."

Evan nodded, but held his tongue. He agreed with her completely on that. Miss Wembley had shown real grace, and that was something to be admired. It was one thing to accept an apology; it was another to honestly forgive. He was quite looking forward to the performance tonight, but that aside, he was pleased that she'd agreed to join them. After spending the past decade floating among the *ton* but never really engaging, it was almost a relief to allow himself to actually be honest with someone. Not that he was in the habit of lying to others, but most of his friendships leaned toward the superficial. It was a means of self-preservation for him, just as isolation was for Julia.

In fact, he'd been much more frank with Miss Wembley than he'd intended yesterday. He had revealed more of himself and of his past to her than he had to anyone in recent memory. Why was that? Was it the inherent sweetness he sensed in her? Those big, innocent-looking eyes that really seemed to see him when he talked to her? Or perhaps it was the fact that, however unintentionally it had come about, she already knew that he was not interested in anything other than friendship. That alone took the pressure off his shoulders.

The carriage slowed as they turned down Miss Wembley's street. Every house looked exactly like its neighbors, each sporting a white door, warm-toned limestone block, and tall, shutterless windows. Even though he'd been to her house, he couldn't have said which one it was to save his life.

Moments later they glided to a stop. Before he could step down, the nearest door opened and Miss Wembley stepped out. As usual, she looked like a ray of sunshine, swathed in a becoming yellow gown and sporting a jaunty beribboned bonnet that tied beneath her chin with a floppy bow. She wasn't a conventional beauty, not by a long shot, but something about her made him smile.

"Good afternoon, Miss Wembley," he said, quickly disembarking and offering a small bow. "You are looking very well today." He paused, surprised when she pulled the door closed behind her. "Will not your mother join us?"

She bobbed a curtsy before shaking her head. "Good day, my lord. I'm sorry to say she has a bit of a headache this afternoon, and wishes to stay abed. Since we are not in London and the event is part of the festival, she felt Lady Julia's presence should be adequate for propriety's sake."

"Really?" he said before he could think better of it. Honestly, Mrs. Wembley didn't seem the sort to pass up the opportunity to join them. He would have guessed she'd jump at the chance to try to push her daughter on a supposedly eligible nobleman. It wasn't a particularly kind thought, but he'd wager it was accurate enough.

Miss Wembley's cheeks reddened as she offered a dimpled smile. "Indeed. Provided the carriage remains open, of course. A happy coincidence that the top is already down; I should hate to cause any delay in our departure. Oh, and lovely to see you, Lady Julia. Thank you so much for inviting me."

His sister gave a little wave from where she sat. "Good day, Miss Wembley. I'm very much looking forward to our afternoon together."

Evan relaxed. At least they were off to a civilized start. Stopping beside the landau's step, he held out his hand to Miss Wembley. "May I?"

She nodded and slipped her fingers onto his palm. "Thank you," she murmured, the words nearly lost in the sounds of the traffic passing by. As she stepped up, the horses shifted, moving the landau just enough to upset her balance. She gripped his hand tightly as she lurched backward, and he automatically steadied her by placing his other hand at her waist.

At least he'd intended it to be her waist.

All at once he realized that, thanks to her elevated position, his hand had landed at her hip instead, just below her stays. She was soft and pliant beneath his fingers, curving in exactly the right way. *Christ.*

As soon as she steadied herself, he snatched his hand away, not wanting to shock her. God above, he knew she had a lovely, voluptuous figure, but seeing vague outlines and actually touching the woman were two *very* different things. She was sweet and innocent, and very much off-limits—something he had never thought he would have to remind himself of. Clearing his throat, he said, "Steady there. Are you all right?"

Stepping up the rest of the way, she nodded. "Quite. Thank you." He tactfully ignored her flaming cheeks.

As soon as they were settled, they set off for the Assembly Rooms, where the duet was to be held. As the ladies chatted, Evan sat back against the cushions, attempting to drag his mind away from the place it had no right going—namely, Miss Wembley's person.

It didn't help that she looked as fresh and sweet as a sunflower, with her cheeks still rosy and her brown eyes alight as she spoke. He'd always thought of her as having a pleasant enough countenance, but today, with the sun shining down on her and the dark curls around her face dancing in the wind, she looked charming. Beautiful even.

Not that it mattered. He hoped she would be a good companion for Julia, and a pleasant friend for him—nothing more.

He blinked, suddenly realizing where his gaze had fallen, and forced his eyes away from the sight of her breasts jostling as the carriage rumbled over the cobblestones. Not as easy a task as it should have been. As if manhandling her hadn't been enough distraction, now the road surface was conspiring against him. Swallowing, he tried to recall what he'd been thinking before his eyes and intentions had wandered. Oh yes—Miss Wembley was to be a *friend*. He just needed to remember that.

Chapter Nine

Sophie could still feel the heat of his hand at her hip. Ridiculous, given the layers of fabric between their skin, but nonetheless, the spot that he'd touched fairly tingled with awareness. No man had ever touched her there before. Her arms, her back, her waist, and even her foot once when dancing with a particularly unskilled partner, but never her hip.

As Lady Julia spoke of her excitement for finally being able to attend a performance by world-class opera singers, Sophie could do little but grin and nod, all the while watching Evan in her peripheral vision. He'd worn a pale blue jacket today, surely knowing how well it complemented his eyes. His hair was tied back with a simple black ribbon, but the wind blew a few mahogany strands across his cheeks and forehead. It looked as fine as corn silk, and she tightly laced her fingers in her lap in order to ward off the temptation to smooth it back from his face.

Not that she could ever imagine doing something so bold, but she knew from experience that she could not trust herself to behave in her usual fashion around him. By the time they reached the Assembly Rooms and made their way inside, she actually breathed a sigh of relief. Yes, she needed to find a way to flirt with him, to be teasing and coy and whatever else young women were supposed to do to land a husband, but first she had to find the wits that he had so thoroughly scattered the moment he'd laid his hand on her.

To her immense relief, May stood by the entry, waiting as her aunt attempted to navigate the steps of their carriage in one of her ridiculously outdated gowns. For some unknown reason, the woman insisted on wearing the much more restrictive and voluminous fashions of her youth. The contrast was striking when compared to May's simple blush gown with white lotus flower embroidery stitched along the hem.

"May," Sophie exclaimed, feigning surprise, "what a happy coincidence! Are you here for the dueling prima donnas as well?"

Her friend nodded before muttering under her breath, "And so is the dragon, unfortunately." Smiling, she said more loudly, "We are indeed. Shockingly enough, I've never attended an opera."

Sophie gestured to Evan's sister as she stepped down to the pavement. "I must introduce you to Lady Julia. She is also new to the experience."

May played her part beautifully, exclaiming over the opportunity to attend the performance with another opera newcomer. She even managed to reposition their little party so Sophie was beside Evan, bless her. With Lady Stanwix in the lead, May and Lady Julia in the middle, and Sophie and Evan trailing behind, they entered the Ballroom.

Despite it being midafternoon, the space was dark, thanks to the series of blinds lining the windows, each painted with classical figures and vases. The chandeliers remained unlit, with only the wall sconces providing illumination for them to find a place to sit. It was surprisingly atmospheric, considering the bright sunshine they had just left. The chairs were arranged in a different configuration than usual, all facing the entrance to the Great Octagon located in the center of the building.

"They must be planning to sing from the musicians' gallery," Sophie said, nodding to the wide alcove with its great arching ceiling perched above the door. Huge swags of flowered garlands were draped from the railing, and several candles flickered from the matching candelabra that bracketed the center section.

Lady Stanwix paused, her mouth turned down in a forbidding frown. "Terrible planning on their part. Do they wish for us all to strain our necks, gauping like peasants from below?" She sniffed, lifting her chin in a way that made Sophie bite her lip to keep from grinning. It seemed as though Lady Stanwix had plenty of experience with her nose in the air. Shaking her head, the older woman sighed. "I suppose we shall have to relegate ourselves to the last row. It will require the least offensive angle for viewing, I imagine." She lifted her skirts an inch and swept down the center aisle, leaving them to follow.

Sophie met Evan's amused gaze. "Will the back row suffice for your sensibilities as well?"

"I suppose it shall have to do," he replied with mock gravity.

May's aunt claimed the aisle seat, and May and Lady Julia filed in next, then Sophie, and Evan on Sophie's right. Sophie allowed herself a little smile. Lady Stanwix's presence may not have been ideal, but sitting in the back row would allow them as much privacy as one could hope for in a crowded hall.

Not wanting to waste even a moment in his presence,

Sophie turned to him and smiled. "It was good of you to accompany us today. I know that it was your sister's idea, but I do hope you enjoy it." It was a little awkward trying to talk without allowing her knees to angle too closely to his. Not that she wouldn't delight in such a thing, but she didn't intend to give him any reason to move away from her.

"Not at all," he said. He, too, seemed to be completely earnest. "I have a tremendous appreciation for opera. If my lot in life had been different, I'd like to think I would have given the stage a go."

"No!" Sophie gaped at him, amazed by the confession. "I had no idea. Are you a very good singer, then?"

Fabric rustled as Lady Julia leaned forward, joining the conversation. "He is. You should hear him when he sings Mozart's *Idomeneo*. I'm eager to hear the prima donnas here today, mainly because I cannot imagine that they are any better than he is."

"*Idomeneo*?" Sophie repeated, looking to Evan with new appreciation. "In English or Italian?"

He pretended to be insulted. "Italian, of course. One does not adulterate a work of art. It would be blasphemy."

"Quite," she replied, at a loss for anything else to say. She was too busy imagining what it would be like to hear him sing—or better yet, speak—in Italian. A more romantic language, she could not imagine.

May asked Lady Julia a question then, and the two resumed their conversation. Oh, right—Sophie was here on a mission. Turning more fully toward Evan, she asked, "Do you speak the language, or only sing it?"

He relaxed a bit in his seat, obviously enjoying the topic. "I have studied several operas, so that I could know what the songs mean and understand the emotions behind them. I've gotten quite good at understanding it, but when it comes to speaking as opposed to singing, I am disappointingly unilingual."

"Well, I can't even sing another language, so you're leaps and bounds ahead of me," she replied with a light-hearted roll of her eyes. "I must admit I'm envious. It would be lovely to understand what they are all so passionate about when they're singing. For all I know, they could be lamenting the temperature of the soup at supper."

He chuckled, lifting his shoulders. "It's possible. I do so hate when my curry soup arrives cold."

"Exactly," she said, nodding sagely. "Alas, I gave my poor governess fits in her attempts to teach me foreign languages. It was all gibberish to me. I'll stick to music as my second language, thank you."

He tilted his head, the corners of his lips turning up. "Do you know, I've never thought of it that way. Music as a second language, I mean. It certainly does speak to us on a different level."

"Yes, that's the perfect way to put it. The spoken word appeals to the mind, but music appeals to the heart, or perhaps even the soul. It elicits emotion much more effectively, since you don't have to find the right words in order to express how you feel."

He nodded, a hint of surprise registering in his eyes. "Yes, I feel that way exactly. If not for the music, I doubt I would ever attend an event during the Season."

She basked in the shared connection, grateful that she had been able to speak so normally to him. She felt like herself for once. "I wouldn't have a choice," she said with a teasing grin. "Mama would never allow me to miss the opportunity to snare a husband."

She very nearly slapped her hand over her mouth.

She was *too* much like herself, apparently. How could she have said such a thing—to the very man she was attempting to snare! But even as heat washed over her in a rushing wave, another, much more distressing thought occurred to her: There would be no more Seasons.

Thanks to her sister Penelope, the family name would soon be dust in the eyes of the *ton*. They had never been of the highest status, and they were certainly not wealthy, but Papa was the youngest son of a viscount, which afforded them entry into the upper ten thousand elite of England. She so loved the energy of the Season, all the wonderful excitement and the whirl of activities. So much to do, so much to see, so much to whisper and sigh about late into the night with her sisters.

A weight settled in her stomach like a stone. This conversation suddenly seemed too heavy for words. She didn't want to think about the fact that her future could rest on how well she entertained the earl. She only wanted to enjoy him.

Oblivious to her dark turn of thought, he chuckled. "You poor thing," he said commiseratively. "Thank goodness you are free of that here. Nothing to do but enjoy the festival."

She nodded, averting her eyes as she fussed with her fan. Hadn't that been her hope? To finally have a venue where she could toss aside the pursuit of a husband and simply revel in the joy of music, her very favorite thing? The anger toward her sister, and all that she had stolen from Sophie and the rest of her family, burned a little brighter. Penelope had always been so strong-willed, so very determined to have her way no matter the cost. But none of them had imagined that she would so callously sacrifice her sisters' hopes in favor of her own desires.

With quite possibly the best timing she could have

hoped for, the master of ceremonies appeared on the balcony and introduced the two sopranos. *Thank goodness.*

Sophie pretended to be absorbed in the proceedings, looking steadfastly ahead. The stone in her abdomen seemed only to grow heavier, making it harder to breathe. May had been wrong. Perhaps *she* was skilled enough to land a husband in a matter of weeks, but Sophie was not. She was far too open, entirely too gauche.

She drew a long, quiet breath, trying to rein in her growing emotions. When the orchestra began to play, Sophie closed her eyes and tried to lose herself in the music. The prima donnas joined in a few moments later, singing words that were entirely foreign, but filled with such polished beauty and overt passion, it was easy to get lost in their voices. The purity of tone was otherworldly, filling the cavernous hall all the way to the ceiling with an almost heavenly sound. When the notes were dolce, they were little more than a caress; when they were forte, it was enough to cleanse the bitter thoughts from Sophie's mind, if only for a moment.

"It's meant to be humorous."

She blinked, startled at the sound of Evan's whispered voice close to her shoulder.

Swallowing, she looked to her right, meeting his concerned gaze. "It is?" It was only then that she felt the tears dampening her cheeks. She quickly dashed them away as discreetly as she could manage. She didn't want to disturb Lady Julia or the others.

He nodded. "They are plotting to expose the countess's husband's infidelity."

His voice was low and smooth, barely rising above the song. She licked her lips, averting her gaze back to the performers as she listened to the way they sang. "What are they saying?"

"The countess, the one on the right, is dictating a letter for her maid, who has been propositioned by the count." He paused for a moment, listening.

Questa sera spirerà . . . "This evening will sigh . . ." *Sotto i pini del boschetto* . . . "under the pines in the little grove."

Sophie sat utterly still, listening to the low murmur of his voice so near her ear. She could feel the warm hints of his breath caress her shoulder and smell the delectable scent of his shaving soap. Of *him*.

"And the rest he'll understand."

Her brow knitted as she tried to work out what the last bit was supposed to mean. He chuckled softly, stirring the fine hairs at the nape of her neck and making her shiver. "She means that he'll understand that the maid is asking for an assignation."

Her mouth dropped open. Did he just say *assignation* to her? Of its own volition, her mind conjured the image of a dark grove of trees on a warm summer night, the breeze carrying with it the sighs of lovers. *Good heavens*.

Without even meaning to, she leaned the slightest bit toward him. He looked at her expectantly, so she said, "And this is to be humorous?"

He shrugged, the rustle of his jacket nearly lost in the sound of the orchestra. "No accounting for humor when it comes to the Italians."

The duet ended, and the audience applauded politely. The orchestra moved on to the next piece, which started with a long instrumental prelude.

Sophie swallowed, unwilling to lose the intimacy of the moment. Stupid thoughts of wooing the man aside, she craved his company. The stone in her stomach had lightened considerably, and she wanted more of the delicious feelings he caused when he was so near. Turning her head a few inches in Evan's direction, she whispered, "I should have known that the last one was meant to be lighthearted."

He subtly shifted so their shoulders were only inches apart. "Why is that?"

"Because of the oboe. Played in the higher ranges, it is impossible to be dour."

His smile was easy, just a smooth lift of one side of his mouth. "Ah. Well, you should know."

"Indeed. Of all the instruments in an orchestra, it's the least likely to take itself seriously."

"Is that why you play it?"

She angled her head, not sure what he meant.

"Because it is small and lighthearted, just like you?"

She almost laughed out loud at that. "I play it because my mother decreed that I would. It took a few years, but I quite like it now." Still, she couldn't help but wonder if he had meant the statement as a compliment or an observation. It rather sounded like the former.

Nodding, he shifted back in his chair a bit, watching the prima donnas with interest. Was that all the stolen conversation they were to have? Her hopes sagging, she exhaled, allowing her shoulders to drop a bit.

"Now this is quite interesting."

She pressed her eyes closed for a moment, relieved to hear his whispered words. "Yes?"

He leaned in close again. "The characters are Poppea and Nerone. Yes, it's written for two sopranos, but Nerone is a man. This is a love song."

"Truly?" She closed her eyes again and listened to the way the music was sung. High and light, their voices twined like ribbons of silk in a soft summer wind, lifting and falling, curling and twisting, harmonizing in a way that made the heart leap.

"I gaze at you."

Her eyes popped open, startled by his words. She darted a glance at him, but his attention was on the singers.

"Possess you," he continued, whispering the words between the lines of the opera singers. "Press you to me. Embrace you."

Her breath caught in her throat. The intimacy of the words was like a lover's touch. Her heart pounded as she leaned toward him, soaking up the sound of his voice.

"No more pain. No more death." He wet his lips, his gaze still directed straight ahead but his body angled toward hers. "O, my life, my darling."

My darling. She sighed, pressing a hand to her heart. Oh to hear those words from his lips for real. To know that he spoke to her, and her alone. She realized with a start that his gaze had shifted to her face, and she gave a shaky little smile. "Beautiful," she breathed, the word tight in her throat.

For some reason, Evan's blood hummed a little faster through his veins. *She* was beautiful. He loved the way she responded to the music with her whole body, her shoulders lifting as the singers' voices rose, and falling as the song grew quiet.

He was suddenly very, very glad that he had studied opera, even more thoroughly than he had admitted to her. It was one of the few things in his life that he possessed true passion for. He wanted to know everything about the songs that tore at his heart and lifted his soul. Most people would likely consider his reaction to opera a little ridiculous, but he knew with absolute certainty that Miss Wembley—*Sophie*—would not.

She didn't just hear the emotion of the music, she felt it and internalized it. He smiled, thinking of her tears of moments ago. Misplaced for that particular song, but endearing nonetheless.

He loved the way she had listened to him, soaking up his translations as dry soil absorbs the rain. "You make me want to learn more Italian," he murmured, offering her a small private smile.

"You make me want to listen to more opera," she replied, her dimples creasing her pale cheeks.

You make me want to spend more time with you. He pressed his lips together, surprised by the errant thought. Not something he would normally think, even of a friend. Still, when an idea occurred to him, he didn't hesitate to share it. Leaning forward, he said, "Then join me for Rossini's *La Cenerentola*. Rossini himself will be here, and it's one of the last events of the festival, but well worth the wait."

Her smile fell a little and she glanced to her lap before meeting his eyes again. "I'd love that," she said softly, her voice oddly thin. "*The Barber of Seville* is one of my favorites, in fact. I'm just not sure if we will still be here."

He was surprised by the force of his disappointment. It trickled down through his chest like a spilled glass of red wine, staining his enthusiasm. "Would it help if you had a note from an earl and his sister, begging your mother's indulgence?" It was as close as he could come to pointing out her mother's matchmaking tendencies. Tendencies that she obviously knew all about.

"Who is to say you won't be sick of me by then?" Her tone was light, even as her eyes seemed hooded. "Four visits in as many days—it's a wonder you're still speaking to me."

Yes, it was, actually. He realized then that she was supposedly there to be a companion for Julia, but he'd monopolized her attentions almost completely.

Oddly enough, that thought didn't bother him as much as it should have.

"What can I say, Miss Wembley? You're uncommonly good company."

Her smile brightened at that, as did, he'd wager, her cheeks, though it was too dark to tell for sure. He really quite liked making those dimples appear.

"Thank you, my lord. The feeling is mutual."

Chapter Ten

"What in the world were the two of you whispering about yesterday?"

Sophie had to give May credit. She had waited precisely three seconds after the maid left them before turning on Sophie and blurting out the question. It was only a few minutes past noon, which meant her friend must have departed her aunt's house the very moment her aunt deemed it acceptable to go calling.

Sophie didn't even try to contain the enormous smile that came to her lips. "First, let me just say thank you for—"

"Yes, of course, you're quite welcome," May interrupted, waving a dismissive hand. "Now, please, my dear little magpie, don't keep me waiting." She raised both eyebrows, clearly anxious to discover how things had gone between Sophie and Evan.

Oddly enough, for perhaps the first time in her life, Sophie didn't want to share every detail of their incredible evening. It had felt . . . special. Intimate. Private. For her, that was really saying something.

Giving a little shrug, she made her way to the sofa and sat. "He's quite knowledgeable about operas, and he was telling me what each song was about." Warm tendrils of delight shimmied down her spine at the mere thought of his lips so close to her ear, his breath fanning across her neck. If, miraculously, they ever did end up as man and wife, she would do everything in her power to encourage him to learn to be fluent in Italian. If she melted at the sound of his voice *translating* the language, she would positively ignite were he ever actually to speak it.

Her friend settled into the chair directly adjacent to her. "Well, it must have been quite a lecture. I could see your blush even in the dark."

Sophie cringed. "Oh, please don't say that. Did Lady Stanwix see? Actually, I can't imagine she did, or she surely would have raised the devil over it. But what about Lady Julia?" They were only just becoming friends. Sophie didn't wish to upset her.

"I don't believe so. She was quite rapt in the performance. I, however, was terribly keen to know how my dear friend was doing." She offered Sophie a sly grin. "I must say, I think you accomplished what you set out to do."

Sophie perked up at this, leaning forward. "Really? And what makes you say that?"

"It was difficult to see Lord Evansleigh past your profile, but I did manage to catch a glimpse right before the last song."

"And?" She held her breath, wanting to know exactly what May had seen.

"Perhaps there are wedding bells in the very near future."

She gasped, a flash of hope igniting like a firework in her chest. Before she could say a word, however, a chuckle at the door made them both whip around. Charity Effington stood with her arms at her hips, a huge grin on her lips. "Are we speaking of my wedding, or is there something else I should know?"

The third member of their trio may have been gone only a fortnight, but with all that had happened, it had seemed an eternity. After much hugging and laughing and exclaiming over Charity's gorgeous ruby ring—"To match my blushes," she had explained with a grin—they all sat down together to catch up. For the next hour, they pored over all the little details May and Sophie had been dying to know about the events surrounding Charity's betrothal.

Sighing dreamily, Sophie leaned back against the cushions, not caring in the least about her posture. "How wonderfully, wonderfully romantic. I can hardly believe it—I would have never thought Lord Cad had it in him," she said with a teasing wink.

"Nor I," replied May, reaching for a cucumber sandwich from the tray they had ordered half an hour earlier. "When he came to speak with me, you could have felled me with a feather."

Charity grinned, her freckled skin fairly glowing with joy. "Well, he certainly managed to surprise me. And speaking of surprises . . ." Charity tossed a pillow squarely in Sophie's lap. "What is this I hear about wedding bells? Has someone actually managed to be worthy of our sweet Sophie?"

No one was more surprised than Sophie when tears filled her eyes. Charity sent an alarmed look at May before scooting over to wrap an arm around Sophie. "Good heavens, whatever has happened? Has someone hurt you? Compromised you?"

Sophie gave a helpless little laugh. "I wish," she said, accepting a dainty lace handkerchief from May and blowing her nose. "It would make things a lot easier if I could simply trap him into marrying me."

Charity cast a bewildered look at May before meeting Sophie's eyes. "Has someone broken your heart?"

Sophie hadn't thought of it that way, but that was exactly what had happened. Nodding, she sighed. "Only my sister." She told the story all over again, from start to finish, leaving out only the contents of the conversation she had shared with Evan.

At the end of it, Charity sat back, her lips pursed in thought. "Perhaps Hugh and I can help. You know that he is not one for parties, but what if we were to host an outing? A picnic, perhaps, or a night of charades? Something intimate that will have fewer distractions than the festival events."

May gave a little snort of laughter. "I can sooner imagine Lord Cadgwith engaging in knitting than a rousing game of charades."

"No, truly," Charity said, though she laughed at the quip. She turned to Sophie, excitement lighting her gray eyes. "A small group at my grandmother's townhouse for a few games might be perfect. A limited number of people, a hard-of-hearing, indulgent chaperone, and at least three of your fellow partygoers with a vested interest in throwing you and Lord Evansleigh together. What could be more perfect?"

Sophie bit her bottom lip, considering the idea. "Yes, but we would need at least one or two married couples, and I can't think of anyone in town who I'd want to have around for something like that." She sighed, shaking her head. "Where is Beatrice when she is needed?"

Charity laughed. "In Scotland with her very handsome Scotsman, last I heard."

May raised a brow. "A friend of yours?"

"Indeed," Sophie said, smiling wistfully. "She married this past winter and is blissfully happy. If I wasn't such a romantic myself, I might be inclined to roll my eyes at her gushing letters. Oh, and Sir Colin is only half-Scottish, Charity, but I believe you are correct that they are spending the summer at his estate outside of Edinburgh. She's probably covered in paints as we speak, capturing the majestic Highlands landscape on canvas."

"Her own personal heaven, to be sure." Charity grinned, then sighed and shook her head. "I suppose you are right about the party. There must be something else that will work."

May sat up suddenly, her face lighting. "The gala! Aunt Victoria was talking about it just the other morning. It's at Sydney Gardens, the Vauxhall of Bath, whatever that means. Believe it or not, she's actually looking forward to attending. Apparently her husband professed his love in the grotto during the fireworks one year, and she hasn't missed a gala since."

Sophie had forgotten all about the gala night at the pleasure gardens. She tapped her fingers on her chin in contemplation. "There will be thousands of people there, but that may work in our favor. And with it being night-time, I might be able to find a darkened corner or two."

"Doesn't it have a labyrinth?" Charity asked, a slow smile growing on her lips. "All sorts of nooks and crannies that one could get lost in." She waggled her eyebrows, a move so unlike her that the other two burst out laughing.

"The thing is," Sophie said when she could breathe again, "that's all well and good, but how do I make certain he attends?"

"Let me talk to Hugh. He may have some ideas on how to approach him. They're around the same age, so they may even already know each other, which will help."

"And you think the baron will go along with helping me? Isn't there some sort of code against a gentleman helping to ensnare a fellow man for the purpose of marriage?"

"Don't worry. I have every confidence I can find a way to convince him." Charity's cheeks bloomed nearly as red as her hair.

Sophie exchanged an amused look with May. One couldn't help but wonder just what sort of convincing Charity had in mind. "Very well, if you think it will help, by all means speak with him. I will keep pondering it in the meantime. Now, I think it's time we set aside my predicament and do something fun. Would anyone like to practice? We could relocate to May's house."

"Oh yes," said May, brushing the crumbs from her skirt and standing. "We have another performance coming up, after all."

"We do?" Charity said, her copper eyebrows lifting in surprise.

May grinned. "Indeed. What good is a trio if not for performing?"

Sighing with great exaggeration, Charity shook her head. "Remind me not to leave you two alone again."

"On the off chance that you are unaware, let it be known that you are simultaneously the best and the worst brother in all of England."

Evan set down his quill and lifted an eyebrow at his sister. She was in a surprisingly good mood this morning. "I'm aware."

Julia grinned, her hazel eyes flashing in the late-morning sunshine as she let herself into his study. "Good.

I can't believe you made all this out to be so tiresome all these years. The performance last night, and the company of those attending, was quite wonderful."

The ancient leather of his chair creaked as Evan leaned back from the desk and crossed his arms, unsure what to make of her happiness, but more than willing to go along with it. Perhaps her time here with him and the friends they had made was succeeding in lifting the weight that had been draped across her shoulders since she had arrived.

"Come now, I didn't keep you from anything. First of all, Bath is a world away from London, I assure you. One is permitted to actually enjoy the entertainments here — unthinkable in our jaded capital." It grated on his nerves that so many took pride in coming up with the drollest, most cleverly snide comments about any given event. Pretending boredom was practically the national pastime.

She waved away his defense with an airy flip of her hand. "Yes, you've said much about the jaded members of the *ton*. So far, the ones I've met have been nothing but pleasant, with the possible exception of you," she added with a teasing lift of her brow.

He thought of Sophie, and the immensely charming personality that she seemed to be revealing bit by bit. "Miss Wembley is hardly representative of the beau monde. In fact, I believe she is the least *ton*ish *ton* I have ever met." Her mother, on the other hand . . .

"Miss Wembley, Miss Bradford, Lord Derington," Julia said, counting off the names with her fingers, "even Mr. Wright, though I'm not quite certain if he qualifies as a member of the upper crust, vicar that he is."

Evan stood and stretched, attempting to shake off the stress of spending the last hour bent over the estate's books. God's teeth, did he hate mathematics. He'd rather do just about anything else, but he made a point of raking over the books every month, without fail.

"His father is an earl, so, yes," Evan answered absently. Leaning a hip against the edge of the desk, he said, "Regardless, I am pleased that you are enjoying yourself. I never wanted you to feel isolated or deprived."

Her smile dimmed to something a little more introspective. "Yes, I know. You were right. We made the decision together."

They'd made a lot of decisions that winter, while shuttered in the family's northern estate, their moods as black as their freshly dyed mourning clothes. They'd been young—entirely too young—but through the years their dedication to a pact made between siblings had never wavered.

The months leading to their father's death would be etched in their memories forever, but God willing, nobody else would ever know what they had endured. When his cousin inherited the title, its vast holdings, and the living it provided for so many, he would do so without ever doubting the noble line from which it had descended.

Clapping her hands together, Julia pasted a determined smile on her face. "Now, as we move past your faults, let us give thanks for what makes you my very favorite brother."

"Which is?"

"Your generosity, of course. After all, this is where you tell me to go out and have a nice time shopping, and to spend as much of your money as I choose." She fluttered her eyelashes expectantly, but he knew she was teasing. Julia was always prudent when it came to spending. In fact, she was more or less in charge of running the estate when he was away.

"Ah, that part. Very well, have fun."

She nodded and started to turn, but then paused and looked back at him. "I don't suppose you'd wish to accompany me?"

He crossed his arms. "That depends. Do you wish to murder your only brother with the seemingly innocuous yet thoroughly insidious weapon known as shopping?"

She laughed and shook her head. "No, I suppose not. The prospect of having to deal with Mama on my own is more than enough reason to keep you in good health for as long as possible."

He felt exactly the same way about her. "Well, then, in that case I should definitely remain at home."

Her lips twitched in a wry grin. "Yes, I suppose that's true. All right, I'll leave you to your numbers." She turned back to the door just as Higgins appeared, silver salver in hand.

"Pardon me, my lord. A Sir Harry Culpepper has just dropped round his calling card."

The baronet was here? "He's in town, is he? I had no idea he had plans to attend the festival." The man's father, the recently deceased Sir Robert Culpepper, had purchased the neighboring estate in Ledbury almost two decades earlier, so their families were well acquainted. "Thank you, Higgins. Just leave it on the sideboard." Glancing at Julia, he said, "Did you know he was planning to come?"

She shook her head a couple of times, a series of short, quick movements. "No. I can't imagine why he'd be here," she said, obviously bewildered. "That is to say, he never struck me as a particular music lover."

"No, I don't think he is. Regardless, I'll invite him over

for dinner tonight. Best to dine with friends in a new city." Evan liked the man. At three-and-twenty, he had the sort of young-pup idealism that Evan had been denied, thanks to the old earl's early death.

Her lips thinned for a moment. "Yes, of course. Unfortunately I forgot to tell you that I agreed to dine with Miss Wembley and her mother tonight. Do give Harry my regrets."

"Are you certain? I could make it tomorrow night instead." Though Harry was two years Julia's junior, they had spent a lot of time together growing up.

"Don't be silly. I saw him only a few weeks ago. Plus, I think you are right—dinner with a friendly face may be just the way to begin his first night in a new city."

"It's settled, then. Should I ring Higgins to have the carriage made ready?"

"No, I've already done so."

He nodded. "Very good. Enjoy your day, sister."

She lingered in the doorway for a moment, her fingers resting against the jam. "Evan?"

"Yes?"

"You're the best brother much more often than the worst."

He smiled. "I love you, too."

Chapter Eleven

"Lady Julia! What a lovely surprise." Sophie rushed to greet her unexpected guest, glad that the drawing room was clean and tidy at least, if a little shabby. What in the world would Evan's sister be doing here, out of the blue? She'd mentioned no intention to visit when they had parted after the opera.

Standing amid the slightly outdated furniture, she looked fashionable and lovely in her smart green-and-white afternoon dress. Still, unless Sophie was very mistaken—and she could have been—the woman's eyes held a hint of worry. Tiny wrinkles marred her normally smooth forehead as she offered a small smile. "I hope it is a welcome one. I don't want to impose."

"Yes, of course! You are always welcome. I only just returned from Miss Bradford's, so I hope you will forgive my appearance." As usual, Sophie's curls were a riotous mess, piled on her head and stabbed through with a dozen pins, not that they helped control the unruly strands. She'd yet to change from her morning gown, and she hadn't even put away her oboe.

"You look perfectly respectable to me," Julia replied,

gracefully lowering herself onto the chair Sophie had offered with a wave of her hand.

Sophie lifted a disbelieving eyebrow. "Leave your spectacles at home, did you?"

This time, a bit of the visible strain seemed to lessen as her guest chuckled. "I only need them to read, I assure you."

Sophie laughed at her quick wit. "If you say so, then who am I to argue?" Taking a seat on the sofa, she couldn't help but wonder again what had brought about this visit. As much as they truly seemed to be getting along, Evan's sister didn't seem the type to simply drop in unannounced. Scooting forward a bit on the cushions, Sophie decided to come right out and ask. "Do tell me, my lady: To what do I owe the pleasure of your visit today? Eager to discuss the opera, perhaps?"

"First of all, please do call me Julia. Second of all, I need to beg a favor."

Sophie blinked, taken aback. "A favor?" What on earth did Sophie have to offer the sister of an earl?

"Indeed. I may have told a little white lie to my brother earlier today when he wished for an old family friend to join us for dinner. I like the gentleman well enough, but as far as I'm concerned, I am here to get away from home, not to dine with the same people we do in Ledbury."

"And the lie?" Sophie asked, properly intrigued.

"I told him that I had accepted an invitation to dine with you this evening. Terribly, terribly presumptuous," she rushed to say, "but that should speak to my level of desperation at that moment. Please forgive me. I am not accustomed to having friends, Miss Wembley, and I do hope that I have not overstepped the bounds."

Not accustomed to having friends? What an odd thing to say. Sophie knew that Julia had tended to stay close to home, but that would be all the more reason to have a handful of friends nearby. "Sophie. And you did not overstep a thing. Mama will be delighted to have you join us." She leaned forward conspiratorially. "Truly, you may regret your decision once she has your undivided attention."

Julia closed her eyes briefly, letting out a quiet breath. "Thank you, Sophie. You are a lifesaver."

"One does what one can. Let me go tell my mother about our plans for this evening, and then we can chat."

"Actually, I was also hoping you could play your oboe for me."

Sophie paused, a little surprised. "Truly? Not many people like to hear it by itself."

"I'd love to. You have heard me play my harp, after all. Evan tells me that you are quite a talented musician, and I find I'd like to hear you play without any other distractions. It is, after all, an instrument that is impossible to be dour, no?"

Sophie's eyes widened. "You heard that?" Good heavens, she had thought her conversation with Evan quite private at the time. What else had Julia heard?

Nodding, Julia gave her a commiserative smile. "I know the experience wasn't enthralling for you since you are so accustomed to listening to performances. Don't worry—you didn't bother me in the least. I only caught that bit in a lull in the music."

Disturbing the woman wasn't at all what Sophie was worried about, and she most definitely had not been bored by the performance, but she quickly grasped onto the explanation. "Well, I'm sorry I disturbed you at all. And yes," she said, rushing on, "the oboe is the happiest instrument I know. Some may say the flute is more so, but they are terribly uninformed, and besides, the flute will cause dreadful wrinkles, what with all that puckering." *Stop babbling,* she chided herself. She always chattered when she was nervous, and discovering that Julia had heard even a small portion of Sophie's whispered conversation with Evan was certainly nerve-racking.

"Does one not pucker with the oboe?"

Good—familiar ground. She shook her head with more enthusiasm than was warranted. "No, the lips are squeezed together very firmly to form an airtight seal. The double reed is quite tricky, and it can be a lot of effort to get the sound just right, so we oboists tend to have exceedingly strong lips."

Julia's jaw dropped open for the space of a second before she slapped a gloved hand over her mouth. Even that wasn't enough to stifle her laughter. Her shoulders quaked as she shook her head, her eyes pressed closed. "I'm so sorry," she gasped when she could speak. Her eyes sparkled gaily, an improvement over her hesitancy when she arrived. "That was quite possibly the oddest thing I have ever heard."

Sophie flushed. "Oh, please, you must forgive me. I do tend to say things as they pop in my head. My mother is forever scolding me for not thinking before I open my mouth, and I must agree it happens more often than not." As many times as she had ended up with her foot in her mouth, one would think she would have learned her lesson.

Julia waved away her explanation with a sweep of her hand. "Think nothing of it. I would much rather know what a person is really thinking. As you could probably tell from our first encounter, I don't tend to mince words."

Sophie gave a teasing, overly dramatic cringe. "Yes, I noticed. Which makes it all the more sweet that you would trust me with your secret now. Although, given my propensity to talk, that may not have been the most prudent choice you've ever made."

Laughing, Julia nodded. "I'm realizing that. Even so, I'm glad I came."

"So am I. Though I do hope you feel the same way once you hear me play. The oboe does tend to work best with others."

"Does it? Does that mean that you don't generally play alone?"

"I don't. Until my older sister married last month, my mother insisted we play together, despite the distinct lack of suitable duets for an oboe and bassoon." She shook her head, glad for the end of those concerts. She loved her sister dearly, but Sarah wasn't the most accomplished musician in the world.

"A very interesting combination, I imagine."

"Yes, but not nearly so much as the trio I play with now." A smile came to Sophie's lips just thinking about the spontaneous moment in which they'd assembled their musical group, all for the purpose of besting the ill-tempered festival clerk who thought to thwart them last month. "May—Miss Bradford—plays the Chinese zither, and our friend Miss Effington is an accomplished pianoforte player and composer. Together we could be described either as 'delightfully unique' or 'dreadfully unusual,' depending on how you feel about exotic music."

Julia's expression teetered between intrigued and confused. "I'm finding it quite impossible to imagine those three instruments engaged in anything that would approach harmony."

"I'm not surprised. We ourselves didn't even know before we committed to play at one of the Tuesday night musicales. Thank heavens it all worked out." And even if there had been a different outcome, it still would have been worth it simply to have gained such wonderful friends.

"Are you to play again soon? I should love to have the opportunity to hear for myself. I even promise to use words like *interesting* and *unique* in place of *terrifying* and *bizarre*."

Sophie laughed. "How very thoughtful of you. As a matter of fact, we'll be playing on Monday for Mr. Wright's little soiree. Perhaps I can see if we can convince him to invite you."

"I'd say I wouldn't wish to impose, but in this case I most certainly would. Are you certain you don't mind?"

"Not at all. I don't know the vicar terribly well, but he does seem quite the affable fellow. I doubt he'd balk at the presence of a lady like yourself."

"I've met Mr. Wright, actually. He was great fun to dance with. I've never laughed so much with a man of the cloth in my life."

Sophie bit her lip, a thought occurring to her. "I suppose I should suggest an invitation for your brother as well. To keep the numbers even, of course." Excitement bubbled up within her—how very perfect! She loved the idea of Evan's hearing her play in an ensemble that was actually good. He'd said he'd heard her play, but that was during the Season at one of her duets with Sarah— hardly the most impressive performance.

Julia raised her shoulders. "If you like. I'm sure he would enjoy hearing your trio, and he's already acquainted with Mr. Wright."

"Then it's settled. I'll send the vicar a note first thing in the morning."

Thank heavens—the clock was ticking, and the more time she could spend with the earl, the better chance she had of properly wooing the man. She almost laughed. By the time all was said and done, Evan would either be in love with her . . . or wish never to see her again.

"How was your little get-together?"

Poor Julia jumped half a foot at the sound of Evan's voice. He hadn't meant to startle her, but she must not have seen him as she walked past the library door. At a few minutes after nine, the waning daylight was still bright enough to read by, so Evan had yet to light any candles.

Backing up a few steps, she peered in and smiled. "Lovely. And yours?"

Evan shrugged and set aside his book. "Uneventful but pleasant. Young Harry has grown up to be a fine man. He'll do very well, filling his father's shoes."

His sister shook her head, amusement lifting the corners of her mouth. "You sound like an old man, talking like that. Young Harry, indeed." She padded into the room and sat in one of the leather chairs across from him. Smoothing a hand over her skirts, she asked, "Did he say what brought him to town?"

"He thought to foray into society for the first time as the new baronet in a somewhat less intimidating manner. He knew I was here and thought the festival might be the perfect place to mingle with those of similar interests and station."

"Eager to claim the perks of his new status, I see," she commented, crossing her arms over her chest.

Evan shot her a disproving glance. When they were children, Harry had often gazed at her with lovesick cow eyes. She'd always been short with him, deflecting his interest as best she knew how, but he was a full-grown man now, long past his childhood infatuations. "Now, Julia, don't be cruel. It doesn't suit you. You know that he and his father were close, and Sir Robert's death was very difficult for him."

"You're right—that wasn't fair. So, did he think to use you as a means of easing his way into society's good graces?"

"He'll make his own way, to be sure. With the title and ten thousand a year, the *ton*—and their daughters—will surely welcome him with open arms." With his passable good looks, intelligence, and young age, Harry would practically be catnip for the beau monde. Good for him, as far as Evan was concerned. He'd have his pick when it came to marriage.

She gave a little sniff of disbelief. "He's impulsive and unreliable—hardly the stuff of young ladies' dreams."

"He's still young. In a few years, I'm sure he'll be steady as Old Time. Speaking of impulsive young men," Evan said, remembering the missive that had arrived while Julia was out, "we've an invitation from Mr. Wright to join—"

"His party?" Julia broke in, sitting up straight.

Evan tilted his head. "You know about it?"

"Sophie mentioned it just this evening. She and her trio will be playing, and I did so wish to attend."

Evan chewed the inside of his cheek. He hadn't thought to accept the invitation, but ever since the opera, he'd had a hell of a time getting Sophie off his mind. The idea of hearing her perform was surprisingly enticing. *Almost* as enticing as that unforgettable figure of hers. His mouth went dry at the thought of her warm flesh beneath his fingers.

Not something he wanted to be thinking about with

his sister watching him. He quickly diverted his thoughts back to Sophie's music. He vaguely remembered attending one of her performances in town, but this was something different. He had gotten to know her now. Liked her.

"In that case, I'll respond in the affirmative." He reached for his brandy and took a drink. That still left him with a bit of a problem: He wasn't sure how he felt about Julia being around the vicar again. Evan liked the man, but he was wary of the look he'd seen in Wright's eyes when he had danced with Julia. Jolly fellow, but too forward by half.

"In fact," he said, setting down the glass as inspiration struck, "I believe I'll beg the good vicar's indulgence in allowing Harry to join us."

Julia's gaze snapped up to meet his. "Harry?"

"Yes," he replied, warming to the idea. After all, he had enjoyed a surprisingly pleasant dinner with his neighbor. Harry had been away at school for the last few years, so Evan hadn't had a chance to really talk with him in a long while. Despite what Julia claimed, he was an open, optimistic young man, eager to share his plans for improving his lands over the next few years. His ideas were sound, and Evan had been quite impressed.

Julia wrinkled her nose, obviously not pleased. "Come now, Evan. Surely you wouldn't be so gauche as to invite someone to another man's home."

He sent a warning look in his sister's direction. "First of all, it's not in Wright's home. It's at a park on the river, near some ruins or some such thing. Secondly, yes, I think I am exactly that gauche. One of the perks of being an earl."

Blowing out a breath, she came to her feet. "Fine, do whatever you like. I think I'll retire for the evening."

He rose as well, and stepped forward to offer her a peck on the cheek. "Good night. Tomorrow is Sunday, so no official festival activities will be held. However, after church I'd like to go spend the afternoon exercising poor Wolfgang. I've neglected him terribly this week. Would you like to join me?" She hadn't brought her mare along, but he was certain they could find a proper substitute.

She gave a decisive shake of her head. "No, thank you. I'll probably just catch up on my correspondence. I'm not used to so much activity in a given week."

"Suit yourself," he said, offering a little wave as she turned and headed to her chambers.

It was just as well. Besides the exercise, he wanted the ride to help clear his mind. He was well aware he hadn't been quite his normal self this week. Why? He leaned over and retrieved his brandy, downing the rest of it in one gulp. The image of coffee-colored brown eyes and a dimpled smile flashed through his mind as he rubbed a hand over his face and exhaled.

Why indeed.

Breezing into Sophie's drawing room with a triumphant smile the next day, Charity spread her arms. "I have good news."

"Oh?" Sophie rubbed her hands together, expectant smile in place. "Do tell, my friend. I could use a very large dose of happy news right about now." Even the weather was depressing this morning, with gray skies and drizzly rain. Charity was a dear for coming to call in the first place.

Charity dropped her arms and angled her head in concern. "I don't think I like the sound of that. Have you had a bad day?"

"If you consider being lectured by my mother about

how very dire my situation is, and her not so gentle urgings to be more dedicated to winning the affections of Lord Evansleigh as bad, then, yes, I have had a very bad day." As if Sophie needed any reminder, for heaven's sake. It was her own future at stake. The supremely uncomfortable conversation had taken place at the breakfast table that morning, and had hung over her like a cloud since then.

Charity's eyes widened in disbelief. "*More* dedicated? From what I've heard, you couldn't be more dedicated if you tried."

"*Exactly*. Unless she wishes for me to propose to *him*, I am quite at a loss as to how to proceed any more boldly than I currently am." Other, more scandalous things came to mind, but Sophie could hardly imagine herself grabbing the earl's lapels and pulling him down for a scorching kiss. On second thought—she most definitely *could* imagine it, she just couldn't actually do such a thing. Still, the passionate thought sent a surge of warmth through her veins.

"Well, then, I am doubly glad to be the bearer of good news. Hugh is actually old friends with Lord Evansleigh— school friends, in fact. He says he is happy to help in any way he can, provided we can come up with a way for him to do so."

"How very kind of him to be so willing." Sophie had to admit she was surprised. The baron was not exactly a social person. For him to be willing to aid in Sophie's efforts meant a lot.

"Yes, I told you I could convince him," Charity responded primly, her smile sly.

Sophie bit back a grin. Perhaps it had been more for Charity's sake than Sophie's, but regardless, it was still sweet. "Kudos to your powers of persuasion. Did he have any ideas about the gala?"

"He suggested we bring it up at Thomas's—Mr. Wright's—party. An easy, casual segue made in the company of friends."

"Yes, it would be so much easier if someone like Hugh could bring it up. I am quite nervous of appearing pushy or overly eager."

"Nothing to worry about with us around. What are friends for if not to make times like these bearable?" Coming around to the sofa, Charity settled into the corner and gestured for Sophie to join her. "Speaking of which, I want to know how you are doing."

Sophie gave a short laugh. "I'm surviving, if only just." She shook her head, her smile fading from her lips. "Do you know, I've been in love with him for over a year, yet I've seen him more in one week than I have in my entire two Seasons combined?" It was strange to think that so much emotion could be wrapped up in so little time with him.

Charity nodded, her eyes pensive. "Now that you've doubled your time with him, do you feel the same? Different? Better? Worse?"

"Yes." When Charity smiled, Sophie sighed and continued. "I'm no longer a nervous wreck around him, which is good, because in the beginning I could hardly get a proper word out. But he's become real to me. Not just a handsome gentleman with kind eyes who asked the less than popular new debutante to dance."

"So, different, then."

"Different, yes. But my heart still pounds whenever he's near, and my stomach flutters like a stack of papers caught in a windstorm. The difference is, I can actually hold a conversation with him now."

"And do you like what you hear during these conversations?"

"Not always." Hearing his lack of interest in her, for one, was less than pleasing. "But I like talking with him, and I think he doesn't mind talking to me."

For a moment, Charity didn't say anything. She sat there, twirling a lock of her copper hair around her index finger as she thought. "Let me ask you this. If your sister had never eloped, if everything were still as it was before I left, would you wish for ways to spend more time with him?"

"Want to? Yes. Be able to? I sincerely doubt it."

"After how things happened for me, I'm beginning to think that everything happens for a reason. No, that's not right," Charity said, releasing the curl and brushing it from her face. "It's more that good can come from any situation. After all, it was through Hugh's suffering that we found each other.

"And your sister did something with terrible consequences. But I have every faith that you can turn this into the push you need to try for what you really want."

"Do you really think that I can do this? Entice the earl, I mean?"

Charity nodded with absolute confidence. "I'd wager you already have. You simply need to let him see that time is of the essence."

Sophie's eyes bulged. "You want me to tell him about the elopement?"

"No. Well, yes, but not just yet. What I mean is, give him a reason to believe the window of opportunity to court you may very well be closing."

It was a suggestion she would never have expected of Charity, the most prudent and thoughtful of the three of them. "You wish for me to lie and tell him I have another suitor?"

"No, silly. I want you to tell him *truthfully* that you

wish that you could have more time together, but that you'll be leaving soon and are unsure as to when you might see him again, since you won't be doing another London Season."

A wisp of regret slid through Sophie's veins. "My, that is forward. But you're right, I think. I can't have him thinking we have all summer to enjoy each other's company. At least I *hope* he's enjoying my company—one never can tell for sure." She gave a nervous little laugh. "Very well. When I see him at the party tomorrow, I shall do my best to tactfully convey just that."

The goals for tomorrow's outing should be simple: Find Evan and somehow separate him from the others; be utterly delightful, charming, and engaging; and somehow casually drop into the conversation that if he hoped to have a catch like her, he'd best hop to it. What could be easier than that?

Chapter Twelve

Given who was hosting the party, Evan was pleasantly surprised by the venue when he, Julia, and Harry arrived shortly after one the next day. Two tents dotted the grassy field, each with a handful of tables and chairs arranged in the shaded area. A buffet was set up under one, with cold meats and cheeses, grapes, strawberries, apricots, and bread artfully displayed on varying tiered platters. What looked to be lemonade awaited at the end, along with half a dozen fruit pies for dessert.

"My goodness—this is quite the spread," Julia murmured. Her eyes darted around the roughly two dozen people talking, playing cards, inspecting the archery setup, or wandering down to the path lining the riverbank.

"Quite nice," Harry said, giving an approving nod. "Wouldn't think a vicar would hold such an extravagant party."

"You're forgetting he's the son of an earl," Julia replied, flicking a disapproving look his way.

Evan rolled his eyes. "Actually, though this is charming and well laid out, I'd hardly call it extravagant. Only a handful of servants and simple fare, no expense of candles or decorations, and entertainment had with little

more than a few packets of cards, half a dozen hay bales
with paper targets, and people's own conversational skills."

It was clever, really. The location was so beautiful, surrounded by woods on three sides and the river on the
other, that it was easy to imagine they were on the finest
of estates.

"Oh, look—there's Sophie." Julia waved, and Evan
followed her line of sight to a small group clustered around
the archery stand.

A yellow-gowned figure waved back, her arm moving
in a wide arc above her head. Evan smiled. He liked that
she favored the color yellow. It certainly made her easy
to find, but it also fit her personality so very well. "And
our host, too, I see," he said, spotting the vicar's distinctive white-blond hair. "Might as well start there."

They made their way down the hill and across the
field. As they approached, Evan could make out the other
people in her group. The tall, willowy blonde, Miss Bradford, stood beside Sophie, talking to Mr. Wright, while
Cadgwith and Miss Effington had their heads together a
few feet away.

Wright smiled when he saw them and lifted a hand in
welcome. "Greetings! So glad you all could come."

Julia returned his smile with a warm one of her own.
"Thank you, Mr. Wright. It's *so* nice to see you again."

Evan caught a slight narrowing of Harry's blue eyes.
Perhaps those childhood feelings weren't as distant as
Evan had imagined. Poor sap. Even if Julia were open to
the prospect of suitors—which she absolutely was not—
she certainly wouldn't give their young neighbor the time
of day.

Stepping forward, Evan began the introductions. After everyone was properly acquainted, Wright clapped
his hands together and addressed the group at large. "I

think some activities are in order. Who here shall participate in our archery contest? It is the only sport at which I have any talent, so I am hoping to have plenty of competitors to trounce."

Harry was the first to speak up. "I am better with a fishing pole than an arrow, but I'm willing to give it a go. Especially if my lady would give me her favor." He dipped into a theatrical bow toward Julia, who looked at him as if he were straight from Bedlam.

"You must be forgetting that I've seen you shoot. I'll be keeping my favor for myself, thank you very much." She looked to Mr. Wright. "Are we to have a ladies' tournament as well?"

Miss Bradford stepped forward, her bright blue eyes sparkling beneath the brim of her bonnet. "Oh yes, please! I've not picked up a bow in years, but I used to be quite good."

"I was the best of my sisters," Sophie said, nodding proudly. "Which means I was the only one who ever managed to hit the target. Still, I think I'm willing to try again, provided no one is within a hundred paces of the target."

Giving a little shrug, Miss Effington grinned. "I'm absolutely terrible at it, but it is great fun. I'm happy to participate."

Mr. Wright put his hands on his hips and looked around at the group. "What say you, stragglers? Hugh, what about you? I vaguely recall shooting some arrows with you and your brother when he and my sister were first married."

Cadgwith snorted, his scarred eyebrow lifting in disbelief. "Vaguely? I imagine you remember very well trouncing the two of us. You crowed for days about it."

The vicar winked, his expression nothing short of devilish. "Then now is the perfect time to redeem your reputation."

"No, I—"

"Please, Hugh," Miss Effington broke in. "It will be fun. Unless you think it's best not to," she added quickly, slipping her fingers into his.

Cadgwith paused for a moment, appearing to give the request serious consideration before finally giving in. "If it pleases you, then by all means, count me in."

Evan almost grinned—he knew the look of a hopelessly besotted man when he saw one.

Rubbing his hands together, Wright turned his attention to Evan. "And you, my lord? Shall we make it an even eight and have four teams of two? Much more fun than splitting the tournament between sexes, I should think."

With seven pairs of eyes on him, Evan spread his hands. "I suppose I could join in."

Julia rolled her eyes. "Oh, don't let him fool you. He's won at least three of the five archery contests he participated in at the county fair."

"That was years ago," he protested, though without much of a leg to stand on.

"Still, it's not as though you've forgotten how to draw a bow. You and I shall be a formidable pair."

"I think not," said Harry, his hand settling at his hip. "We should be evenly distributed over talent in order to be fair."

"I agree," Miss Bradford added, looking between them. "A fairly matched spread will make the outcome less certain, therefore much more exciting."

Wright nodded. "Excellent point. Very well, let me see. If Lady Julia is the best female archer, then I think it best you partner with Sir Harry."

Julia's shoulders sagged, but she didn't balk. "Very well," she grumbled. "Do try not to hurt yourself," she tossed in Harry's direction.

Moving on, the vicar pointed to Miss Bradford. "I think you and Cadgwith should do well together, and Miss Effington, I'm honored to offer myself as partner. That leaves Miss Wembley with Evansleigh."

Sophie turned to Evan and offered an apologetic smile, her normally dark eyes looking bronze in the bright sunshine. "Apologies, my lord. I shall strive to actually hit the target."

He shrugged, not at all sorry for the pairing. "I have faith in you, Miss Wembley. So long as you don't hit me, I think we shall do just fine."

"I shall do my best, but no promises. All I can say is that you would do well to stay behind me." Her self-deprecating grin was endearing enough to make him chuckle.

After a flurry of working out equipment, each team chose a target, and they started with a few practice shots. Evan and Sophie had ended up on the second-to-last target, which situated them nicely beneath the shade of a wide oak. Sophie removed her bonnet and set about donning the protective brace and glove while Evan tested out the borrowed bow. It was completely different from the one he was used to, but after a few shots, he was able to compensate for the difference. He'd always liked the feel of a well-made bow in his hands. The balance, the curve, the tension—it was the perfect mix of beauty and function.

"Julia was not exaggerating," Sophie said, admiration coloring her words. "You're quite good. And to think I had no idea you were an archer. Although I guess I wouldn't, seeing as how we've only met in ballrooms before this week, and you'd hardly wear your quiver to a dance."

Her compliment had him standing a little straighter. "Thank you. My uncle taught me when I was young, and I've always enjoyed the sport." He drew another arrow, paused to evaluate the wind, and aimed to the left of the bull's-eye. When he released, the arrow struck the white space an inch to the right of where he'd intended. Not bad.

Turning back to Sophie, he said, "My mother has never liked visitors at Leighton Hall, so archery was a sport in which I could engage on my own, if I chose. Julia tagged along quite a bit when I was younger. She's practiced more and more in recent years, whereas I have practiced less."

She tugged at her leather vambrace, pulling it higher on her wrist. "My father attempted to teach his daughters the sport, but quickly gave up. I wasn't being facetious when I said I was the only one to hit the target. And I'm being *very* loose with the interpretation of the word *target*; it was twice as big as the ones here."

She fiddled with the lacings on the brace, but couldn't seem to get it properly tightened. "Allow me," he said, holding his hand out.

She smiled and offered up her arm. He adjusted the brace's position before tightening the laces. The dark leather was supple, but not nearly so much as her pale skin. Not wanting to leave any marks, he checked to make sure the strings weren't too tight before tying them into place. When he was done, he released her arm with surprising reluctance.

"Thank you," she said softly as she pulled her hand back.

"Of course," he replied, dipping his head in a shallow

nod. It seemed so easy to be with her. He'd always been overly careful not to spend too much time with any one female, but somehow their rapport seemed to come naturally. He simply didn't feel as though he needed to be on his guard with her. Clearing his throat, he tipped his chin toward the bow. "Let's see if your skills improved, shall we?"

"Don't get your hopes up," she warned, but pulled an arrow from her quiver anyway. After carefully positioning it, she drew the bowstring taut and closed one eye in order to sight down the shaft. Right away, he could see that her form was terrible: the bow underdrawn, her fingers too high, her aim too low. He held his tongue, though, waiting to see how she would do. When she released, the arrow flew wildly through the air, flirting to the left and landing short by at least ten paces.

She cringed and looked back at him, the very picture of sheepishness. "I think it is safe to say my skills, such as they were, have actually managed to worsen."

"Right," he said, stifling a laugh. "I think perhaps a lesson in form would help."

"I think perhaps we are too late for that," she said, pointing to the vicar.

Wright lifted a mallet and rapped it against a small gong. When he had everyone's attention, he spoke. "Ladies and gentlemen, we are about to have a small, friendly archery competition. The rules are, each member of the team will shoot four arrows. Whichever team has the highest points by the end will win bragging rights for life, or until such time that we compete again."

With that, the competition began. As host, the vicar took the first shot, hitting a respectably short distance from the bull's-eye. Miss Effington followed, winging the petticoat of the target, but still close enough to count. A little cheer went up from the spectators, and she bowed prettily.

Harry and Julia were next, and between them they managed to earn five points. "Not bad," Sophie whispered beside Evan. "I think Sir Harry isn't near as bad as Julia made him out to be."

"Not surprising," he responded, shaking his head. "Julia has always been harsh to poor Harry. He was a bit of a besotted fool in our childhood, and she's never let him forget it."

"Really?" Sophie raised her brows, watching the pair with increased interest. "But he seems so young."

"He's only two years her junior. Still, she'd best learn to be nice. He's a gentleman now, and she needs to treat him that way."

"In her defense, sometimes it's hard to change one's opinions after they've been formed." She glanced over to Evan, her smile wry. "It's a wonder you're even talking to me, after the way things started with us."

His lips curled in a slight smile as he shook his head. "I can't imagine anyone ever being cross with you for any amount of time—myself included."

She tilted her head, surprised by his comment. "Why is that?"

"You, Miss Wembley, are the very picture of irrepressibility."

"Am I to assume that is a good thing?"

"Absolutely. It's a very admirable trait." The girl reminded him of a glass of champagne. Effervescent, light, and sweet.

Her dimples belied the smile she tried to hold in check. "In that case, thank you. Oh," she said, standing at attention. "It's our turn."

His first shot was the best of the round, nicking the

bull's-eye and earning them nine points. He nodded in acknowledgment of the applause, then turned to Sophie. "Are you ready?"

"That depends," she answered, lifting her bow in place. "Are you safely behind me?"

He chuckled. "Well out of harm's way."

This time her arrow managed to flirt in the other direction, nearly hitting the target Julia and Harry were using. Sophie's nose wrinkled in dismay as she dropped her bow to her side. "Well, that was embarrassing. At least I can make the others feel better about their own shots."

Julia laughed merrily, the sound clear despite the fifteen paces between them. "A little more to the left next time, if you please. We're happy to take any points you'd like to give us."

Sophie's hand went to her waist, even as she laughed in response. "Go ahead, mock away. Even with my terrible shot, Evan's still better than the both of you."

Evan? He looked at her in surprise. Granted, he'd been thinking of her as Sophie for days, but he hadn't called her that.

"What?" she said, noticing his expression.

"Nothing. I was just thinking we need to go over that form of yours if we are to have any hope of earning bragging rights."

"Yes, I know—oh!" Her hand flew to her mouth as her cheeks flamed pink. "I'm so sorry! I cannot believe that I just called you Evan. In front of everyone, no less. It's just that that's how Julia speaks of you, and I wasn't thinking, and it just popped out. I'm dreadfully sorry."

He put up a staying hand. "Think nothing of it. Evan is what my friends and family call me, so I see no reason why you shouldn't as well. It's not as though it's my

Christian name, so we should be safe from anyone's moral outrage."

She peered past him to the area where the tents were set up. "Just so long as the chaperones didn't overhear. I can just imagine what my mother would think if she heard. Now then, about my form?"

Her form? For a split second, his mind flashed to the moment when he'd laid his hand on the generous curve of her hip. Except that was *not* the form they were talking about. Drawing a breath to settle himself, he nodded. "Nock your arrow and pretend you are just about to shoot."

She complied, getting into the exact same position that had sent the other arrows winging far from their targets. He pointed to her fingers where they held the arrow against the bowstring. "Your grip is all wrong. Go ahead and relax."

When she did, he pulled the arrow from her hand, set it aside, and lightly gripped her wrist. Turning her hand palm up, he slid his finger along the highest joints of her middle three fingers. "You want to cradle the string here, not here." He moved to her second joint. "The way you were doing it, the string drags against your fingers and throws your aim off, not to mention robbing the arrow of some of its energy."

"I'm not entirely sure my fingers are strong enough at that point," she said, looking doubtfully at their joined hands. "I'd hate to lose my grip and really mess things up. Not that I could do much worse than I already am, but I'd prefer not to end up with an arrow in the river."

"I'd wager you're stronger than you think. Here," he said, placing the fingertips of his left hand over the fingertips of her right so they locked together. "Curl your fingers and resist my efforts to pull them straight."

*   *   *

Sophie sucked in a quick breath, her eyes flitting back up to Evan's. Thankfully his gaze was directed at their hands. Their *joined* hands. It didn't matter that she wore a stiff shooting glove, or that his hands were encased in the buff leather of his own gloves. Their hands were still linked, and that was good enough for her.

He tugged his fingers, trying to pry hers open. She held steady, keeping her fingers curled just as he had instructed. She almost laughed. He wanted her to keep their hands from separating? *That* she could do. Letting go would be the hard part.

"There now—just as I had suspected. You are stronger than you look, Miss Wembley." He met her eyes, smiling triumphantly. He didn't pull out of her grip right away, and she kept her own hand completely still.

"Thank you, Evan. I hope you're right."

He was standing close enough to her that she could smell the crisp, slightly musky scent that she'd grown to adore. He blinked, looked down at their hands, then quickly pulled away. "All right, moving on. There is a slight breeze coming from the river. That air will push your arrow, throwing it out of the line as it travels. If you move your aim in the direction from which the wind originates, it will compensate for that push and hopefully help you to actually hit your target."

She lifted the bow again, getting back into position, careful to hold her fingers just so. Starting with her arrow pointed directly at the target, she shifted a few inches to the left. "Better?"

He moved to stand directly behind her, so that he could sight down her arrow's shaft. She closed her eyes for a moment, imagining she could feel the heat of him at her back. It was easy to imagine his hand sliding along her waist from behind, his lips finding the sensitive skin at the nape of her neck, his—

"Your lateral aim is good, but you need to move up slightly."

Her eyes popped back open. Yes, the lesson.

Unaware of her daydreams, he continued. "The arrow is not immune to gravity, and it will fall as it flies. It is up to you to compensate based on how far away the target is."

Forcing herself to concentrate, she tilted the bow up just a hair. "Like this?"

"A smidge more," he murmured, his breath caressing the side of her neck.

She shivered, causing her grip to slip. The arrow sailed off, arcing gracefully through the air. It hit the very edge of the paper, well outside of the target, but a thousand times better than her previous shot. She gasped, whipping around to face him. "I did it!" She bounced on her toes, so thrilled she could hardly contain it. "I can't believe I hit it! You are a genius, the best tutor ever to have lived, I'm sure of it."

He chuckled, obviously amused by her. "Or perhaps your last tutor was simply the worst. Regardless, well done."

"Miss *Wembley*," Mr. Wright called, the merriment in his voice ruining his stern expression. "I know you are eager to lose to us, but do try to wait your turn."

"I was merely reenacting your last shot, Mr. Wright," Sophie replied tartly, making the vicar hoot with laughter.

"Such insolence," Evan said, his voice low and teasing. "You'd better play nice. I won't have you getting us tossed from the competition. If they are going to compel me to play, then I fully intend to win."

She grinned hugely, not even trying to temper her delight. "I know, I know. But still, did you see the way it flew straight at the target? I could be the next Robin Hood. Or Robinette . . . Robina? Never mind, just call me Sophie Hood."

His gorgeous blue eyes danced with amusement. "I don't suggest taking up residence in Sherwood Forest just yet, Sophie Hood."

She laughed and turned her attention back to the others, trying not to linger on the way he had said her name just then. It was a very ordinary name, but hearing the way he wrapped his tongue around the word made her wish he'd call her by her Christian name all the time. Why must etiquette always get in the way of the things she wanted?

The contest continued, with Julia and Harry scoring lowest, Hugh and May only a few points above them, and Evan and Sophie neck and neck with Mr. Wright and Charity. While Sophie's second arrow lodged in the hay bale just inches from the target, the third had actually hit the outermost ring. Evan hit the bull's-eye twice, but his third shot had strayed left and landed in the second ring, much to his dismay.

"Oh, dreadful luck, Evansleigh," Mr. Wright teasingly taunted. "Must be losing your touch in your dotage. 'The Lord giveth, and the Lord taketh away.'"

Lord Cadgwith gave a short snort of laughter. "Careful, Thomas. 'Pride goeth before destruction.' The Lord may taketh from you yet."

"Touché, old man. I can only hope the Lord continues to show favor to his humble servant."

The men continued to taunt one another, their lighthearted jabs amusing them all. When the fourth and final round began, Evan turned to Sophie, earnestness written all over his face. "All right, Sophie Hood, this is your chance to best each and every one of your friends, and earn eternal bragging rights for us both. I have no intention of allowing that wolf in vicar's clothing to defeat us."

She quirked an eyebrow. "Wolf in vicar's clothing? My, aren't we a competitive soul."

"Yes, quite, which is why you *must* hit the target."

"I must?" She fluttered her eyelashes in mock confusion. "Surely you are mistaken, because I am thrilled simply not to be in last place." It was great fun to banter with him like this. His spirits were as high as she had ever seen them.

He scoffed. "Second place is practically last place. Surely you want to win and be able to hold it over your friends' heads for the foreseeable future?"

"Not at all. I'd be thrilled for Charity, were she on the winning team."

He made a face. "Yes, but I cannot lose to an upstart clergyman who is half a decade my junior."

"Hmm. It sounds as though you're in a predicament. Perhaps if there were proper incentive, I might be more driven to succeed." Her mind whirled with all the ways he could entice her. A carriage ride alone? Another waltz, preferably one where she kept her feet about her? Or, perhaps a promised kiss? The mere idea had her stomach fluttering.

"Incentive?" he repeated, his hand going to his chin. The wind rustled the leaves above them, causing bright spots of sunshine to dance over his face. "Shall I promise to buy you a new oboe? Play the role of your servant for the rest of the day? You've only to name it."

A cheer went up from the small crowd, and they turned just as Mr. Wright let out a triumphant whoop. His arrow still swayed where it had struck the target directly in the bull's-eye. With a sweeping hand in their direction, he called, "Your shot, Evansleigh. *If* you wish to take it. You may prefer to save yourself the trouble of losing and simply forfeit now."

"Not a chance, Wright," Evan responded, the sentence almost jovial. His jaw tightened as he lined up his shot, taking his time. He held the string against the smooth skin of his cheek, one eye squinted as he sighted his target. Respectable, modern clothing aside, he looked like some sort of medieval warrior, poised with leashed energy at the moment right before battle.

At the exact instant he released the string, a gust of wind blew up from the river, pushing his beautifully aimed arrow to the right. It thudded into the third ring, more than a foot off from the center. Sophie gasped aloud, her hands flying to her mouth.

He stood there, blinking at the target in disbelief. Mumbling what she was sure must have been a curse, he turned to her, his eyes flashing silver. "Name it."

"I'm sorry?" she said, taken aback by his abrupt command.

Teasing taunts and sounds of dismay came from the other competitors, but he ignored them completely as he pinned her with his gaze. "Name your incentive. And make it good, because you must hit dead center if we are to win."

"The bull's-eye?" she squeaked. "Good heavens, Evan, I couldn't hit it for all the money in the world."

"Why not? The arrow has to go somewhere. Why not to the center of the target?"

She laughed, shaking her head. "Why not, indeed. You do remember to whom you are speaking, yes? The girl who tripped on her own skirts? Nearly hit our competitor's target? May or may not have managed to fall *up* the stairs yesterday?"

"I know whom I am speaking to. Now, Miss Eternally Optimistic Sophie Hood—name your incentive."

He was quite serious. She nibbled on her bottom lip, deciding whether or not she wanted to play along. As far as she was concerned, the competition was over, and they had earned a very respectable second place. Because really, there was optimistic, and there was deluded. She started to tell him as much, when suddenly inspiration struck. What had she to lose?

"Sing for me."

His brows came together. "I beg your pardon?"

She hadn't realized just how much she had wanted to hear him until that moment. "If I hit the bull's-eye, I want to hear you sing. *Opera.*"

She smiled up at him, batting her eyelashes for good measure. It was incredibly far-fetched that he would ever have to follow through, but it was certainly as good an enticement as she could imagine . . . other than asking him for a kiss, which she couldn't have brought herself to suggest in a million years.

Surprise flashed across his features. His lips turned up in a sort of disbelieving grin as he nodded and extended the bow to her. "This shall be your only chance, so I suggest you hit your mark."

Even knowing the hopelessness of it, a thrill still raced through her belly. If hearing him sing in Italian wasn't incentive enough to make the impossible happen, then nothing could. "Very well, we have a deal."

Drawing a nervous breath, she accepted the bow and lifted it into place. Evan stepped up behind her, his presence making the hairs on the back of her neck stand up.

"Wider stance," he murmured. "Good. Now draw a little further back. A little more, so that your left arm is fully extended and your fingers rest at the apple of your cheek."

Her lips were parted, her breaths coming in short draws through her mouth as she listened to the low, encouraging tones of his voice. He sounded so mellow, so calm and confident.

"Aim a little higher, and when you release, hold the bow absolutely still. The follow-through is what propels the arrow."

Taking one last long breath, she concentrated all her energy on the three fingertips holding the string. One, two, three, *release.*

Chapter Thirteen

Sophie closed her eyes as the arrow whipped from her fingers and whispered through the air. *Please, please, please . . . Thump!* Hope erupted along with the spectators' enthusiastic applause. Opening her eyes, she held her breath and looked to the target. There, her arrow wobbled, firmly embedded in the white space just outside the bull's-eye.

The air whooshed from her lungs in one disappointed rush. It was so tantalizingly, tauntingly close! She groaned, dropping the bow to her side as she glared at the game-losing arrow. "I'm so, so sorry. I tried, I really did."

"Surely you're not serious," he said as he came around to her side.

"I swear I did! I'm just no good."

His eyebrows lifted in disbelief. "What are you talking about? That was incredible. Yes, it wasn't perfect, but that's the best shot you've ever had. I'm proud of you, Sophie Hood."

She turned to face him fully, surprised to hear the excitement, the *pride*, in his voice. But . . . "Evan, I just lost the competition for us." And she'd lost the promise of hearing him sing. Of the two, she was much more disappointed by the latter.

"Yes, I know," he said, pausing to wave to the victors. Mr. Wright clasped Charity's fingers and raised their joined hands above their heads in exuberant victory. He was the least modest vicar Sophie had ever met, but it only served to endear him to her.

Evan rolled his eyes. "Damn pup. Apologies," he said quickly, offering her a contrite smile. "And *we* lost. Good thing, too, because I am a terrible winner. Boastful, self-satisfied, exceedingly annoying to be around. Much like the vicar will be, I'm sure."

Sophie chuckled, shaking her head. "Give him a chance—he's not as bad as all that. I quite like him, in fact."

Sighing hugely, he nodded. "Yes, I'm sure I'd like him, too, if he'd steer clear of my sister. The man is too engaging by half."

"And that's a bad thing?"

"For a brother? Absolutely. But I suppose we should go congratulate them anyway." He offered her his elbow. "Shall we?"

She held up her arm, which still was confined by the brace. "Let me just get these off." She started tugging at the laces, but Evan brushed her hand aside and set to work loosening the strings for her.

"While I know it's not Sherwood Forest," he said, pulling the vambrace free and dropping it beside the bows, "perhaps we may go for a walk by the river after your concert. We can call it our victory lap."

Sophie only just managed not to gape at him. Purposely spending more time with her, without a bit of prompting from her or anyone else? Pressing her lips together to hold back what was sure to be an enormously gauche grin, she nodded her assent. Time alone with the earl was all the victory she needed.

Evan didn't know what he had expected from the concert, but it certainly wasn't what was unfolding before him.

The vicar had managed to have a small pianoforte delivered to the site, along with the long stringed instrument Miss Bradford referred to as a zither, though it was unlike any zither Evan had ever seen. At the center was Sophie with her little oboe. From the first notes, it was clear this would be a performance unlike any he had ever heard.

The music was utterly unique, but it wasn't just because of the exotic sound of Miss Bradford's instrument. It was the way the three instruments blended together. From the silence of those around him, he knew that he wasn't the only one enchanted by their performance.

Evan recognized the piece as being a variant of Mozart's Sonata No. 11, but it was by no means a literal interpretation. It was whimsical, mysterious, and charming, all at once. Each of the women brought her own strengths to the piece, but it was Sophie who most held his interest. He loved watching her play, if for no other reason than the fascination of seeing her so focused and solemn.

How had he not paid attention the last time he attended her musicale? She was almost a different person when she was playing. There was no self-consciousness, no laughing, no bubbly words. She exuded serene confidence. He could actually sense all the hours she must have dedicated to practicing. The oboe was notoriously difficult to play, yet she pulled it off with complete capability. She knew her instrument, she knew her part, and by Jove, she was going to make it perfect.

Evan tilted his head, considering that thought. Not perfect, actually. That was the wrong word. More like beautifully and meticulously executed. She took an odd-sounding instrument and made it compelling to listen to.

Not unlike herself.

She was sweet, but at times peculiar, yet she managed to take that part of herself and make it an asset. When he had suggested the walk, it was because of the look on her face when she realized they had lost. It had been wrong of him to suggest the incentive, because it had set the burden of success at her feet, and that had been unfair.

But even though it was her comfort he had been thinking of at the time, he found he was actually looking forward to it. When the last note of the piece came to a close, he clapped along with everyone else, hands out-stretched in honest enthusiasm.

From the seat beside him, Julia applauded just as earnestly. "That was extraordinary," she said, leaning toward him to be heard above the noise. "I feel as though I've visited Vienna and the Far East in the very same day."

He nodded. It was the perfect description of the experience. As the applause quieted, he came to his feet and offered her his hand.

His sister waved him off, smiling up at him. "No, thanks. I think I'll sit in the shade a little longer."

"As you wish. I promised Miss Wembley a promenade along the river to soothe the bitterness of defeat."

"Defeat?" She gave a soft snort. "You do realize that I came in last place, thanks to our terrible shot of a neighbor." She tilted her head toward Harry, who sat two seats over.

Harry rolled his eyes when he heard her, leaning back in his chair. "I don't know if you can lay all the blame at my feet. I saw Evan helping Miss Wembley with her form, but you offered no such assistance. A little guidance might have made the difference."

She lifted an eyebrow, clearly unconvinced. "Don't expect me to drop everything to help you simply because you've not got the skills. Perhaps next time you won't insist on participating in something you have no business doing."

"Julia," Evan said, the single word a warning. "Can you be civilized long enough for me to leave you alone?"

"Yes, of course," she answered, lifting her chin. "I thrive on being alone."

Shaking his head, Evan clapped a hand on the baronet's shoulder. "I believe that's our cue. Why don't you go join a card game while I take my walk? I can almost guarantee the company will be more agreeable."

As they walked together to the makeshift stage, Harry lifted his hat and ran a weary hand through his hair. "I wonder if I shouldn't find my own way home. I wouldn't wish to impose my company on her any more today if it distresses her so."

"No, of course you shouldn't. Someday she'll find her manners when it comes to you, but in the meantime you may rely upon mine."

"Somehow I doubt she will," Harry replied. "But there are plenty of interesting people here today, and I shall enjoy spending time with them." With a tip of his hat, he headed off toward the card table, holding his shoulders straight and proud.

Evan shook his head. His sister had best sort her moodiness out, before he sorted it out for her. Turning his attention to the makeshift stage, he watched as Sophie and the other two girls laughed with one another as they finished up tending to the sheet music and instruments.

Cadgwith strolled up beside him and tipped his chin toward the stage. "They're something to behold, are they not?"

Evan hadn't realized the man had caught the performance. He had seen him wandering off toward the food tent when the rest of them had been taking their seats. "Very compelling," Evan answered, offering a relaxed smile. "I'm glad I was able to see them perform. I only just missed it at the Tuesday recital they played."

Cadgwith smiled, wrinkling the silvery scars along the left side of his temple. "The one and only recital of the series I happened to catch. Can't say I'm sorry to have missed the others. Speaking of which, are you and your sister planning to attend the gala tomorrow night? Supposed to be quite the event."

"I hadn't thought, but it might prove an enjoyable evening. Will you and your betrothed attend?"

The baron gave a half shrug. "Charity is exceedingly excited about it, as are the other two," he said, nodding to where Miss Effington stood with Miss Bradford and Sophie. "I'll come to see the famous lamps, but I doubt I'll make it to the fireworks. Had enough artillery explosions to last me a lifetime in the war."

Evan slid his gaze to his old friend. Beside the scars at his left temple that stretched down to his neck, there were faint purple circles beneath his eyes. Curiosity flared as to what had happened to him in the war, but Evan wasn't willing to pry. Too many men had endured far too much during that dark time. Offering a half smile, he said, "I'm sure Julia will love it. Shall we meet there?"

Shooting Evan a wry grin, the baron nodded. "Yes, please. God knows I could use another man to help even the odds."

They worked out the details, deciding to meet at Sydney House at the eastern edge of the park an hour before sunset. Sophie saw him then and waved. Closing the clasps on her case, she set it aside and walked over to join him. "You survived the concert, I see."

The baron nodded to them both and went to join Miss Effington. Evan turned his full attention to Sophie and smiled. "Quite. It was very different. Refreshing. I know I've heard you play before, but somehow I had no idea just how talented you are."

She ducked her head as if embarrassed. "Charity is the one who made it all work. She rewrote the parts of the piece in a way that made us all sound good. Quite an accomplishment, really."

He gestured toward the river path, and they started walking together. "And she did a lovely job, but she had nothing to do with your talent. You should be proud."

"Charity is talented. May is talented. I merely practice within an inch of my life and simply try to keep up."

"All the more impressive, then." Natural talent was one thing, but to train oneself to be as accomplished as Sophie was when it didn't come naturally was something to be admired.

Her cheeks bloomed with a hint of soft color as she bit back a smile. "You, sir, are too easily impressed."

"I'm not, actually. I'm a great lover of music, so I know when something falls short. Take Miss Harmon, for example."

"I'd rather not," she replied, wrinkling her nose.

He laughed, cutting an amused glance her way. "Bear with me. Miss Harmon is not a natural talent. She is accomplished, but her music is calculated and cold. If I were to guess, I'd say she has much more interest in being accomplished than she does in the music itself."

It was bad form to speak of her this way, but after the

way she had treated Sophie at the ball last week, she deserved that from him and more. "You, on the other hand, are accomplished as well, but more importantly, you manage to be engaging when you play. You are invested in the music, and you therefore pull your audience in as well."

"I can scarce imagine more lovely praise—it nearly makes the eight million hours of practice worth it," she said with a wink. "However, I think we have reached the compliment quota of the day. Should you go forth, I fear I shall get a terribly big head, and with hair as wild as mine, I'd best not chance looking like an ogre."

"Ah. Excellent point." He laughed out loud when she grimaced. "What? If I had said 'terrible point,' you would have accused me of complimenting your lovely hair."

"I would have done no such thing. I am well enough acquainted with my hair to know that any such compliment would purely be Spanish coin," she said, her tone full of wry humor. "Now then, allow me to thank you for your excellent tutelage today, so the deficit of flattery may be righted."

"Deficit of flattery? Are we supposed to be keeping count?" He made a face. "I despise mathematics, just so you know. The only tallies I'll be keeping are the ones in the estate's ledgers. Blood—er, dreadfully dull business, that."

A breeze from the river gusted over them, and she rubbed her arms idly. "How can one despise mathematics? It's neat and orderly and utterly predictable. Much like music, it is the universal language."

He sent her a disgusted look. "If you tell me that you are accomplished at numbers as well, I may very well have to escort you back to your mother."

She held up her hands. "Fine, fine, I won't say another thing . . . except that you look very handsome in that color jacket, and that is it. We're even now and I won't say another word." The sentences ran together in a blur, ending with a definitive slash of her hand.

He chuckled, shaking his head as they followed the curve of the path where it ran alongside the riverbank. She was damn good company, he'd give her that. They continued along in silence for a while. The trees lining the path provided shelter from the afternoon sun and, with the breeze blowing up from the river, it made for a pleasant excursion.

When they'd gone a few minutes in silence, she suddenly blew out a pent-up breath. "I fear there is something you must know about me, my lord."

Evan slowed. That sounded rather ominous. "All right," he said, his curiosity piqued.

"The truth is, I am a talker. A terrible gabster, in fact. So much so that my father says in a race between my mouth and my mind, my mouth would win by a mile every time, and truly, I can't say I disagree."

Certainly not what he might have expected her to say. "I see. And you're telling me this because . . . ?"

"Because long silences and I don't get along well. And I feel as though I've been lying to you by keeping my mouth shut. Well, at first it was because I was too nervous to talk to you, and then because I was afraid I would make an even worse fool of myself around you than I already had, but now I feel as though the truth must come out." She inhaled and exhaled in short succession as though relieved to have it out.

He stopped, turning in order to face her. Her smile was sheepish, apologetic even. "What on earth would you have to be nervous about around me? I make a point of being nice to all the young ladies at the events I attend."

"Do you make a point of being handsome, too?" As soon as the words were out, she slapped her hand over her mouth and groaned. Dropping her hand, she widened her eyes at him. "Do you see why I thought it best to keep my mouth shut? A lady does not say the first thing that pops into her head."

"I wouldn't say that. Before she died, my grandmother was quite a plainspoken woman. Everyone knew exactly what she thought of them. As the Dowager Countess of Evansleigh, she was most definitely a lady."

She glanced heavenward as though he had completely missed the point. "Yes, an *old* lady. Such things are permitted among the elderly. They've quite given up on worrying what others think of them, I believe." She gave a little half-shouldered shrug. "Try as I might to practice restraint, I shall always be adept at ending up with my foot in my mouth. I suppose that means for the next thirty or so years, I have to get used to being uncouth until such time I can be labeled eccentric."

They were all just keeping up appearances, weren't they? Saying and doing all the correct things so society wouldn't brand them unfit to be part of their stratum. Sometimes it seemed to Evan as though all he ever did was pander to social correctness. Go to so many parties, dance with the proper number of women, spend an adequate amount of time at the club—all in the name of avoiding the roving eye of the *ton*, ensuring that no one narrowed their eyes and noticed that things were not as they seemed. He couldn't risk anyone seeing past his cultivated façade.

He and Sophie had more in common than she probably realized. "Well, you may always count on me to ask you to dance, couth or not."

Sighing, she shook her head. "You shan't have to

worry about asking me to dance after next week. Mama and I will be on our way back home to Appleton by then."

An unexpected pang of disappointment thumped in his chest. "Ah, so the decision to return has been finalized. I had hoped you'd be able to stay long enough to attend the opera with me."

She pushed a wayward curl back from her temple, her gaze flitting out over the water. "Sadly, no. I fear I don't know when we might see each other again after the week is out."

He dipped his head, catching her eye and offering a small grin. "Not just talkative, but dramatic, too, I see. You forget that there will be opportunities aplenty during the Season, especially now that we are such great friends."

It was nice, knowing that she'd be there. Someone with whom he could shed a bit of his mask and simply enjoy the company. No ulterior motives, no pretenses, just friendship and mutual regard.

But she didn't return his smile as he expected. Instead, her humor slipped away even more. "I'm not making myself clear," she said quietly, glancing down at her hands. When she looked back up, the regret in her eyes made his heart sink. "There will be no more Seasons for me, I'm afraid. When I go home, it will be for good."

He blinked, caught off guard by the announcement. "I don't know what to say. Has something . . . happened?"

In his experience there was only one reason that a debutante would step away from the matchmaking frenzy that was the Season: marriage. He swallowed, unable to believe that could be the case.

Had she accepted a proposal that he was unaware of? If she had, she sure as hell didn't seem happy about it. A forced match, then? The idea of her sweetness being soured by an unwanted marriage made his fists tighten at his sides.

Her chin ticked up a notch, proud but not haughty. "Yes. Let us just say that my family's situation has changed."

Ah. Christ, now he felt like a proper jackass. He knew her family was purse-pinched, but he hadn't realized they no longer had a feather to fly with. Damn tactless of him to even inquire. All the joy seemed to have leached out of her, leaving her cheeks pale and her eyes lacking their usual spark. She didn't hold his gaze, instead peering out over the swiftly moving water.

Damn it all, he had asked her here to make her happy, not to make things worse for her. "In that case, I think some allowances can be made."

She looked up sharply, her brows pinched together. "Allowances? But I'm not asking for anything."

"Stop pestering me, or I'll change my mind," he teased, knowing full well he was confusing her. She opened her mouth to speak, but he stopped her with a raised hand. "Fine, fine, you've talked me into it."

"Talked you into *what*?" she asked, completely at a loss now. At least there was a spark of interest lighting her dark eyes. That little glimmer within her that made her so unique in his circle of acquaintances.

"Were it not for the wind, you and I both would have had perfect scores in the last round. Therefore, since you put up such a convincing argument, I shall make good on my promised enticement, Sophie Hood, and sing for you."

Chapter Fourteen

Sophie gaped at the man, not entirely sure if he was joking or not. "You wish to sing for me?" It was such a monumental leap from what they had been talking about, she couldn't quite follow his reasoning.

"No, but since you insist, and since I am such a gentleman, who am I to refuse?"

From discussing her family's fall from grace, to an impromptu concert? "All right," she said slowly, unable to think of anything else to say. Was he attempting to cheer her up? Or did he simply wish not to dwell on her family's misfortune? She pursed her lips, watching his face closely. She didn't see any mocking in his expression, not even the first hint of ridicule. All that she could perceive was his light teasing and genuine intent to follow through.

"Let's see," he said, glancing past her shoulder. She turned too, peering down the empty river path. They'd walked farther than she'd realized, and she could only just make out the others through the trees and up the hill.

He nodded once. "Yes, I think we are far enough that no one will hear me embarrass myself, especially with the sounds of the river. Well, no one but you, of course."

He *was* trying to cheer her up. Her heart melted as

the corners of her lips curled up in a small smile. "If you embarrass yourself—and I sincerely doubt you will—then it will only serve to make us somewhat more even in terms of having humiliated ourselves in front of the other."

"There you go with the tallying again. I *will* march you back to your mother, young lady."

Where was this silliness in him coming from? He was making it impossible not to grin, not to let go of the darkness that weighed on her heart whenever she thought of her family's situation. Putting her hand over her heart, she said, "I promise, not another word. Now, I'm ready whenever you are, my lord."

His shoulders rose as he drew in a deep breath, looking genuinely nervous for the first time. "Very well. I shall sing an aria from *Idomeneo*. Since it is only the two of us, I'm not going to sing at full volume. Consider this a softer, more dolce interpretation of the song."

He rolled his shoulders a few times and licked his lips. Sophie bit back a smile—he truly was nervous. It was adorable, really. It was nice to know there was something out there that made that composure of his slip. She waited patiently as he shifted his feet, opened and closed his fists at his sides, and then cleared his throat.

She was just about to give up on him when he drew a breath, closed his eyes, and began to sing.

He started very quietly. So much so that she found herself leaning forward, wanting to hear him over the sounds of the river beside them. But as the song began to build, his voice opened up, sounding rich and pure and so lovely it brought gooseflesh to the exposed skin of her arms. The words rolled off his tongue, unintelligible to her in literal terms, but beautiful and stirring nonetheless. Slowly she began to realize that he was repeating phrases. He'd sing it first one way, and then again in a totally different way, his chest rising and falling with the music he so clearly heard in his mind.

She closed her eyes, listening to every rise and run, every vibrato, every deftly changed key. She could feel the lightness of the song. It was hopeful and happy, and just being witness to his interpretation of it made her feel the same.

Sighing, she gave herself over to the experience. She couldn't have ever imagined his singing to be so beautiful, so wholly moving. He didn't need an orchestra or a grand hall with carefully designed acoustics. His singing wasn't meant to be perfect; it was meant to be an expression of the music within him. It was meant to be sung in the forest, among the trees and the wildflowers, with an interloper like her somehow being lucky enough to hear it.

When the last note ended, he drew a great breath and finally opened his eyes. He looked at her, a hesitant smile on his lips. She stood there, awed, so impressed and honored that he would share this part of himself with her that she couldn't come up with a single thing to say. She, of all people—completely at a loss for words.

Shifting, he gave a little lift of his shoulders. "I believe applause is customary." His words were teasing, but she saw the hint of self-consciousness lurking in his tentative gaze.

Sophie smiled, but didn't raise her hands to clap. "I'm terribly sorry, but I'm afraid applause is quite beyond me right now. I am still paralyzed with shock at the exquisiteness of your voice, which you have cruelly kept entirely to yourself until now."

Pleasure at her words reflected back to her in the depths of his eyes, blotting out the momentary insecurity. "I like to have a few surprises up my sleeve."

She shared a grin with him, enjoying the warmth with which he watched her. "What did it mean?" she asked quietly. "The song, I mean. Can you translate it?"

He nodded, relaxing his shoulders and taking a step closer to her. "*Torna la pace al core*: Peace returns to my heart. *Torna lo spento ardore:* Extinguished ardor is re-kindled. *Fiorisce in me l'età:* Youth is reborn in me. *Tal la stagion di Flora*: Thus does Flora's season, *l'albero annoso infiora:* make the old tree bloom again, *nuovo vigor gli dà:* and give it fresh vigor."

A shiver of delight went through her at the way he spoke the Italian lyrics. Heavens, what she wouldn't give to attend the opera with him and hear his whispered translations again. Step One and Three-Quarters of wooing the earl seemed to be him inadvertently wooing *her*. . . .

Nodding as though she wasn't imagining his lips at her ear again, she said, "So the song *was* as hopeful as it sounded. It made me feel as though mountains were conquerable when your voice rose to its high range. It gave me gooseflesh, in fact," she said, rubbing her arms.

His smile was as wide as hers. "Now, now—I'm certain that was just the result of the river breeze," he said, all humbleness now that he was certain of her enjoyment. "Shall I go and fetch your wrap? It wouldn't do to leave you chilled."

She quickly shook her head. The very last thing she wanted was for him to leave her. "Not chilled, my lord—awed. And you may deflect my praise all you want, but that was by far my very favorite opera performance, and before you make any remarks about how many I have attended, I'm not entirely certain, but I can assure you it was enough to know yours was truly wonderful."

"Now you've gone and done it," he said, his hands going to his hips.

"What?" she exclaimed. "I haven't done anything."

"You've clearly upset the balance of compliments, and I cannot call myself a gentleman if I allow it to stand. Let me see," he said, slowly circling around her. She crossed her arms and grinned, shaking her head as he inspected her. He tapped his lips with his gloved finger. "If you are to praise me so highly, I must do the same. That rules out your gown, your countenance, and your hair, as those would all be ordinary compliments."

She could hardly believe his playfulness. He seemed as happy as she had ever seen him. "Very ordinary, and quite unbelievable," she agreed.

He paused in his circuit and raised a questioning eyebrow. "Unbelievable?"

She inwardly cringed. Perhaps she shouldn't have said that out loud. Ladies were not supposed to point out their shortcomings, as others would see it as fishing for praise. She had simply been stating the obvious. "It's just that a woman prefers an honest compliment," she said, feeling heat rise in her cheeks. What kind of ninny reminded the man she was attempting to woo that she was in possession of average to passable looks?

For a moment, he simply considered her, his brow furrowed, as if trying to work out a riddle. "Are you of the belief that a compliment to your appearance would be insincere?"

If she could snap her fingers and return to the conversation of a minute earlier, she would happily and eagerly do exactly that. "Evan, please. There is nothing wrong with being average, and we shall leave it at that."

He didn't respond right away. Instead, he resumed his

circuit, his footfalls soft on the packed earth of the dirt path. "When you are resting, perhaps."

She angled her head, trying to work out what on earth he meant. "I beg your pardon?"

"When you are simply sitting quietly, as one might do in front of a mirror, I can see how you might see your features as ordinary."

"Oh," she said, lacing her fingers awkwardly. She was oddly disappointed to hear him agree with her. Why, oh why hadn't she kept her mouth shut? She almost rolled her eyes. Because she was Sophie, that's why. Talkative, silly, ordinary Sophie, who never could manage to keep her tongue behind her teeth.

He stopped directly in front of her, his brilliant, icy blue eyes holding hers hostage with their earnestness. "It's when you speak, and listen, and laugh, and smile, and even frown that your beauty comes alive. When you are you, unable to be still or even quiet, you have a luminosity to your countenance that could never be considered ordinary." His lips relaxed into a soft, almost tender smile. "Which, in my very educated opinion, makes you rather extraordinary, Sophie Hood."

She gaped at him, unable to believe what he was saying. It was the loveliest thing anyone had ever said to her. Butterflies danced to life in her belly, stealing her breath with the force of the sensation. "You certainly know how to even a score," she breathed, doing her best to smile normally.

He stepped closer to her, tilting his head down to meet her gaze. "I know how to speak the truth, that is all."

Her heart hammered a staccato beat within her chest, and she moistened her lips as she exhaled shallowly through her mouth. No man had ever spoken to her like that before. Even more remarkable, he seemed to mean every precious word.

Her gaze fell to his lips, those lovely lips that had said such beautiful things to her. They looked soft, and supple, and more inviting than any man's lips had a right to. Swallowing, she looked back and met his gaze. Was it just her imagination, or was the look in his eyes inviting as well?

"Evan," she whispered, desperate to know if she was imagining the look he was bestowing on her or the unbelievable magnetic attraction between them. Almost of their own volition, her fingers slipped into his, and instead of pulling away, he closed his hand to hold hers tighter. She didn't move, hardly even breathed, as she relished the warmth of the touch and savored the inherent strength of his body, evident in little more than that whisper of touch between them.

Light laughter from around the bend startled her out of her trance. Someone was coming! Sophie's body went limp with disappointment, and she dragged in several breaths, trying to recapture her composure. Blast their miserable timing!

Evan stepped back, breaking their contact as his eyes darted down the path toward the sound. "It looks as though we have company," he said, straightening his shoulders. He sounded nonchalant about it, as if the intruders hadn't just ruined a perfectly wonderful moment.

By the time Miss Paddington and her chaperone rounded the bend, Evan and Sophie were a respectable distance apart, both staring out over the scenic river. They murmured greetings to the others as they passed, and stood silent as the pair continued out of earshot. When

Evan turned back to her, it was with a polite smile that made her heart sink. "I think perhaps we should rejoin the group," he said, holding out his elbow.

Trying valiantly not to show her disappointment, she nodded, placed her fingers on his sleeve, and allowed him to guide her back toward the party. It was hard to believe now that he possessed the sort of passion she had glimpsed in his singing. Yet even with the frustrating interference upon their time alone together, at least now she knew there was hope.

"You are awfully quiet tonight."

Evan blinked and glanced up. He hadn't even heard Julia come into the library, let alone walk over to his seat. Closing the unread book in his lap—a translation of *The Barber of Seville*—he set it on the table beside him and smiled. "Busy day."

The ride home had been quiet as well, with Evan, Julia, and Harry all lost in their own thoughts. Julia had steadfastly ignored the baronet before they had deposited him in front of his inn, but that was preferable to the little jabs she'd been taking at him earlier. Evan had been distracted by his own thoughts, idly considering the unexpected progression of the day.

"Indeed it was," his sister responded, a tired grin tugging at the corners of her mouth. "I fear I may have gotten a bit too much sun on my face, but it was well worth it. Did you enjoy yourself?"

Nodding slowly, he said, "Yes, I did, actually. The archery was particularly entertaining, even without winning." He couldn't remember ever enjoying the sport quite so thoroughly. Having Sophie as a partner had been an unexpected delight. She had the unique ability to be happy and lighthearted even when she was failing.

She had tried as hard as she could, and when she had fallen short, she had no thought of herself, only for him. He got the impression that she was the sort who kept getting up, no matter how many times she was knocked down.

Julia settled herself on the chair at the other side of the table. "It was absolutely priceless seeing Sophie's face when she hit the hay bale that first time. One would have thought she'd hit the bull's-eye."

He grinned. Sophie's exuberance was one of her best traits. Today she had proven remarkable company, making him laugh and banter in a way that felt more genuine than he could ever remember. He was glad they had fallen into friendship over the last week. Being around her seemed to lift something inside him, that invisible weight that had been his constant companion all these years. She was a sweet person, and he was happy to know her.

And no, he had no intention of analyzing the moment he'd had distinctly *un*friendly thoughts about her, when her fingers had tucked into his and he'd briefly considered tugging her flush against him. It was a simple lapse. An understandable one, given her loveliness and the intimacy of the moment. She was a friend, and that's all there was to it.

It was a damn shame she would soon be sent back to Appleton because of her family's circumstances. He knew all about living a life that one had never asked for. Knowing what lay ahead for her made him want to make the rest of the time that she had in Bath all the more enjoyable.

He looked back at his sister and nodded in agreement. "If only she had—and not just because the vicar will hold that victory over us until the day we die."

"Nonsense," Julia said, amusement tickling the word.

"You're the one who will hold on to it, I'm sure. Mr. Wright was simply enjoying the moment. Speaking for myself, it made my defeat somewhat less crushing to know I lost to a man of God."

Evan sat back against his chair, eyeing his sister. "I noticed you spent quite a lot of time talking to him. Discussing the Good Book?" He liked to see his sister enjoying herself, laughing without the strain that so often tightened her features. But what he did not approve of was a far too forward young peacock making eyes at her whenever she was near.

She lifted an impertinent brow. "I'll tell you all about what we discussed just as soon as you tell me what you and Sophie were discussing on your walk."

"Opera, mainly," he replied, calling her bluff. "A little of my dislike of mathematics and her unaccountable like for it." It was true enough. She didn't need to know that he had sung anything for Sophie. There was absolutely nothing wrong with doing so, but he simply didn't feel the need to share that particular detail.

After seeing Sophie's spirits sag when she spoke of her circumstances, he had wanted to make her happy again. He was by no means a master, but she had clearly enjoyed the impromptu performance. There was something special about a person who was easily pleased by something so simple. Some people wanted baubles or favors; she simply wanted music.

Across from him, Julia smiled, all innocence. "Then, yes, we talked all about the Bible."

He scowled at her, knowing full well that she was holding out on him. "I do wish you would keep your distance from him. He's about as close to a saint as I am." Julia was a strong person, but he worried about her ability to withstand a true Lothario. It was easy to be swayed by one so skilled at the art of flattery.

"Oh, quit posturing. He is actually a very nice man beneath all that charm."

"I'm not posturing; I'm keeping your best interests at heart."

Her amusement faded a bit as she sighed. "I wonder — is it he that you don't trust, or I? You should know that I am perfectly capable of taking care of myself."

It wasn't that he didn't trust her; it was more that he didn't trust her lack of experience when it came to members of the *ton*. "Yes, I know," he said, not wanting to make it a big issue. "But I don't see why you don't spend more time with someone like Harry. He at least can be counted on to be a gentleman."

Harry had been around their whole lives. Evan hadn't expected to see their neighbor here this summer, but with Julia showing up on his doorstep, Evan was glad for the man's presence.

Julia rolled her eyes with all the dramatics of a stage actress. "If you're so keen that someone should spend time with the man, might I suggest you do the honors?"

"I spent the entire evening in his company only two days ago. *Happily*, I should add."

"Well, it appears you are a saint after all," she replied, a patronizing smile stretching her lips as she came to her feet. "We should all strive to be so tolerant."

He held up his hands, surrendering. "Fine, fine. I shall trust your judgment, just as I have for years. I'll thank you for continuing to be trustworthy."

"See?" she said, coming around to kiss his cheek. "You really are a saint."

He sighed and shook his head. "A martyr is more like it."

As she started for the door, he swiveled in his chair, a thought occurring to him. "Would you like to go to the gala tomorrow? Cadgwith invited us to join him and the ladies of the trio."

"Absolutely," she replied, nodding eagerly.

It would be good for her to spend more time with the other females. He suspected that her lack of close friendships was half the reason she had traveled to Bath.

He angled his head, stuck on that thought. "Are you ready to tell me what brought you to my doorstep last week?"

She bit her lip and gave a little shrug. "Just needed to escape. Funny how some things tend to follow us wherever we go, though."

"Yes, I know what you mean." His secrets—*their* secrets— would always be with them. Hopefully her time here would show her that there was still much they could enjoy in life.

"Still, I'm so glad I came. If nothing else, it's good to see you laugh." She winked before taking her leave.

He settled back against his chair, considering what she'd said. He really had enjoyed being here this summer. The music, the friends—the whole atmosphere of the place was exactly what he hadn't known he needed. And the burgeoning friendship with Sophie Wembley, of all people, was a particular surprise.

It was rather unfortunate that tomorrow might be one of the last times he saw Sophie for the foreseeable future. He was glad for the time they'd had today, especially when he'd had the chance to dispel her notion that she was ordinary. It wasn't right that she should think herself average—she was so much more than the reflection in the mirror.

He chewed the inside of his lip, thinking. Though he

could do little to change the fact that she was departing soon, he could at least make certain that she enjoyed her remaining time in Bath. She was a good friend to him and his sister, and she deserved to leave here knowing that she'd be missed.

"I've a letter from your father," Mama said, sailing into the drawing room and closing the door with a firm click. She came to sit beside Sophie on the sofa, the letter in question clutched in her fingers.

Sophie's mind had been a million miles away—actually, it was more like two miles away, on the river path—and it took her a moment to come back to the present. "News of Penelope?"

"Yes," her mother said, her nose wrinkled in distaste. "They're returning from their so-called honeymoon in Scotland. Oh, the blasphemy of the word. I'd say their illicit holiday, but your father has made it quite clear that the church will recognize the union whether we like it or not."

Sophie pressed her lips together, anger and worry colliding in her chest. So they thought they could slide right back into their lives, did they? As if their actions hadn't permanently damaged both of their families, and blackened their own reputations? "I'm sure whatever funds they had ran out, and they think to return to their families' bosoms."

"Yes, I imagine you're right. Oh, the nerve," Mama said, throwing her hands up. "If they had to go off and do such a reckless, selfish thing, they could have at least had the decency to stay away longer. We need all the time we can get."

The knot of tension that had loosened in recent days yanked tight again in Sophie's stomach. She nodded, not trusting her voice to answer.

Mama eyed her, her lips pursed as she worried the paper in her hands. "How goes your husband hunt? I noticed you spent quite a bit of time in the earl's presence yesterday."

Not a topic she wished to discuss with her mother. The words *husband hunt* alone made her feel like a fraud. Her feelings for Evan had nothing to do with her sister's foolish actions, and everything to do with the earl himself. "Well enough, I think."

"Have you managed to get him to kiss you? Don't think I don't know exactly how much time you spent on the path with him yesterday. I'm quite willing to be a lenient chaperone, but I expect you to show some results."

Sophie's cheeks flared red-hot. What a horrible, horrible topic to discuss with one's parent. She lifted her chin, clinging to whatever dignity she had left within her. "He was a perfect gentleman. Though I do feel that we have a connection between us. I can talk to him quite easily, and he to me."

Mama's eyebrow lifted beneath the lace of her mobcap. "Talking never landed an earl in the parson's mousetrap, I'm sure. You must make certain that his interest is captured. Use your feminine wiles, such as they are, and make him see that you are the perfect bride for him."

Setting down the letter, she pulled both of Sophie's hands into her own. "Sometimes a woman is most interesting when her mouth is *shut*, my little magpie. Push back those shoulders, bat your eyelashes, and smile at him as though he is the cleverest man in the world. We're running out of time, and I don't want to see your hopes dashed forever."

Embarrassment aside, it was actually one of the sweetest things her mother had said to her. Sophie nodded, swallowing against the despair that rose up at the thought of living her life not only without the man she loved, but as a cast-aside spinster as well. "I'm doing my best, Mama."

A pleased smile crinkled the corners of her mother's dark eyes. "Excellent. Whatever it is the earl sees in you, I'm grateful for it. If you can secure his promise, then no one will dare snub the family of a countess."

Sophie's heart fell. Blast it all, she hadn't even thought of that. Just what she needed: not only her own hopes pinned on a match, but those of her entire family. She exhaled and tried to return her mother's smile. The stakes for tonight's gala had just gone up.

Chapter Fifteen

"If either of you has a brilliant plan for getting the earl and me alone tonight, I would be ever so grateful," Sophie said, collapsing onto her bed like a sack of flour.

May chuckled, coming over to perch on the edge of the mattress. "You did a jolly good job of it yourself, yesterday. I've been on tenterhooks all day waiting to hear what happened."

Both May and Charity, bless them, had converged upon Sophie's house after she had sent out notes begging them to come help her prepare for the gala. She wanted to look absolutely perfect tonight, and heaven knew she'd need reinforcements for that. Sophie had no eye for fashion, and while poor Lynette was perfectly adequate as a lady's maid, her strong suit had never been taming Sophie's unruly hair.

Coming up onto her elbows, Sophie sighed. "He was very sweet, and ever the perfect gentleman—which, of course, was the problem. We had quite a lovely conversation, and he complimented me quite wonderfully, but there weren't any stolen kisses or embraces." She sighed, blowing a wayward curl out of her eyes. "It figures that with all the dire warnings about protecting our tender sensibilities from men who are unable to contain their ardor, I would choose one who wants to actually *talk* when we are alone."

It hadn't just been talking, of course. Hearing him sing just for her had been very special, but it wasn't something she was about to share. Like his whispered translations at the sopranos' performance, those were precious moments between only the two of them.

Smiling from her seat at the dressing table, Charity shook her head. "I'm rather disappointed in you, Sophie. I was sure you, of all people, would have had him wrapped around your little finger by the time you returned from your excursion. No one is as effortlessly charming, in my book."

"That is a bag of moonshine, but thank you nonetheless," Sophie said with a grateful smile in Charity's direction. "Honestly, I might have, had Miss Paddington and her chaperone not strolled down the path and interrupted a very promising moment." At least it was easy enough to tell herself that.

"Oh, there was a moment?" May's blond eyebrows lifted with interest.

Sophie couldn't hold back an embarrassed grin as she nodded.

"Well, the plot thickens. In that case, we must be certain not only that you find time alone with the good earl tonight, but that you are not interrupted." She crossed her arms and thought for a moment. "I think it should be the labyrinth. My aunt said that even if one knows the proper route, it is still half a mile long. Without knowing, it can take hours to find one's way through."

"That is promising," Sophie replied, trying not to think of what in the world she would do once she got him alone. How did one go about using one's feminine wiles?

"I can hear the worry in your voice," Charity said, her gray eyes sympathetic. "Just remember that we will be there with you the whole time . . . until you don't want us, that is."

"Yes," May added, her smile sly. "At which point we promise to scatter like mice so you may have your moment."

Charity wrinkled her nose. "Like mice? I'd rather not."

"Fine—like cockroaches then?"

"May!"

As they laughed and teased one another, Sophie couldn't help but feel the tiniest bit better. She was running out of time to capture the earl's heart, but at least she had her allies to help her through.

"All right, ladies," she said, calling them back to order. "Now for the most important decision of the day: What shall I wear?"

Hours later, as Sophie stood nervously just outside the elegant hotel at the entrance to the park, she was beginning to wish she had ignored her friends' advice. They had decided on one of her best gowns, a pale pink confection with flounces at the bottom and two rows of blond lace at the bodice. It was truly lovely, but it just didn't feel like *her*. She wasn't the frilly-gown-and-lace type; she was just plain Sophie, who preferred simple styles done in sunny colors. No use gilding a lily, after all.

She did at least love her hair, thanks to May's intervention. Apparently a lady's maid hadn't always been available in the outer reaches of the East Indies, and she had learned to be quite good with dressing her hair. She had pulled Sophie's long locks into stylish plaits that coiled around her head, locking away the wiry strands that normally sprang free from her hairpins on warm summer evenings like tonight.

Of course, all of her efforts would be for nothing if Evan didn't show up.

Sophie resisted the urge to ask Lord Cadgwith for the time yet again, and instead scanned the faces streaming past as they entered the park. From where she stood, she could see hundreds of attendees blanketing the gravel paths and spilling out over the well-manicured grounds. Thousands upon thousands of unlit lamps lined the paths and hung from the trees, all waiting for the dark of twilight to unleash their magic. The vegetation was lush and mature, obscuring much of the park past the principal walk, so there was no way to tell just how many people were actually present.

Sophie sighed. No wonder May's aunt had been so willing to relax her normal watchfulness and join Charity's grandmother and Sophie's mother at the pavilion seating area. There were so many people around, it would be impossible to get into any real trouble.

"Don't worry," Charity said, slipping her arm through Sophie's. "Once the sun sets, the concert will begin in earnest. People will congregate by the pavilion, and the park won't seem nearly so crowded."

"If you say so." She wasn't so sure—the idea of privacy in this crush seemed absurd—but she squeezed Charity's hand in thanks for her support anyhow.

When Sophie turned back to the crowd, her eyes immediately landed on a tall, broad-shouldered man pulling ahead of the cluster of people walking toward the park. She sucked in a short breath, her hand going straight to her heart. She'd know that long-legged stride anywhere.

Evan was there at last, and he was emerging from the crowd like Triton from the boiling sea. She dropped her hands to her side, silently berating herself for her silliness. Obviously she was anxious if she was comparing the man to the god of the sea. Although, in her defense, he did rather have the bearing of a Greek god, thanks to his fine, straight nose and chiseled jawline. It was in his walk, too. He was always so self-possessed, so sure of himself.

He was impeccably dressed, wearing a dark green coat and handsome tan breeches. His cravat was crisp, his shoes polished, and his bearing was exactly what one would expect of an earl. She waved, grinning in welcome. He returned her smile easily—warmly, even—as he tipped his head up in a nod of acknowledgment.

Sucking in a nervous little breath, Sophie stepped forward to greet him. "Good evening, my lord. Welcome to the gala."

He nodded in return. "And to you, Miss Wembley. Good evening, all," he said, smiling at the others. "What luck to have such perfect weather for the festivities."

For the first time, Sophie noticed that Julia was at his side, looking splendid in a mulberry gown with dainty puff sleeves and a matching fringed shawl. Her cheeks were a vibrant shade of pink not far off from the hue of the gown.

"Yes, how fortunate we are," Sophie said as she grinned at Julia. "I'm so glad you both could join us."

"We're delighted to be here," the earl's sister replied, though she put a self-conscious hand to her cheek. "I stayed inside for most of the day since I managed to get far too much sun yesterday, so I was feeling dreadfully cooped up."

May cringed, offering a sympathetic smile. "I know all

about the dangers of the summer sun. I have burned more times than I can remember when on board my father's ship."

Julia's eyes lit. "Oh, I can only imagine what it must be like to traverse the ocean. I haven't even *seen* a ship, let alone been on one. Is it as terrifying as it looks in paintings?"

"It is the most free and marvelous feeling you could imagine—assuming you don't succumb to mal de mer." May made a face at the mention of seasickness.

Charity held up her hand, mirth crinkling the corners of her eyes. "Before we further explore that delightful thought, perhaps we should decide what we would like to do first."

Seizing the opportunity, Sophie clasped her hands together. "I, for one, am quite resolved to try my hand at the labyrinth."

"Will it be open?" the baron asked, glancing to the sky, where the sun was already dipping to the trees.

"I don't see why not. Heaven knows they have enough lamps to light half the city. And it will be good escape from the crowds, since I imagine most shall attend the concert." Sophie knew that Charity's betrothed couldn't countenance loud music or noise, so he would likely be gone before the concert, and most certainly before the fireworks.

May nodded, betraying not a hint of having suggested the maze hours earlier. "I think that is a marvelous idea. And I imagine we'll still be able to hear the orchestra, if only just."

Evan lifted his brows, sending a mischievous look around the group. "Shall we make a race of it? First one out reclaims lost bragging rights from the tournament?"

"Hold on," Charity said, putting her hands on her

hips. "I'm not giving up my hard-won rights, thank you very much."

"More like *stolen*, if I remember correctly," the earl replied, winking at Sophie.

For some reason, the heat of a blush rose up her cheeks. He seemed in a good mood today, which made things slightly easier, but he still made her heart race with a single look. Pursing her lips, Sophie said, "Perhaps we should have an entirely different set. Charity, you may retain archery superiority, and I'll soon boast directional."

Cadgwith chuckled, shaking his head. "We'll see about that. I am a trained army officer, after all. I should be able to find my way through a maze blindfolded."

"That can be arranged," May replied, her blue eyes filled with good humor. "I've no problem accepting any advantages I can find."

Sophie laughed before looking to Evan. "And you, my lord? Are you as good at labyrinths as you are at archery?"

He lifted his shoulders in a good-natured shrug. "Couldn't say, as I've yet to subject myself to one. However, being a proper English lord, I have every expectation that I shall conquer the thing by sheer force of will."

Shaking her head, Sophie grinned. "This is one thing that I can say with a hundred percent confidence that your title will not help you do. Actually, I'll even go so far as to say my female intuition gives me the advantage in this case."

"Such confidence. Well, I suppose there is only one way to settle the matter," Evan said, gesturing toward the path in front of them. "Shall we?"

After the ladies had informed their chaperones about their plans, the group headed off for the maze. Evan was

glad to see that Sophie was in good spirits today, not that
he would have expected anything less of her. If there was
one thing he had learned from their recent encounters, it
was that she was always willing to look for the best in
any situation.

And it was impossible not to notice how exceptionally well she looked today. With her dark hair done up
the way it was, she reminded him of some sort of Greek
temptress—something he would have never thought to
associate with her before. The gown itself went a long
way toward furthering that impression, with a low swoop-
ing neckline that seemed custom made to draw the eye
to the generous rise of her breasts.

He may be a gentleman, and this was Sophie, but he
wasn't blind. His mind flashed back to the memorable
moment his hand had landed on the curve of her hip the
night before the opera. He swallowed, dragging his thoughts
away from her figure.

He turned his attention to their surroundings. Colorful flags lined the path they walked, strung from tree to
tree like Christmas garlands. The smell of roasting nuts
and sweet buns fragranced the air as they passed vendor
carts and costermongers, all eager to relieve the attendees of a few shillings.

He held his silence as they headed down toward the
canal. It felt awkward, unnatural even, but at that exact
moment, he couldn't think of a thing in the world to
talk about. The others were no help, having broken off
into pairs, chatting as they walked ahead. Cadgwith led
the group, with Miss Effington on his arm while Miss
Bradford and Julia had their heads together, probably
discussing world travel, God help him. By way of de-
fault, Evan and Sophie merged closer and closer as they
brought up the rear of the group, until finally he sighed

and did as any good gentleman would, offering his elbow.

"Why, thank you," she said, easily accepting his assistance. "I always dislike walking on gravel in slippers. More than that, I'd hate to trip again. One does try to keep that sort of thing to a minimum, especially when I'm so looking forward to beating all of you in the maze."

Her enthusiasm brought a small smile to his lips, thankfully unlocking his frozen brain. "I don't think you were half so competitive about the contest yesterday. Have we awoken your inner competitor?"

Her dimples appeared as she threw him a wry look. "Yes, I think so, though please don't tell my mother. She believes that in mixed company, a lady should always allow a gentleman to win. That way a man can feel accomplished, and the woman can have reason to heap praise upon him." She gave a light roll of her eyes. "In her opinion, no man likes to be bested, and a woman shouldn't jeopardize his good opinion of her by doing so."

"Hmm—she may be onto something."

She lightly tapped his arm with her gloved hand. "Don't think I'm going to take it easy on you or Lord Cadgwith in order to protect your masculine sensibilities. A win isn't worth having unless it is achieved honestly."

He chuckled, shaking his head. "There are many who would disagree with that. Victory at any cost, no matter the means. Take Miss Bradford, for example. Happy to blindfold poor Cadgwith in order to seize the prize for herself."

The woman in question turned, sending him an arch look. "I heard that," she said, "and I'm not the least bit repentant. You may count me in the 'ends justify the means' camp, thank you very much."

"Very good to know," Evan said, nodding gravely. "I shall gird my loins whenever we do battle."

May patted Julia's arm. "As well you should. Your sister and I have just decided to double our odds of winning by teaming up together for the labyrinth."

"The devil you say. Julia, if you were to partner with anyone, shouldn't it be your own brother?"

Lady Julia gave a decisive shake of her head. "Miss Bradford is the only daughter of a sea captain, and spent many an hour at his side. I'm betting she'll have ten times the sense of direction you ever could."

He grinned, despite himself. This was exactly what he wanted for her. "The betrayal cuts deep, sister. You'd best hope your gamble pays off, for I may very well send you back to Ledbury for such an offense."

Her tinkling laughter continued even after she turned back around. They crossed the footbridge at the canal and Cadgwith steered them to the left, following a smaller path that meandered along the waterway.

Sophie looked at him, her smile mischievous. "Your sister and May appear to be combining forces against us. Shall we do the same, in hopes of redeeming ourselves? We were robbed of victory yesterday, but I think if we have our heads together, we can emerge triumphant."

They reached the entrance of the maze, where an attendant stood collecting admission. Cadgwith turned and shook his head at Evan. "You might as well accept, old man. Charity has already informed me that we must be a team, so the pair of you are already at a disadvantage."

Miss Bradford tsked, rolling her eyes. "They are *supposed* to be at a disadvantage. How else are Lady Julia and I to have an unfair advantage? They beat the both of us rather handily yesterday."

"There, you see?" Sophie said, gesturing toward her friends. "You cannot let me flounder alone when they have so clearly teamed up against us both."

"I wouldn't dare," Evan said, pulling away in order to dig a few coins from his pocket to pay his and Julia's admission. "Victory is so much sweeter when one has a partner with whom to share it."

Sophie's grin was wide and a bit impish. "My thoughts exactly."

Chapter Sixteen

If Sophie didn't already love her friends, she would have positively adored them after the way they had helped her manipulate the earl into being her partner. Even Lord Cad, who had no reason to help her other than to help his betrothed's friend. He was a dear, and she was glad for whatever small part she had played in helping to get Charity and him together.

Luckily, the labyrinth was much less populated than the body of the park. Or at least, the parts that she could see were. The hedge rose at least seven feet high, making it impossible for participants to cheat their way out. When the group came to the first fork, May, Julia, Charity, and the baron turned right, and Sophie and Evan went left. Laughter could be heard through the hedge as other maze-goers encountered dead ends or found themselves back in the same spot.

Evan walked quickly, surprisingly focused given the silliness of the task.

"I see you are eager for your first labyrinth experience," she said, hurrying to keep up. "The competitiveness has resurfaced, it would seem." She loved the way his lips curled up even as he concentrated, not unlike an eager boy.

He lifted a single dark eyebrow even as he laughed at himself. "You did say this was our chance to recapture our honor after yesterday's defeat. I don't intend to squander the opportunity."

Sophie glanced up to the sky, which was just beginning to show the first streaks of the coming sunset. Hopefully they wouldn't be successful too soon. She was counting on the cover of darkness to bestow some privacy on them. "I approve of your dedication, but I'm not sure my slippers agree with your speed."

He immediately slowed, sending her a sheepish look. "My apologies. I forget how flimsy ladies' footwear can be."

"Yes, I know," she said, breathing a sigh of relief. "They more hinder than help, but at least they are pretty. Now I must know: Is this really your very first maze? I thought everyone in the world had been through the one at Vauxhall."

He paused at another fork before choosing the right path. "Everyone but me, I suppose. The odds of being cornered by a marriage-minded miss were never in my favor, I'm afraid."

She cringed. That one stung a bit, though he clearly had not intended to disparage her with the comment. She'd never considered herself a hunter, but that was suddenly exactly what she felt like. The much-maligned marriage-minded miss, chasing after the handsome, rich, titled gentleman. It would be laughable if she weren't so serious about it.

"Well," she said, her voice determinedly bright, "thank goodness we are not in London. I'd hate to have fellow females jumping out of the bushes at you." *Jumping out of the bushes?* She gave a mental roll of her eyes. Sometimes she said the most asinine things. If she hoped to woo the man, she needed to find something else to speak of.

Evan managed not to look at her as though she were mad, bless him. "You and I both," he agreed, hints of humor lifting his tone.

A group of three young men rushed past them on the left, their faces flushed from the exertion and their eyes bright with merriment. Sophie grinned and shook her head. "I imagine you'd rather be with them, running past, unfettered by your slippered and gowned companion."

He let out a little laugh. "I'm with the person I wish to be with, slippers or not. Besides, I have a feeling that this will be more of an endurance event. They will succeed in wearing themselves out, no doubt, and little else. When one rushes like that, it is impossible to pay attention to where you are going, and where you have already been."

Sophie was still quite stuck on his first sentence. Hope and delight flitted through her, bolstering her spirits. "Such sage advice from a first-time maze-goer."

"In my experience, it is a truth applicable to nearly all things."

She bit the inside of her cheek, considering his words. No doubt he felt the same way about marriage. Some of the thrill of his earlier remark fled. Was it even possible for her to persuade him to throw caution to the wind and take a chance on her? She was betting everything she had on it, but the outcome was doubtful at best.

She sighed inwardly. She never would have thought she could be so comfortable with him. Not even two weeks ago, she could hardly string together a proper sentence in his presence, and now look at them, side by side, chatting idly together like old friends.

Better than old friends, really. Old friends didn't make her pulse flutter like hummingbird wings, or her stomach dance with anticipation. Old friends didn't make her heart leap at the thought of sharing a kiss. A *real* kiss, where the entire world disappears, and it's just two people lost in the joy and passion of being together.

"Did you say something?"

Sophie blinked, startled from her daydream. Had she sighed aloud? "No, nothing," she replied, her voice a little breathless. She smiled as normally as she could manage, as though she hadn't just been imagining them locked in a passionate embrace.

"Are you well? Your cheeks are looking a little flushed. We can slow down a little more if you'd like."

She nodded. "Yes, that would be nice." Anything to prolong their being alone together. "I wouldn't want to wear myself out when we've only just begun—especially if this is to be a race of endurance."

He adjusted his pace, his eyes focused ahead on the next junction. "Left or right, do you think?"

"Have you been employing a method thus far? Or are we just going about it havey-cavey?"

His smile was easy as he cut his icy blue gaze toward her. "As far as I'm concerned, there are two methods: havey-cavey, or making only left turns. Since we have already ruined the latter, then clearly we are employing the former."

"Ah," she said, nodding with exaggerated approval. "The age-old, tried-and-true method. In that case . . . I say we go right."

They made the turn, almost running into a pair of women who were probably older than Sophie's mother. The grins on their faces were priceless, however, and Sophie couldn't help but smile back. She opened her mouth to say something to Evan, when she noticed a glow of orange light dotting the tree canopies visible over the top of the hedge.

"The lanterns!"

"What's that?" Evan said, looking back at her with raised brows.

"Do you see the light? They are lighting the lanterns. From what May's aunt said, there are thousands of them all across the park." Even within the labyrinth, she could see them now. Small, variegated glass domes were set on thin black rods spaced roughly every twenty paces.

"That's good. At least we won't be blind when the sun goes down. Who knows when we would have gotten out then?" As he spoke, an attendant came into view, making quick work of lighting the candles.

"How very clever. They look like little fairy houses. Well, if fairies ever lived so close to the city."

Evan tapped a finger to his chin, watching the man go about his job. "Should we cheat and follow the attendant? I bet he'll know the way out." A devilish grin lifted Evan's perfect lips. "Seeing how we've all agreed that victory may come by any method."

She scrunched her nose. "That sounds like a dreadful plan. You do realize that he'll be going down every nook and cranny, lighting every lantern in the whole maze, yes?"

"And yet, he'll still probably get out of here sooner than any of us." Evan set his hands on his hips and looked up and down the aisle. "I didn't imagine it would be so effectively disorienting. If it weren't for Merlin's Swing rising from the middle, I doubt I could say what end of the maze we were on to save my life."

Which was exactly what Sophie was hoping for. "And it seems so tantalizingly close, does it not? As though a simple turn here and there could spit us out right where we want to be. And yet . . . still we walk."

"And walk and walk and walk. So which way should we go now?"

Sophie pursed her lips, looking down the two corridors. "Left?"

As they walked, the sky grew deeper and deeper blue, until the first signs of stars appeared above. The warm glow of the multicolored lanterns, combined with the towering walls of the hedge, added an almost magical feel to the place. They passed others every now and then, but as the first strains of music wafted out on the warm night air, the frequency declined.

"Are you ready to give up?" Evan asked, pausing at yet another intersection. "The attendant did say they would rescue us if need be."

Beyond his shoulder, Sophie caught a glimpse of May, but she quickly turned and darted out of view. Biting back a smile, Sophie shook her head. "You will find, my lord, that I will almost never give up a worthy fight."

His eyes cut to hers, the colorful lamplight staining his irises a watery green. "An admirable trait. Doesn't surprise me, really."

"It doesn't? I daresay you're the only one, then," she said with a small laugh. Little did he know he was praising the exact trait that she was currently employing to bring them together. Good to know he approved.

"I very much doubt that. For one thing, you seem to have eager supporters in your fellow trio members."

"Who handily abandoned me not half an hour ago," she countered with a smile. "Not that I mind—it will be all the more satisfying when they emerge from the maze to find me waiting."

She was only bluffing, of course. She could not care

less about getting out of the labyrinth. Not until she finally recaptured the moment they had shared yesterday. Why was it proving so blasted elusive? How hard was it to lock eyes, have that intangible, indescribable *something* pass between them, and have him be overcome with his suddenly forthcoming ardor for her?

The ambiance couldn't be more perfect, they were alone, at least for the moment, and her hair and dress were perfect. What was missing?

They turned round another bend, and before them stood a small pavilion. "Oh, thank goodness! Would you mind if we sat for a few moments?"

"Not at all. At this rate it could be hours before we find our way out."

The pavilion was made of stone and housed three benches arranged in a circle. Sophie chose the closest one, and gratefully lowered herself onto it. She hadn't expected wooing to be such hard work. Evan came and sat beside her, keeping a respectable distance between them. He stretched his long legs out in front of them, and arched his back for a moment before correcting his posture.

Sophie glanced down, wondering what he would do if she scooted over a few inches, closing the distance between them. Would he allow it? Move away? Smile at her? Scowl? She swallowed a frustrated groan. All the uncertainty was driving her mad.

Taking a quiet, calming breath, she glanced up at his lantern-lit profile. "Isn't the sky lovely tonight? Not a cloud in sight to obscure the stars."

He tipped his head back, exposing the pale length of his throat as he looked to the heavens. "Brilliant. That would really come in handy if I had any knowledge of constellations whatsoever. Perhaps Julia chose her partner well, after all."

As he watched the sky, she watched him, shamelessly exploiting his averted attention. The light flickered across the smooth skin of his cheeks, casting the hollows beneath his cheekbones in shadow. His mouth was relaxed, making the soft Cupid's bow of his upper lip seem more pronounced than usual.

More kissable, too.

Nervous energy kept her frozen in place, unable to say or do anything as she waited for him to look back at her. Lud, why must he always be so handsome? As far as she could tell, he was practically perfect. Wealth, station, angelic voice, natural athletic ability, kindness, general likeability—he was unfairly blessed with all the best in life. Although, if he hadn't been, would she be so hopelessly enamored with him?

Impossible to say. She did know that the kindness was essential; it was what she loved most about him.

As much as she enjoyed his handsome features, as much as that had originally caught her eye, it was the least important of his traits. One's looks never lasted, but all the goodness in him? That would always be a part of who he was.

Still, he *was* handsome, and her heart tapped a wild beat at his closeness as she waited for him to look down. To make eye contact. To press his lips to hers . . .

At last. Her heart slammed to a stop as he finally lowered his gaze. Their eyes met and held, her breath coming in little puffs as she waited for him to move nearer. Time seemed to stand still as his gaze dropped to her mouth. She shifted the slightest bit, lifting her chin barely a fraction as her lips parted. The music played softly in the background, like the whisper of a dream come to life.

"Well, then," he said, abruptly coming to his feet and

offering an overly bright smile. "If we are to win, we must keep moving."

She gaped at him, astonished, as her hopes crashed to the ground and shattered before her like fine porcelain. But . . . but it had been the perfect moment! Not a soul around, the magical lighting, the soft music—what in the world had gone wrong?

"Evan, I . . ." She trailed off, having absolutely no idea what to say. What *could* she say?

"Fear not, I think we could still win yet," he said, looking up and down the path as though nothing had ever happened. "Perhaps a little cheating is in order."

She watched, dumbfounded, as he stepped onto the bench, and stood on his toes in order to see over the hedge. He turned in a little circle, his chin tipped up as he eyed the course. She could hardly believe it. One minute they were so close, the next, he was scaling furniture in order to find escape. It was almost like a dream that had suddenly veered off course.

After several seconds, he jumped down and offered her a wide smile. "I should have done that ages ago. Come on, this way."

"Evan, wait."

"And lose our opportunity at victory? I should think not." He held out his hand, and Sophie allowed him to pull her up. She had the impression that if she refused to join him, he would simply leave her there. With her properly on her feet again, he started forward, his steps brisk.

Blast, blast, blast! She set off after him, her dainty pink slippers offering little protection against the hard ground. Yet the pounding of her feet was nothing compared to the battering of her pride. He was as good as running from her.

He turned right at the next intersection, then left at the one after that. His strides were confident; he knew where he was going now. Desperation settled deep in Sophie's gut, seeming to grow with every step they took. This was supposed to be her chance. She had only days left before the world would know about her family's shame. She *had* to make him see her differently—to see her as desirable—before then.

She had no illusions like her mother. The marital contract couldn't be written quickly enough for him not to learn the truth. And truly, she wouldn't want it to be. What she did want was for him to see her—*really* see her—and understand the perfect couple they would make before his view was tainted by the scandal.

Then, and only then, would she have a chance at happiness with him.

The way he saw her shouldn't be based on her selfish, reckless sister. If she couldn't turn his head before the news broke, then there was no chance in the world she would turn it after.

Evan's strides were long and purposeful, carrying him ever closer to the end of the maze, with her scurrying along behind him. Her heart rebelled, pounding loudly in her ears as she cast about for a way to stop him. He paused, and she gratefully leaned over to catch her breath, willing her heart to slow down. He poked his head forward and looked both ways, then turned to her with triumph lighting his eyes.

"The end is in sight! We're almost there."

Perfect. In a matter of moments her chance would be lost. "Just a minute, please. I need to catch my breath."

He nodded and paced away a few steps, as though sensing that she wanted him closer, not farther. "My apologies. I do have that competitive streak. I want this win for both of us, after the way things went yesterday. Are you all right?"

Sophie exhaled before offering him a wan smile. Was she all right? Not in the least. He had to have recognized the look in her eyes, yet he couldn't get away fast enough. "I'll live," she said, unable to keep the hitch from her voice.

Tilting his head, Evan watched her for a moment, his expression unreadable. Letting out a soft breath, he stepped forward and held out his hand. The kindness that she so loved in him was reflected in his firelit eyes as he smiled. "I'm a beast for rushing you. Allow me to regain my status as gentleman."

She looked down to his proffered hand, his strong and capable fingers stretched out to her in invitation. What if this was the most encouragement she would ever get from him? What if she stopped waiting for him to be moved by his heretofore unseen ardor, and instead seized whatever opportunity fate gave her?

Her body tensed in excitement and fear. Terror, really. Did she have the nerve to actually do such a thing? To set aside everything she had ever been taught and take control? Moistening her lips, she straightened to her full height and met his gaze. The stakes were too high. She couldn't leave her destiny to chance.

Stepping forward, she slipped her fingers into his, curling them as he had shown her yesterday. His naturally followed suit, bending to provide resistance.

She took a deep breath, tightened her hold, and tugged him sharply forward.

His eyes went wide in the quarter second before their bodies met, but after that his reaction was lost to her as she closed her eyes, lifted on her toes, and pressed her lips to his.

Chapter Seventeen

Evan couldn't have been more shocked if the king himself had jumped from the hedge. One second they were racing to the end, and the next Sophie's lips were pressed against his. They were warm and petal soft, not at all unpleasant but so unexpected he didn't move a single muscle as he tried to figure out what the hell he should do.

Their joined hands were trapped between them, her fingers still gripping his tightly. She smelled of roses and lemon and something uniquely her that he couldn't quite pinpoint. As his mind reeled, she moved, leaning into him more fully. Honest to God, it was impossible to think clearly with the feel of her soft, full breasts pressed against his chest and her breath warming his cheek.

Of its own volition, his free hand slid around her waist, pulling her more firmly against him. She made a breathy little sound against his lips, surely the most enticing sound he had ever heard. Her kiss was unschooled, but driven by a passion that the deepest part of him recognized and responded to. He tilted his head and parted his lips, allowing the tip of his tongue to slip along the seam of her lips. *So sweet.*

He'd never experienced a kiss so honest and real. One that he felt all the way to the pit of his stomach, like the sensation of stumbling down a step he hadn't known was there. One that made him long for so much more from her. The rest of their surroundings seemed to fade away, the soft light of the lanterns little more than a muted glow, the music far away, as if heard from underwater.

God, but she felt incredible. He could sense her curves and the danger of letting himself get carried away with her—something he suddenly desperately wanted to do. He pulled his hand free of her grasp and slid it behind her neck, holding her to him more firmly. Her fingers slipped up his shoulder and delved into his hair, her fingernails scraping lightly along his nape. Chills cascaded down his back, and he pulled her tighter still against him, reveling in the feel of her softness pressed against his chest.

Even as his body cried out for more, his conscience whispered at the back of his mind. He struggled to pull his wits together, so much of him not wanting to release this moment and face the consequences.

Consequences.

With an act of willpower that he hardly knew he possessed, he drew back his hands and broke the kiss, forcing his eyes open and stepping back. *God have mercy.* He needed space to think. A moment to figure out how in the hell that had just happened.

"Miss Wembley, I . . . that is to say . . ." He shook his head, unable to think of a single coherent phrase to describe how ill-advised their kiss was. It was hard to think with the rush of desire still thrumming in his veins and his heart pounding in his ears.

Her hand went to her mouth, her fingertips gliding over her lips in exactly the way he wished his own lips were. Drawing in a steadying breath, he said sternly, "That was exceptionally unwise of me. Please accept my apologies."

He gritted his teeth together, steeling himself against the hurt that flared in Sophie's dark eyes.

"Should I apologize as well? Is that the proper protocol after one's first kiss? I'm sorry to say I haven't the experience to know." Her words were fast and low, nearly a jumble in her haste to get them out.

How on earth had he allowed things to come to this point? She'd heard from his own lips that he wasn't interested in her that way. It was one of the reasons he felt so at ease with her, in fact. Had he been leading her on without even realizing it?

"No, of course not. I am merely saying that we are in public, and we have no agreement, and such behavior is highly ill-advised. If we'd have been caught, I'm sure your mother would have had the first banns read by the end of the week." Something his muddled brain should have thought of first thing, instead of being distracted by how perfectly she fit against him. He backed up a few more steps for good measure, should his brain decide to take another hiatus and leave him vulnerable again.

She visibly worked to pull herself together, lifting her chin and affixing a completely false smile in place. Her dimples were conspicuously absent, further driving home her upset. "Well, good, because I'm afraid I couldn't apologize if I wanted to. Sometimes in life, we have to take a risk. Sometimes those risks are worth it, and sometimes we're haunted by them for the rest of our lives. The thing is, you never know which outcome you'll get unless you actually take that leap."

The lantern light shimmered precariously in her eyes, and he knew she was valiantly trying to hold back tears.

Her first kiss, and he had completely decimated whatever hopes she had pinned on it. He felt like an ass and a heel and every other horrible thing possible, but he hadn't asked for any of this, for God's sake. He was simply extending a helping hand, trying to show a bit of kindness when she was obviously less than pleased with him.

He shouldn't have stopped. When he'd seen that flicker of something different in her eyes earlier, he should have kept on walking until they were out of this damn place.

What made him even more convinced of that than anything was the fact that once her lips had touched his, he had *wanted* the kiss. He had liked the feeling of her pressed against him immensely. He'd even wished he didn't have to stop things there, God help him. He'd enjoyed every minute they had spent together this week, and the kiss felt like coming home. She was everything he hadn't known he wanted in a woman.

Sweet, a little daring, open, guileless—who would ever have thought those traits could be so endearing? That he'd find himself wanting to laugh with her, and sing to her, and teach her to shoot a bloody bow and arrow. If he were free to marry, she was exactly who he'd want at his side. Her animated face was exactly the one he wanted to see across the breakfast table as she regaled him with some story or another. Her dimples were exactly the ones he could imagine on his daughters, and her daring spirit would make his sons adventurous. Her body was exactly the one he wanted in his bed every night for the rest of his life.

But damn it all, he *wasn't* free to marry. He wasn't free to imagine a family of his own because there could never *be* a family for him.

Drawing a dark, cleansing breath, he straightened his

jacket and addressed Sophie as he might a business associate. "It is always difficult when risks don't lead to what we wish, but there will be other times, other opportunities." *Other people.* "Now, if you'd like to follow me, I believe I've had quite enough of this labyrinth."

Her eyes fluttered closed, and a tear slipped down her cheek. She brushed it away quickly before facing him again. She gave a quick nod, sweeping a hand down her skirts. "Very well. Lead the way."

His heart ached at the pain she tried to hide, but there was nothing he could do about it . . . other than making damn sure that their paths did not cross again anytime soon.

By the time he arrived home that evening, Evan had descended into a foul mood. Julia had been bewildered at first, unhappy that he had cut the evening short and departed the gala without ever having stopped at the concert. On the way home, her mood had deteriorated with each of his sharp responses until they were both brooding in silence when the carriage came to a stop.

As Higgins opened the door and accepted their gloves and hats, Julia sighed long and hard. "Home again. So much more fun than remaining at the gala with friends."

Evan threw her a less than pleased look and stalked up the stairs.

"What?" she said, following behind him. "Clearly something happened in the labyrinth, and you had to run away like a spooked foal instead of allowing me to stay and enjoy myself."

He didn't bother to slow or turn around. "You've been enjoying yourself since you arrived. One early night will not be the death of you."

"Easy for you to say. When I go home, I won't have

the luxury of attending such events again. While you're out gallivanting around London, I'll be stuck at home, with little more than Mama and Harry to keep me company, God help me."

"Harry is as good company or better than anyone you'll find here." He stopped inside the doorway of the drawing room and poured himself a glass of brandy. His mind was whirling with all that had happened with Sophie today, and he was in no mood to argue about their damn neighbor again. Since arriving on his doorstep, Julia had been unreasonably temperamental, and he was done with it.

She breezed past him and draped herself across the settee. Her eyes were narrowed, her jaw set defensively. "Is that so? Well, you could always have offered to switch companions yesterday. Sophie would have been vastly preferable company."

Evan paused with the glass at his lips, then quickly downed a large swallow. What was he doing? Sophie's company had been vastly preferable, all right—so much so that he had seemed to forget what he was about. How could he have allowed himself to get so carried away with her? He felt vulnerable, transparent. He wanted to be alone so he could think through the knot of emotions twisting in his gut.

Tightening his grip on the glass, he lowered himself into his preferred chair. He swirled the drink in his hand, watching the amber liquid chase itself around the glass. "It's not about switching companions. You were rude to our friend yesterday, and I won't have you speaking ill of him or to him anymore."

She scowled, sitting up a little straighter. "I don't need judgment from you, thank you very much. At least I make it clear that there is no hope of any sort of future. You think he's being friendly, but I see the way he looks at me. If Harry gets hurt, then he does so knowing full well what my feelings and wishes are on the matter. Can you say the same?"

Evan's jaw muscles worked as he clenched his teeth. He knew exactly what his sister was saying, but his decisions were no business of hers—especially when he hadn't yet worked out his own thoughts. "We *all* know your feelings on the subject. Have a heart and try not to be so bloody obvious about it."

"I *am* having a heart. That's the point. And since we are being so honest here," she said, raising her nose in the air imperiously, "I consider Sophie to be a friend and I don't want to see her hurt. Don't kid yourself that she is unaffected by you. I've seen the way she looks at you when you aren't watching."

He didn't answer, taking another sip of his drink instead. He wasn't unaware of the look Julia was referring to. He had convinced himself it was nothing, just Sophie's normal sweet self, all the way up until the moment her lips had touched his. He had been such a damn fool to think that he could simply enjoy having a true friend for once. He'd let his guard down around her, and she was the one who suffered for it.

So had he, but at least he deserved whatever suffering he caused himself.

As if sensing the direction of his thoughts, Julia pressed her lips together and shook her head. "The more I think about it, the more I'm convinced she's harboring some sort of *tendre* for you after all." She shook her head, her hazel eyes judging him. "It's cruel, leading her on like that. She's a sweet girl, and I don't want you hurting her."

He couldn't have said it better himself. Still, his sister's admonishment rankled. She was much closer to the truth than he wanted to admit. Guilt tightened like a fist in his chest as he narrowed his eyes at her. "That's enough, Julia."

"Is it? Because I'm not sure that it is." Kicking her skirts aside, she came to her feet, suddenly restless. "All these years, I took you at your word that you were being careful, not allowing others to get too close. I believed that you were as dedicated as I, because God knows I was holding up my end," she said, pacing back and forth in front of the fireplace. She stopped, shooting Evan an agitated glare. "I'm five-and-twenty, and I've only ever been out of the county of my birth twice, for God's sake."

He slammed down his glass with enough force to rattle the table. "I *have* been careful. If I hadn't, do you think we would be invited to bloody garden parties by your beloved vicar? Or balls, dancing the waltz and nodding to our peers as we sip warm lemonade? Do you think we would be accepted by *anyone*?"

Looking down to her fingers, she shook her head. "No, I don't imagine we would."

Her concession didn't make him feel any better. He *had* been careful all these years, but today he had allowed himself to slip more than his sister could imagine. He scrubbed a hand over his face. "I've skimmed the surface of life all these years, Jules. There are no close friends to ask questions we don't want to answer, no true enemies to wish to bring us low. I have walked a damn thin line because I know that we cannot afford the attention."

It was a speech as much for him as it was for her. In a little over a week's time with Sophie, he'd experienced the most real connection he'd ever had with anyone. He'd opened up to the diminutive, endearing, guileless young woman who had effortlessly managed to slip around his carefully erected walls. And look what had happened as a result.

"Do you ever feel damned?"

Evan's gaze jerked back to his sister. "Don't say things like that. Our souls have as good a chance as any."

She came and sat on the end of the sofa that was closest to his chair. "But do you worry for your sanity?" Her voice was quiet. Bleak, even.

It was not a rhetorical question.

It was a concept he didn't want to think about. It was hard to believe that she had even voiced the question, and he knew all too well that she wasn't being facetious. He wilted back against the stiff cushion of his chair, giving a humorless, rusty laugh. "What do you think, Jules? Our father belonged in a bloody madhouse." Words he'd never spoken aloud before, given now with a sort of stark, detached honesty.

She dragged a hand over the back of her neck. "Sometimes I wish he would have been. Then at least we wouldn't be stuck in this eternal purgatory."

He glanced over at her, lifting an eyebrow. "Living on one of the finest estates in the country, eating the best foods and enjoying the respect of all who know you is hardly purgatory. You have everything you could want right at your fingertips."

"Everything except what matters," she said quietly.

He sighed, offering her a tired smile. "You have me. And our mother, for what it's worth. But you know we can't risk damning a spouse to what Mother endured. Or worse, putting innocent children through what we endured, or even passing Father's madness on to them. It's best this way."

Something he needed to remember. The slip that he'd

had today couldn't be repeated, for Sophie's sake. Sharing a friendship was one thing, but when it slid into the murky waters of flirtation, that's when people got hurt.

He didn't want to think about what she was feeling at that moment, but he couldn't help it. She was sweet and entirely too quick to think the worst of herself. He wished he could boost her spirits, but what the hell could he do? He no longer knew how to walk the line between friendship and, well, *more* than friendship. He couldn't trust himself not to make things worse.

"Thank you for not sending me home, Evan."

He blinked, refocusing on the present. Working his lips into a smile, he dipped his head in a shallow nod. "Truth be told, I rather like the company. Though I mean it about being more civil. Tomorrow I want you to send Harry an apology—something I should have had you do yesterday. There's discouraging attention, and there is downright rudeness. He doesn't deserve the latter."

Just as Sophie didn't deserve a cold shoulder. But what could he do about it? It would be impossible to apologize to her without encouraging her.

As much as he wished he could make things better between them, his duty to his own family came first.

Chapter Eighteen

"Begging your pardon, Miss Sophie, but Lady Julia has come to call."

Sophie sat up in bed, blinking in surprise at her maid. "Lady Julia? Did she say what brought her here?"

Lynette lifted a shoulder, her green eyes kind. "Can't rightly say, Miss, but your mother said you must come down. Can I help you dress?"

Sophie sighed, knowing full well that her mother would not let her get away with turning the earl's sister away. "Well, I suppose I can't greet a lady in my night rail. Could you choose something simple, please?"

As the maid hurried to the armoire, Sophie tossed off the bedclothes and swung her feet around. It was well past noon, but she had pleaded a headache this morning, just as she had last night after the horrendous rejection from the earl.

Fresh humiliation washed over her, and she pressed her hands to her temples. She still didn't know how things had turned out so dreadfully. When she had kissed him, it may have taken a moment, but he *had* kissed her back. Not merely politely, either, if there was such a thing. She hadn't imagined it, yet here she was, still exhausted from a sleepless night wondering what had turned him against her.

Less than ten minutes later, Sophie hurried downstairs and let herself into the drawing room. Mama and their guest both sat on the sofa, tea in hand. Julia looked more than a little relieved to see her. Offering an apologetic smile, Sophie went and sat in the chair closest to her friend. "Good afternoon! I'm so sorry to have kept you waiting."

"Think nothing of it," she replied, grinning as she set her tea down. "Mrs. Wembley kept me fully entertained, I assure you."

Mama beamed, no doubt delighted to have had their guest to herself. "You are such splendid company, Lady Julia. I do hope you'll feel free to call on us again." She came to her feet, depositing her teacup on its saucer before grabbing a biscuit from the small plate in the center of the table. "I'll just leave you ladies be."

Sophie waited as she bustled out, then turned to Julia when the door had clicked shut behind her. "My apologies if she held you hostage while I was dressing. She does mean well."

Waving a hand airily, Julia said, "Not at all. My own mother isn't nearly so easy to talk to, so I found it rather entertaining. However, I am ever so glad to see you."

"And I you. It was lovely of you to join us yesterday. I'm only sorry we didn't have more time together then. Or at the vicar's party, for that matter." Sophie had been too preoccupied, not that it had done her any good in the end.

"Yes," Julia said slowly, sending Sophie a sly look. "It would seem my brother has quite monopolized your time."

The sting of a hot blush swamped Sophie's cheeks,

and she quickly looked to her lap. She was still too tender to bear speaking about it now.

"Oh dear, I see I've upset you."

The rustle of fabric was followed by the splash of liquid filling a cup. Two plops and the clink of silverware against porcelain, and then a teacup appeared at Sophie's hands. She sniffed and smiled, accepting Julia's offering.

"Thank you," Sophie said quietly, then took a sip. It was sweetened just the way she liked it. Rallying, she looked up, her smile wobbly but in place. "Please forgive my silliness."

"There's nothing silly about one's feelings." Julia smiled kindly as she pushed the plate of biscuits in Sophie's direction. "I had a feeling something may have happened between the two of you last night, and I wanted to make sure that all was well with you."

Something had happened, all right. All of Sophie's hopes for love and happiness had been dashed in one fell swoop. She nodded, not knowing what else to say to Evan's own sister. Honestly, Sophie didn't even know why she had ever thought she'd have a chance with the man.

"Whatever happened, I'm sure it wasn't your fault. Evan is not only oblivious—he's also a bit of an idiot sometimes."

Sophie reached for a biscuit and took a bite, desperate for the comfort gingerbread always brought. It didn't help. "No, in this case, I was both the idiot and the party at fault." She shook her head, suddenly wanting Julia to understand. "But I've been in love with him since the moment I met him, and I didn't want to lose my chance to turn his head."

Julia's eyes showed nothing but sympathy. "Oh, Sophie. I'm so sorry. But you are most certainly not an idiot. Evan, confirmed bachelor that he is, should have never allowed things to progress as far as they did. It was very badly done of him."

Sophie breathed a hopeless little laugh. "Evan didn't do anything. I fell for him when he hardly even knew my name. He was so kind, and we had the same love of music, and every time I looked at him my heart would leap from my chest." She buried her face in her hands. "I cannot believe I am telling you this. What you must think of me."

"I think you are a sweet, sweet person who had the misfortune of falling in love with the wrong man." There was such kindness in her words, it was hard to believe she had ever spoken so harshly to Sophie at their first meeting.

Sophie nibbled her lip, considering Julia's words. "Do you know, I don't look at it that way? I don't think I could ever regret falling in love with him." It didn't make sense, she knew, especially after the awfulness of yesterday. Even so, she meant what she said.

"But he hurt you," Julia said, confusion knitting her brow.

"Not on purpose. Any time we fall in love, there will always be risk. Romeo and Juliet taught us that much," she said, a fleeting smile crossing her lips. "I'm teasing, of course, but still, every great love story on earth started with a risk.

"Even the ones that worked out have no guarantees. Look at Lord Cadgwith's brother, who died much too soon, leaving behind a young wife and infant. If his widow had known his fate, would she still have married him? If she loved him, then I would think yes."

Julia angled her head, genuine interest flickering in

her hazel eyes. "Very thought-provoking. I hadn't quite considered such a thing."

Sophie scooted forward, relieved that her friend wasn't dismissing her thoughts out of hand. "The way I look at it—or at least the way I am trying to look at it—is that even if my gamble didn't pay off, at least I tried. At least I know that I put all my cards on the table, even if my hand lost."

"That's very . . . profound. You surprise me." Julia's eyes were no longer sympathetic or even apologetic, which was an improvement, as far as Sophie was concerned. She didn't want to be some sort of tragic figure, no matter how upset she still was.

"Yes, well, I had a lot of time to think last night. That's not to say that I'm not very, very hurt, but I did everything I could to pursue my own happiness, and that is all I can ask of myself." Her mother was a different story, but Sophie would face her mother's wrath later.

Julia lifted her spoon and idly stirred her tea, her lips pursed in thought. "What if you knew that, even if you both felt the same way about each other, your love could only lead to heartbreak? Wouldn't you be happy knowing he had helped save you from that?"

Giving a helpless little shrug, Sophie grinned. "In case you hadn't figured it out, I'm a terrible romantic. As far as I'm concerned, if two people love each other, then their love will always triumph." She blinked, realizing what she'd just said. What did that mean for her sister? Had Penelope pursued her love in the only way she felt she could? Sophie pushed the thought aside, resolving to reexamine it when she was alone.

"Well," Julia said, setting the spoon on the saucer and straightening her shoulders, "I had come here with the intent of offering my support, yet somehow I feel as though you're the one with all the insight. You've given me quite a lot to think about."

Sophie had given *herself* a lot to think about. She felt a thousand times better than when she had come downstairs. When Julia stood, Sophie did the same. Giving her friend a heartfelt hug, she said, "I'm so glad to have met you. I do hope that you will write once we are back in our respective homes."

"Yes, of course," Julia replied, smiling broadly. "I consider us to be great friends by now." She started for the door, but stopped and swiveled to face Sophie again. "And for what it's worth, Evan feels very, very badly for whatever happened yesterday in the labyrinth. He hasn't said as much, but it is plain as day to me."

After she had gone, Sophie sipped her tea, thinking about Julia's last words. As odd as it was, she felt bad that *he* felt bad. He may not have handled things terribly well, but to be fair, she had more or less assaulted him. Only she could turn a first kiss into an ambush.

She put a hand to her heart, directly over the ache that she knew couldn't be soothed. This time, when she thought of her sister and the fate she had damned Sophie to, it wasn't with anger or fury. It was with sadness. Sadness for herself, for her family, and for the sister who had, for whatever reason, felt she had no choice in following her heart.

The question was, would love be able to triumph for any of them? Despite what she'd said to Julia, this time even Sophie's romantic, eternally optimistic soul couldn't be sure.

After Evan and Julia had spent most of their meal in relative silence, he was mildly surprised when his sister dabbed her mouth, put down her napkin, and smiled at him across the polished surface of the dining table. "I wrote a letter to Harry."

Evan set down his wine goblet and nodded. "Excellent. I'm sure he will be very appreciative." Despite his directive, he hadn't been certain she would actually put pen to paper.

She leaned back as the footman swapped her empty plate for her dessert course. "I imagine he will," she said, smiling almost contritely. "I thought a lot about what you said, and I realized that I haven't treated him either fairly or kindly of late. That was not very well done of me."

He knew exactly what she meant. He still felt the sting of guilt when he thought of Sophie's expression the night before. She had looked absolutely crestfallen. Neither could he stop thinking of the way she had felt in his arms, or the softness of her willing lips pressed against his. He couldn't forget the taste of her tongue, or the sweet lemon-and-roses scent of her skin.

With effort, he dragged his thoughts away from his desire for the girl and stretched his lips into a thin smile. "I'm proud of you for attempting to make amends. It is never easy to admit when we are in the wrong." He forked a piece of his dessert and lifted it to his mouth. He almost closed his eyes when he tasted it: lemon cake with rosewater infusion. Apparently his cook was conspiring against him.

Across from him, Julia nodded as though he had made a very compelling point. "Interesting you should say that," she replied, pausing to pop a small strawberry in her mouth. "I went to visit Sophie today."

Evan nearly choked on his cake. "Whatever for?"

She shrugged, her hazel eyes glinting mischievously in the evening sunlight angling through the dining room's

wide windows. "She's a friend. It was clear that something had transpired between the two of you yesterday,
and if it put you in such a dreadful mood, I worried how
she might be doing."

An unexpected rush of emotions welled up from deep
within him. Had Sophie been upset? Angry? Humiliated? It was hard to imagine his ever-positive friend being any of those. What would she have shared with his
sister?

On the one hand, he hated how he had handled things
yesterday, but on the other, he still didn't know what else
he could have done. Yes, he should have pulled away the
moment she kissed him, but that hadn't been his instinct,
damn it. Could a man be faulted for an honest reaction
to a woman's advances?

That was the question, wasn't it? He felt more strongly
for Sophie than he'd ever expected. His body hummed
at the possibility of being near her, his mind lingered over
thoughts of her, and his heart seemed to ache with the
hope of seeing her again. He couldn't help any of these
things, and that was the real problem.

Sending Julia a sideways glance, he said, "And how
was she?"

"How do you think she was?" she countered, keeping
a perfectly straight face.

"How am I to know? I'm not the one who visited
her."

"Mmm," she murmured noncommittally. She dipped
a strawberry in the lemon icing and held it to her lips.
"Hurt, to be sure. But not resentful." She bit the strawberry in half and watched him as she chewed.

He didn't know what to think about that. It was
Sophie—had she ever been resentful a day in her life?
The hurt part didn't surprise him, but it did make him

feel that much more guilty. "I'm sorry to hear that," he said, very much meaning it.

"I was right about her having a *tendre* for you, but I imagine you already knew that."

He didn't answer. Of course he knew it. He also knew—as did his sister—that pursuing anything with the girl would be impossible.

No matter how much he found himself thinking about her. Like when he was alone, attempting to deal with mundane estate matters. Or when he was in bed, imagining things he had no right imagining.

She set down the uneaten portion of her strawberry and met his eyes straight on. "All I have to say is that I did right by Harry and apologized to him. I think it's only right that you should treat Sophie with the respect she deserves."

Evan's jaw tightened. What the hell did she want him to do? If he could think of something that would make things better, without risk of hurting Sophie further, then he would do it. "I'm not writing Sophie a letter, Julia."

"Good—we are in agreement." Her smile was swift and determined. "It's so much easier to convey one's thoughts in person, don't you agree?"

"No, I—"

"*Yes*, you do." Her voice rang with an authority that made him straighten in surprise. "Sophie is a good and honorable person. She may have taken a chance on something that wasn't meant to be, but she doesn't deserve to feel badly about doing so."

Yesterday his sister had condemned his relationship with Sophie, and today she wanted him to go make amends? Where was this coming from? "I agree that she should not feel that she did anything wrong. However, I don't believe going to see her will solve anything."

Julia held his gaze for a moment, her eyes softening. "Call it a closure of sorts, if you will. Do her the kindness of assuring her that you still think well of her. She deserves that much."

That much, and more. Sighing, he offered a reluctant nod. "Very well. If you think that it will be a kindness, then I shall call on her tomorrow. *Briefly*," he added, more for himself than for her. The problem was, it was entirely too easy to be drawn into Sophie's light. Now that he knew her feelings toward him, he couldn't afford to make that same mistake again.

Chapter Nineteen

"Well done, child," Sophie's mother crowed, hurrying into the drawing room with her eyes positively glowing with delight. "I was beginning to wonder, but clearly you've done something right."

Sophie paused, her oboe lifted halfway to her lips. "I have?" As far as she was concerned, she hadn't done anything right in days. Months, perhaps.

"No time, no time," her mother responded, examining Sophie from top to bottom. "Yes, you look quite nice today, thank goodness. The earl has called and asked for you to join him on a carriage ride through the city. He's outside with his handsome matched chestnuts as we speak—they're worth a mint, to be sure," she exclaimed, pressing her hands to her round pink cheeks. "This is your chance, my little magpie!"

The oboe slipped from Sophie's fingers, and she only just managed to catch it before it fell to her lap. "The earl? He's here?" There was no catching her dropping stomach—it seemed to plummet clear to her toes.

Mama plucked the instrument from Sophie's hands and plopped it on the sofa. "Yes, yes, that's what I said. Hurry now, you mustn't keep him waiting." She tugged

Sophie to her feet and brushed at her skirts like a mother hen.

Sophie stood rooted in place, dumbfounded at the unexpected upheaval of her perfectly dull morning. What in the world? Why would Evan be here? Hadn't he made it abundantly clear that she was an unwanted companion? Before she could get her wits properly about her, Mama had hustled her downstairs and out the door. Sure enough, Evan stood beside a smart little curricle, the ribbons loosely clasped in his fingers.

Without even meaning to, Sophie came to an abrupt stop, her heart pounding furiously in her chest. The day may have been overcast and cool, but the sight of him sent heat rushing through her body. His lips were turned up in the slightest of smiles, but his eyes watched her with a quiet reserve that made it impossible to know what he was thinking.

"Sophie," her mother hissed, giving her arm a little pinch.

She flinched and pulled away. At least it had served to pull her from her frozen state. With both her mother and Evan watching her, she couldn't seem to remember how to properly act. "Good morning. *Afternoon*," she quickly corrected. Drawing in a fortifying breath, she walked forward, moving carefully so as not to trip or otherwise embarrass herself.

Evan dipped his head, his features trained in bland welcome. "And to you, Miss Wembley. I hope you don't mind me calling unannounced like this. The weather just seemed perfect for a nice ride about town."

"Oh, it is, quite," Mama said, her voice jarringly bright. "No danger of sunburn with all these clouds, and not a bit of wind to worry about. You are so very thoughtful, my lord."

Sophie tried not to cringe at her mother's pandering, but it wasn't easy. The best course of action was to leave, as soon as possible. "Well, then," she said, her voice coming out entirely too high. She cleared her throat and tried again. "Thank you, my lord. A ride would be lovely."

Moments later they were pulling away, leaving her beaming mother behind them. The smart *clip-clop* of the horses' hooves on the street mirrored Sophie's own heartbeat. What on earth was she doing, sitting beside the man as though nothing had happened between them? Did Julia say something to him? Sophie's cheeks burned at the thought.

"I hope you don't mind the imposition," Evan said, his voice smooth and low, the way a rider might speak to a spooked mount. "I wanted to be able to speak without being subjected to prying ears, and a ride seemed like the best option."

"Not at all," she said, offering him a nervous smile. "A very clever decision, for I can assure you my mother would be quite keen to hear whatever it is we have to say."

She clasped her hands tightly in her lap, not quite sure what to do with herself. Curiosity burned bright in her chest. What was it that he wished to speak of? What was it that he had to say that he wouldn't want overheard? She wanted to ask, but at the same time she was afraid to know. Both hope and dread took turns unsettling her stomach.

They carried on toward Prior Park Gardens, which had quite a nice driving lane, without a lot of traffic. It was only two miles from the city center, but was located up the surrounding hillside, so it had marvelous views overlooking Bath. *Not* that Sophie could focus on anything other than her nerves.

After they passed the park's stone gate, Evan slowed the horses to a walk. Glancing over at her with a small smile, he said, "I feel as though I owe you an apology. I fear I mishandled things the other night, and I want you to know that I value our friendship."

Friendship. She didn't miss the emphasis. "You're very kind. Thank you." The words felt stilted on her tongue. Here she was, sitting so close beside him her shoulder bumped his whenever they turned, and yet he was more distant from her than ever.

No, that wasn't true. He had been leaps and bounds more distant after the kiss. It was . . . kind of him to do this. She had to give him credit for wanting to settle things between them.

His shoulders relaxed, subtly, but she still noticed. "You are a lovely person, Sophie, and I don't want you to believe I think otherwise. I hold you in the highest regard."

She blinked and looked over at him. *Sophie?* It sent a shiver of delight through her to hear her name on his lips. Not Miss Wembley, not Sophie Hood—just Sophie. Now of all times. There had to be some sort of irony in that.

"It's very noble of you to say so. It's a relief to know I didn't irreparably damage things between us. I'd have a devil of a time finding someone else to sing to me—or translate Italian operas, for that matter." Her grin was somewhat self-deprecating. She knew things would never be the same between them, but it didn't make the butterflies that swarmed in her stomach whenever he was near stop fluttering.

He chuckled lightly. "And I couldn't find another who would be interested in hearing it."

They plodded along for a minute, neither of them speaking. It could very well turn out to be the last time she spoke to him, but for the life of her, she didn't know what to say to the man. Of course, the beauty of it being the last time was, well, did it really matter what she said? Her brows came together.

No, it didn't. Just as it wouldn't matter what she did. She glanced at his profile, her pulse fluttering faster as an idea formed.

After a moment, he looked over to her, his eyebrows raised. "Yes?"

"We're friends, are we not?"

He nodded, a hint of wariness creasing his forehead.

"And you know that very soon, my mother and I will be returning to Appleton for good?"

"I do," he said, his voice softening with compassion.

She forged ahead. "Since there will be no more Seasons or festivals for me, it is unlikely that we will meet again."

He nodded, his eyes trained on the path. "Unfortunately, yes. Though if your circumstances were to change, I would always be glad to see you again."

Drawing a tight breath, she turned to him. "Then may I ask you a question?"

He flicked his gaze toward her, then slowed the horses to a stop and turned to face her. "By all means."

"In the labyrinth, before you thought better of it, you kissed me back . . . did you not?" She could hardly believe she was even saying the words, but she didn't look away. She held his gaze evenly, wanting him to see her earnestness.

He shifted uncomfortably. "Sophie—"

"Please, Evan," she said, interrupting what was sure to be a clever dodge of the question. "Please just say yes or no. I promise it is in no way a trick question, and there is no one to hear us but your matched chestnuts, and I'm fairly certain they are more interested in eating the grass than listening to our conversation." She clamped her lips together, attempting to stanch the torrent of words before she made a fool of herself. *More* of a fool, anyway. Still, she pleaded with her eyes, willing him to be honest in this one small thing.

He blew out a breath, but didn't look away. "Yes."

"So it wasn't completely awful, was it?"

A fleeting smile brushed his lips. "No, not at all. But—"

She didn't let him say whatever qualifier lay at the tip of his tongue. "Then may I ask one more thing?"

He glanced out over the path briefly, shaking his head, before meeting her gaze again. "Why do I feel it would be prudent to say no?"

"Consider it a last wish?" she said hopefully, pouring her heart and soul into her eyes.

"You make it sound as though you're ready to stick your spoon in the wall. You're simply going away for a while. I imagine you will have family and friends aplenty to grant your every wish." He adjusted the ribbons in his hands, but didn't look away from her.

She shook her head. "No one can grant this wish but you. Evan, I know you don't think of me as anything but a friend. We'll be parting very soon, and before you know it I—and this time we have had together—will be but a distant memory."

"Sophie—"

But she didn't slow down, didn't let him say whatever logical argument he was building. "But for me, this will always be one of the most magical summers of my life. I'll never forget it, or you, or all the wonderful things I have experienced.

"I know I'm destined to be a spinster. I know that the

best part of my life has been lived. So I ask you, as a friend and a wonderful man whom I not only trust, but admire greatly . . ." She paused, licking her lips and inhaling a steadying breath. "Would you please do me the honor of giving me my last kiss?"

He sat there, watching her with a wealth of unreadable emotion darkening his blue gaze. "Sophie," he said at last, raspiness touching his normally smooth voice, "I hardly think such a thing would be proper."

"Good! A lady needs a little adventure to look back on in her life." She leaned forward, wrapping her fingers around his forearm. "Wouldn't you like to look back and say that you didn't always do the exact proper thing? That once, just because, you took a girl up on her offer and kissed her soundly, knowing full well that you both would walk away with nothing but fondness for one another?"

"And here I thought you were a romantic," he said dryly.

"I am! The absolute worst, in fact." She shook her head and sighed. "But the thing is, I've had exactly one kiss. It was entirely of my doing, as will this be, but at least this time you'll be kissing me, as opposed to a rather clumsy ambush on my part."

"It wasn't clumsy."

"It was, terribly, and don't try to change the subject. I shan't be diverted."

He opened his mouth, then shut it, then opened it again. "You certainly know how to craft an argument, do you know that?"

She grinned, the heady buzz of triumph lifting her heart. "Anyone who talks as much as I do will occasionally manage to wear down the listener."

Pursing his lips, he glanced about the park. Though not crowded, there still was the occasional passerby. He flicked the reins, setting them back into motion. Sophie didn't dare speak, not wanting to upset the tentative agreement she had seen in his eyes. Her nerves hummed with anticipation as she tried to remember how to breathe.

Another kiss from Evan; a proper one this time. Well, as proper as a begged-for kiss could be. Still . . . She bit her lip, doing her best to keep her giddiness at bay.

The curricle slowed as Evan eased back on the reins. Ahead, the path wound around a small copse of trees. The low-hanging branches would be the perfect cover for obscuring them from casual observers.

Her blood raced, making her a little light-headed as the carriage pulled to a stop. Evan turned to her, his pale gaze serious. "Are you absolutely certain? Knowing we will soon part ways and perhaps never see one another again?"

She nodded, a rapid movement of her head that answered him when her suddenly tied tongue couldn't. He jumped to the ground, then turned to hand her down. She stood and reached for his hand, but instead he grasped her by the waist and lifted her. *Good heavens!* Her heart roared in her ears as her hands went to his shoulders, and she clung to him as he slowly lowered her to the ground. His eyes never left hers, and she couldn't have looked away if her life had depended on it.

When her feet touched the ground, he didn't release his grip on her. She held her breath as his hands tightened at her waist, holding her securely in place. He didn't pull her against him or step closer to her. He simply held her, his elbows locked at his sides while his gaze skimmed over her face, making her heart race even faster with the intimacy of the moment. His fingers were gentle but firm, his eyes more intense than she would have expected.

His gaze dropped to her lips. She could hardly take the suspense, nearly coming out of her skin with anticipation. His clean, light musk surrounded her, torturing her with his nearness.

"Sophie," he whispered, shaking his head. "We shouldn't." But he didn't relax his hold. If anything, he seemed to draw her the slightest bit closer.

"Please, Evan," she breathed, unable to bear the thought of him pulling away now, when her whole body was aflame with the need to feel his lips on hers. "Just this once."

Blowing out a breath, he gave the barest hint of a nod. She stood with her head tipped back as she waited for him to move. Wetting his lips, he lowered his head, inch by tantalizing inch, until he was close enough for her to feel the heat of his skin. Then, just when she thought she might die from suspense, his hands flexed at her waist as he dipped down and pressed his lips to hers.

Chapter Twenty

Sophie's head swam with the intense rush of desire that washed through her at the feel of his mouth against hers. Her fingers found their way to his hard chest as he kissed her once, twice, three times, each kiss firm but chaste. After the third kiss he pulled back slightly, watching her with a sort of half-lidded look that made her fingers curl into the fabric of his lapels.

She gazed up at him, her lips parted as she struggled to draw a proper breath. In that moment, she held absolutely nothing back from him. She poured all of her heart into her eyes, all of the love and desire and longing that filled her every time she looked at him, or even thought about him.

With a sharp exhale, his mouth swooped down to claim hers once more, only this time he didn't pull away. This time he tugged her flush against him while his lips parted against hers. There was nothing chaste about this kiss, thank God. She didn't hesitate for even a moment, eagerly opening to him, anxious to touch, taste, experience him any way she could.

The kiss was everything she could have wanted, everything she could have possibly dreamed. The invisible barrier that always seemed to stand between them evaporated beneath the heat of their passion, leaving him so very accessible to her.

Her fingers stole up to the back of his neck, pulling them even closer together. His chest was solid against her breasts, an unyielding wall that somehow felt exactly right. She relished the foil of his hardness against her softness, his strength against her weakness.

The kiss was so much more than the touch of lips and dancing of tongues. It was the moment she had dreamed of since she had laid eyes on him that very first time. He wasn't holding back as she feared he might; he was sharing himself with her in a way she could never forget. In that moment, she could believe that he loved her back. She could believe that he was every bit as affected by their kiss as she, that his body sang with desire as hers did, that his heart pounded every bit as hard.

His hands slid down over her back and settled at her waist, pulling her hips soundly against his, if only for a moment. Her blood raced with desire so acute, she moaned out loud. She knew with absolute certainty that she would never forget this moment, or the way she felt in his arms.

When he pulled away at last, it was with a lingering reluctance that brought their lips back together twice before he breathed deeply and leaned his forehead against hers. She stood there, panting, unable to believe what had just happened. He released her waist and she followed suit, dropping her hands limply from his neck. But instead of pulling away, he wrapped his arms around her shoulders and held her in a sweet embrace for a few thundering heartbeats.

Finally, he pulled away, his chest rising and falling as he took several deep breaths. "Will that sustain you, sweet Sophie Hood?"

Sustain her? She could live on that for the rest of her life. Swallowing, she nodded. "Yes. Quite. Very much so." She pressed her lips together, trying to bring her soaring heart back into her chest where it belonged. "Thank you."

There was no levity in his gaze, no teasing or dismissive rolls of his eyes. If she hadn't known better, she'd have guessed that he was just as affected by their kiss as she was. "You are welcome." Drawing a deep breath, he stepped back and held out his hand. "I think perhaps we should head back. I wouldn't want to worry your mother."

He helped her back into the carriage before climbing up behind her. Within minutes, they were back on the road, headed down the hill to Bath. She found it almost impossible to believe that he would soon deposit her at her house and ride away from her for good. How was it possible to share that much passion and simply walk away from a person? She thought of a thousand different things to say to him, a thousand different ways to beg him to stay with her, but no words passed her lips.

The truth was, there were only three that really mattered, and those were the three that cut through everything else. *I love you, I love you, I love you.*

If only she could say them out loud.

After leaving Sophie's house, Evan made it as far as the next corner before pulling the horses to a stop and raking both hands through his hair. His heart was still thundering against his ribs, his breathing still erratic.

God's teeth, he deserved to be horse-whipped.

First of all, he should never have agreed to such an outlandish request. No matter how pleading her big brown eyes had been, no matter how oddly logical her argument, he should have bloody well told her no—just like any sane person would have.

But no, he'd let himself be swayed, convincing himself it was a kindness when in reality, he had *wanted* it. He had wanted to kiss her again, from the moment she had emerged from the front door with such an endearingly adorable look of shock on her face. That desire had only grown when she'd sat so close beside him, her sweet, lemony-rose scent teasing him anytime they slowed.

Cramming his hat back on his head, he snapped the reins and set the horses on a very roundabout way home. He needed time to gather himself. Time to shake the odd feeling that had settled deep in his stomach. No kiss had ever been so intense for him. No woman had ever addled his brain so thoroughly. For him, there was no such thing as matters of the heart, only matters of the body. Impersonal, pleasant, forgettable. He'd never allowed himself to care so much for a woman before. Damn it all to hell, he hadn't *wanted* to drop her off at home. He hadn't wanted to bow to her, to nod politely to her mother, and to go on his merry way.

Yet it didn't matter what he wanted, damn it. He had no choice but to leave her behind. In fact, the whole incident had only driven home the fact that it was time to leave. He needed to go back to Ledbury, where he could purge himself of all these unwanted emotions. As the horses' hooves pounded the cobblestones, Evan gave up on trying to clear his cluttered mind and decided to attempt to sort it, instead.

When it came down to it, there was really no reason that he and Julia should remain in Bath.

The festival no longer held his interest. Anywhere he went would simply remind him of the events he had attended with Sophie, and how far he'd inadvertently—and then not so inadvertently—allowed things to go between them. The joy of music wasn't even there for him anymore, not with the awareness that she was having to leave it all behind as well.

The worst of it was, if he were free, he could so easily imagine himself pulling her into his arms and offering his hand in marriage. As his wife, she wouldn't have to relegate herself to the country, never to enjoy the delights of the Season or the entertainments of festivals like these again. She could buy any gown she wanted, throw as many balls as she pleased, and never again be looked down on by wretches like Miss Harmon.

For the first time ever, he could picture a woman by his side as his wife, her gay dimples brightening his day, and her lush body warming his nights. If Sophie were his, he could imagine singing to her by the lake at his estate, grinning at her over coddled eggs and buttered bread at the breakfast table, or offering her much-more-hands-on private lessons for archery.

He bit down hard on the inside of his cheek, forcing away the image.

Damn it all, he *wasn't* free, and he couldn't pretend that he ever would be. Yes, returning to the estate was the only thing that made sense now. Julia wouldn't be happy, but that was too damn bad. He'd be sure to spend the rest of the summer with her and their mother, so she would have plenty of company. He'd even throw a bloody party, if that would make her feel better.

Having made up his mind, he changed directions and headed back to the house. By the time he strode through the door and handed over his hat and gloves to Higgins, Evan was feeling at least a little more settled. He had a plan, which meant he was in control. Mostly.

"Thank you, Higgins."

The butler nodded. "Will that be all, my lord?"

"Please inform Lady Julia that I'd like to see her in

the drawing room at once. And see that we are not disturbed."

When the butler dipped his head in the affirmative, Evan went straight to the drawing room, or more accurately, to the sideboard and its impressive selection of spirits. He chose his favorite brandy and filled a glass. After taking a long draw, he walked to the window overlooking the street and sighed. It was a fine city, regardless of the talk of its decline recently. The festival had breathed life into the place, and Evan had easily lost himself in the excitement of it all. If things had gone differently, he might have stayed for quite a bit longer.

He sipped his drink, idly watching the carriages rumble by. Tonight was the concert featuring works by Thomas Linley the younger at the Assembly Rooms. He was Evan's favorite composer, but with all he needed to do to prepare for the journey home, it wouldn't make sense to go to the concert even if his heart was still set on it.

By the time the scratch at the doorway made him turn away from the window, his drink was nearly gone and he was beginning to grow impatient. He glanced toward the corridor, fully expecting to see his sister, but came up short when he laid eyes on Higgins instead. The man's face was pale, his shoulders unusually taut.

Evan set down his glass and hurried forward. "What is it? You look as though you've seen a ghost."

Uneasiness trickled down his spine as the butler wrung his hands. "I'm not sure how to say this, my lord, but it appears that Lady Julia has gone missing."

"Missing?" Evan repeated, the word harsh on his tongue. This house was not a fifth of the size of their estate in Ledbury. How on earth could one go missing in it? "I don't understand. Have you checked the gardens? The library?"

Higgins nodded, his eyes sober with concern. "Yes, my lord, but I fear I may have misspoken. I'm not certain she is so much missing as she may have decided to . . . leave." He stepped forward and extended his hand. In it was a sealed missive with Evan's name scrawled across the front in his sister's hand. "The maid found this on the escritoire in her room."

Evan snatched it from his hands and yanked it open, trepidation making his heart pound. Taking a breath, he read the short text, his blood turning colder with each word.

My dear brother,

A friend recently taught me that sometimes, we must follow our hearts, no matter how daunting the risk. Today, I am taking the biggest risk of my life: I am marrying Harry. It is a very long story, one that I will be happy to recount when we return in a few days, but for now, let me just say that I learned I couldn't keep running from love. Please don't be angry with me. I simply couldn't live in fear and regret anymore.

Julia

Evan reread it, disbelief burrowing a hole straight through him. How . . . how could she do something so unbelievably reckless? After all they'd been through, after all the years of acting for the good of the family, and she simply decided to throw it away for *Harry*, of all people? Evan cursed, sick to his stomach. He crumpled the paper and lobbed it at the wall, making the butler flinch.

He turned on the man, barely managing not to lash out with all the fury burning in his gut. "When was she last seen?"

Visibly shaken, the butler cleared his throat and straightened his shoulders. "After breakfast, my lord. Lady Julia told her maid she wished for quiet today and that she would ring when she wished for anything. My lady closed the door to her chambers, and we assumed she had been there the rest of the day."

Evan counted back. That was what, five hours ago? God help them, it was almost certainly too late to do anything. Where would they have gone? Who would have married them? A thousand questions somersaulted in his mind, none of them finding purchase. "Has she talked with anyone recently? Sent or received correspondence?"

"Only the letter to Sir Harry and the visit to Miss Wembley, my lord."

Sophie. Turning on his heel, Evan began pacing the room, trying to think. Julia was the one who had wanted Evan to go see Sophie today. Had she and Sophie somehow conspired about this yesterday? It was impossible to imagine sweet, innocent Sophie misleading him, but really, what other leads did he have to go on?

He dragged his fingers through his hair, furious but impotent to do anything about it. He thought of all the times he had implored his sister to be nice to Harry. Be kind; don't be such a shrew. Was she fighting whatever was between them all the while? Had he somehow had a hand in this as well? He gritted his teeth. They had deceived him. Julia, Harry, and possibly even Sophie.

But what could he do about it now? What if it wasn't too late after all? There was a chance, even if it was infinitesimal. With precious few options, he whipped back around to face the butler. "Have my horse saddled at once."

In less than ten minutes, Evan was on his way back to

Sophie's townhouse, pushing his horse faster than was prudent on the city streets, but not nearly as fast as he wished. He hadn't expected to see her again anytime soon, and certainly not under such circumstances as these, but he steeled himself as he approached her street.

If she knew something—anything—then Evan intended to uncover it, by whatever means necessary. Arriving in front of her door, he jumped to the ground, threw the reins over the nearest post, and rushed to the house. Three harsh bangs later, the door was pulled open and Sophie's maid appeared in the doorway. Her eyes widened to saucers and she quickly dropped into a curtsy. "Begging your pardon, my lord, but Mrs. Wembley and Miss Sophie aren't at home."

Stifling the urge to push past the girl to make sure for himself, he said, "Where are they?" As rude a question as had ever been asked, but right about then he didn't give a damn.

"Assembly Rooms, my lord. The concert."

Offering brusque thanks, Evan turned on his heel and hurried back to his horse. It would appear that he was to attend the concert after all.

Chapter Twenty-one

Sophie would much rather have been at home, dissecting every minute of her afternoon excursion with the earl, but she had already planned to attend the concert with her mother, and more importantly, Sophie knew that May would also be in attendance. If ever she needed to talk with a friend, this was the time.

As soon as they arrived, Sophie had scanned the audience, searching for May's blond hair and distinctive style. She was nowhere to be found in the Ballroom, nor the Great Octagon, nor the Card Room. The master of ceremonies had already announced the five-minute warning, and the Tea Room was emptying as people started moving to the Ballroom, where the concert would be held. Blast it all, she *really* wished to talk with May before it became impossible to do so.

Mama patted her arm. "Shall we go in, dear?" She was still floating with happiness over the earl's visit, and Sophie hadn't said anything to disabuse her of whatever assumptions she had made.

Sophie glanced toward the entrance again, stalling for a moment. "I was rather hoping to find May before we did. Perhaps just another min—" Sophie gasped, stopping in midsentence as the earl strode through the doors.

He paused, his eyes sweeping the corridor before landing on hers with enough force to steal her next breath.

"Whatever is the matter with you?" Mama asked, her brows coming together. She followed Sophie's line of sight, and excitedly reached out to squeeze her hand. "Oh, my dear, you have certainly piqued his interest. Look at the way he watches you!"

Sophie couldn't have responded to her mother for anything. She was far too busy trying to remain in an upright position. Evan's gaze was intense, his lips unsmiling. His long-legged stride closed the distance between them before she truly even had a chance to gather her wits about her.

As he arrived at their sides, the first strains of music drifted from the Ballroom—the concert was about to begin. "Good evening, Mrs. Wembley. I wonder if you would mind my stealing Miss Wembley away for a moment. There is a matter of some importance that I would like to discuss with her."

Mama's eyes bulged with surprise. "Oh. *Oh.* Yes, yes, of course, my lord." She abruptly dropped Sophie's arm and took a step back. "Why don't the two of you take a turn about the Tea Room while I find us seats?"

Moving surprisingly fast for a woman of her age and girth, she scurried off into the Ballroom. Sophie simply stood there, unable to think of a single thing to say. He was here. He was standing right next to her, after she had already given up on seeing him again at all. The memory of their kiss not even two hours ago assailed her, sending a shiver down the back of her neck.

He held out his arm, and she laid her hand upon it.

There was something odd in the way he held himself that brought the first hint of unease to her stunned excitement. His posture was stiff, his body nearly vibrating with a sort of raw energy that she didn't recognize. He led them to the Tea Room, where only two servants were left, busily setting the room back in order. Evan paid no mind to them at all as he came to a stop, turning so that he faced her directly.

"What did you and my sister speak of when she came to visit yesterday?"

Sophie blinked. The question was so far outside of anything she would have expected, she floundered for a moment. "Um, I—I don't know."

He blew out an impatient breath. "You do know. Why did she call on you? What did she want?"

Where on earth was this coming from? And why was he looking at her with such intensity, as though this were the Spanish Inquisition and her answers meant life or death? "She was worried about me. She wanted to know if I was well after . . . the way we parted at that gala."

"And what did you tell her?"

Sophie flinched at the barely leashed anger that simmered beneath his quiet words. "Evan, please, what is the matter?"

"Answer the question, please."

This was not the way she had wanted things to be between them—especially not after the passionate kiss they had shared, the kiss to end all kisses. "I said that I would be fine. That I took a risk, and it didn't pay off. I told her that it had still been worth it, because at least I had tried. At least I hadn't left my happiness completely to fate."

Blowing out a harsh breath, he scrubbed a hand over his face. He seemed to wilt before her eyes, as though the anger had been holding him up. Dropping his hand to his hip, he said, "Did she mention Harry?"

Sophie's brow wrinkled. "The baronet? Not that I remember." She took a step toward him. "Evan, what is all this about? Will you tell me what has you so terribly upset?"

The rising music echoed from the Ballroom, the melody entirely too exuberant for their conversation. Looking to the floor, he shook his head. "Julia's gone."

She gasped, her hands flying to her heart. "Gone?"

"She left a note stating her intention to marry the baronet today. I can only assume they somehow procured a special license." He looked so defeated, so angry, she couldn't resist reaching out and placing a hand on his arm. He stepped away, then turned toward the servants. "Leave us," he called, his voice ringing with the kind of authority only a peer seemed to know how to command.

The two men exchanged glances, but quickly filed out of the room, leaving Evan and Sophie alone in the huge space. He paced away from her, his movements clipped and agitated. "I thought you might know of her plans. I want to find them, to bring her home, but I have no idea where to start looking."

She wanted so badly to help him, but she could offer him nothing. "I'm so sorry. As far as I knew, she didn't even like the man."

His laugh was harsh and devoid of humor. "At least I wasn't the only one. She played us all for fools." He raked a hand over his already windblown hair, muttering something that sounded suspiciously like a curse. "Very well. Thank you for your time."

Without another word, he turned and began to stalk away, but she rushed forward, grabbing him by the arm. "Evan, wait. Please don't go like this."

"Like what?" he said, whirling around to face her. "My sister has brought disgrace to herself and her family — how am I supposed to go?"

"If it's by special license, it may raise eyebrows, but it won't bring disgrace," she said, attempting to reason with him. She would have given anything for her own sister to have married that way instead of eloping, but of course they hadn't the funds nor the connections for such a privilege.

"You don't know anything about it," he growled, raising his eyes to the ceiling. "She never should have been so reckless, so utterly self-absorbed. And Harry . . . I've half a mind to make my sister a widow before the night is over."

"Don't speak that way," Sophie said sharply, causing him to look to her in surprise. She put her hands on her hips, not allowing him to intimidate her. "I'm assuming he is the man your sister is in love with?"

He snorted. "So she says. I don't care if he's her bloody soul mate, she never should have done such a foolish, foolish thing."

"I agree," she said, ignoring his curse. If ever there was a pass on coarse language from a gentleman, this was it. "But perhaps she felt she had no other choice. Would you have consented to her marrying Harry?"

His eyes turned to stone as he crossed his arms. "No. Never."

Never? Why would he want to deny his sister the life she wished to pursue? "And you wonder why she took such drastic measures."

"I don't *care* why she took such measures. It's unforgivable to turn her back on her family like that."

Sophie knew exactly how he was feeling. She nodded, compassion filling her heart for both Evan and his sister.

"I know you feel that way now, but trust me, when your shock subsides, you'll find your way to forgiving her."

He seemed more distant than ever as he shook his head, his eyes shuttering. "You don't know anything about what I'll do, or what I'll feel."

"But that's just it. I *do*. I know exactly how you're feeling." Her heart began to pound in her chest, making her palms sweat. The last thing she wanted to do was reveal her own sister's scandalous marriage, but at that moment she longed to let him know that he wasn't alone in this. She *did* know what she was talking about.

"You can't possibly," he said, his hand slicing through the air with the vehemence of his response. Two rooms over, the jaunty music continued, providing an incongruous backdrop to their quarrel.

She stepped closer, laying a hand along the fine wool of his coat, wishing there weren't so many layers between them. "I can. I, more than anyone, know what it's like to be in your shoes."

His mouth still set, he shook his head. "You know nothing, Sophie. Nobody does."

Blowing out a breath, she looked him straight in the eye, wanting him to pay attention. "I do. My own sister eloped not three weeks ago. If anyone knows the devastation of a sister's betrayal, I do."

Evan gaped at her. "What's that?" he said, his voice taut with his incredulity.

She closed her eyes and took a long breath before meeting his gaze again. She looked vulnerable, fragile almost. "My sister Penelope eloped several weeks ago. That's why I must return home."

"Sophie, I . . ." He trailed off, at a loss for what to say. Giving a shrug, he said simply, "I'm so sorry."

"In another week or so, the whole of the *ton* will know of my family's downfall. Penelope's decision will effectively ruin any chance Pippa and I have of marriage and family."

There was such aching regret in her voice, such profound disappointment, he longed to wrap his arms around her. "I'm sure you'll still have the opportunity, once the scandal has blown over." Despite his own riotous emotions about Julia, he couldn't help but want to comfort Sophie.

Her smile was heartbreaking. "Perhaps if my father had wealth or rank . . . We are already on the outskirts of society, however. The possibility of regaining our standing is practically nil."

And yet . . . she had shared her situation with him. She had spoken the truth that would soon bring her pain so that he might feel better. Tenderness, and something more, washed through him like rain after a drought.

The promise of all those things he had wished he could have with her assailed him all over again. Love, marriage, children, *happiness.* He wanted it all, and he resented more than ever that it couldn't be. He wanted her to know how he felt, how much he wanted her, and that he would marry her tomorrow if he could. He wanted to tell her, so damn badly.

But unlike Julia, Evan knew it was impossible. And to tell Sophie how he felt about her, knowing that nothing could ever come of it, seemed like the cruelest possible thing to do.

Pulling himself up to his full height, he looked down at her with what he hoped appeared to be gentle neutrality. "I'm very sorry for your family's difficulty, just as I am sorry for mine. Neither one of us deserves what our siblings have done."

She must have heard the coldness in his voice. Her brow knitted, concern clouding her dark eyes as she stepped still closer to him. "But that's what I was trying to say. You'll forgive your sister, just as I have forgiven mine. I came to realize that Penelope did what she must have felt she had to in order to grab hold of the love that she felt she couldn't have any other way."

She shook her head, raising her shoulders. "How can I begrudge my sister's being in love? Knowing, as I do, how all-consuming love can be, how unbearably wonderful and perfectly breathtaking it is, how could I want any less for her?"

Evan's blood ran hot, then icy-cold, as he realized what she had just said. *Knowing, as I do . . .* He knew she harbored a *tendre*, but *love*? Was she in love with him as well? The truth of it kicked him squarely in the chest, leaving him breathless.

He couldn't do this. He had far too much to deal with already—how could he handle both his and Sophie's heartbreak on top of everything else? With effort, he drained his features of anything but polite detachment. "I suppose you have a right to react to your sister's choices any way you wish. Now then, if you will excuse me, I must be on my way. If I can't locate Julia, then I want to be home when she returns."

He held out his arm expectantly, ready to escort her to her mother. She stared at it for one blank moment. "Evan . . ."

"My apologies, but I really must be on my way. Your mother will be waiting, as well."

The pained expression in her eyes was nearly his undoing. He held strong, though, raising an impatient eyebrow. Her cheeks flared bright pink, and for a moment he thought she might protest. Her eyes shimmered suspiciously in the golden candlelight, and he steeled himself against the threat of seeing her tears.

She blinked rapidly several times, then set her fingers against his sleeve. In silence, he escorted her to the door of the Ballroom, where Linley's masterpiece *Let God Arise* was being performed with impressive enthusiasm. With a final bow, he turned and left her, cursing his father, his sister, and most of all, himself, the entire way home.

Chapter Twenty-two

For several minutes, Sophie stood outside the concert, listening to the rise and fall of the symphony as her inner turmoil raged. She had reached out to Evan, told him her most devastating secret, and all he could do was offer his apologies and be on his way?

Had he known that, in her own way, she was telling him of her love for him? For a moment, she'd thought he had, but then the frost had descended over his eyes and she had been completely shut out. She felt . . . betrayed. How could he not care about her emotions? How could he not care for his sister's? What kind of man would prevent his only sister's chance for happiness and love, forcing her to marry in secret without his consent?

Unable to bear the thought of going inside and joining the crowd, she moved to the cluster of chairs situated opposite the doors and crumpled onto the closest one. The last thing she wanted to do was go sit beside her mother and attempt to smile her way through the performance.

For the next twenty minutes, she sat in silence, surrounded by the muted strains of Linley's vaunted works as they echoed in the otherwise empty corridor. Just when she was beginning to relax, the squeak of the Ballroom door made her jerk upright. She quickly dashed any remaining moisture from her cheeks and patted at her hair, trying to at least look normal. To her vast relief, it was May who slipped through the door. When her eyes landed on Sophie, her brows snapped together and she hurried over to the conversation area.

"Sophie, what are you doing here? Your mother asked me to check on you and Lord Evansleigh since you've been gone so long." She paused, sympathy softening her eyes as she took in Sophie's doubtlessly tearstained face. "Oh, my dear. What is the matter?"

Sophie leaned back, shaking her head. "I told him. I told the truth about my sister. I told him how I feel, I laid everything on the table, and . . . nothing. He simply walked away."

It was validating, at least, to see the indignation flare in May's sapphire eyes. "Then he's an idiot. Not surprising, given his sex, but still, I am sorry that he so clearly hurt you."

"Could you please go tell Mama I want to go home? I simply can't sit here another moment longer."

May nodded. "Yes, of course. And I'm coming with you. No woman should be alone after something so wretched as this."

"No, really, you needn't worry about me."

"Whyever not? Is there some other pressing matter holding my attention?" She looked around, as though searching the empty corridor for the matter in question. "No, not a thing that I can see."

It was very, very tempting to take May up on her offer, but Sophie knew she had to tell her mother where things stood with the earl. It wasn't the sort of conversation one wanted to subject friends to. She shook her head. "No, tonight I must have a long, dreadful talk with my mother. Tomorrow, however, I shall expect you first thing, extra handkerchiefs and gingerbread biscuits in hand."

Nodding, May squeezed her hands and offered an encouraging smile. "Very well, if that is what you want. Now, chin up, darling—I shall be back in a trice."

As she stood, the music rose in an enthusiastic crescendo, followed by polite applause. Sophie cringed and came to her feet. "Never mind—it appears my mother, along with everyone else, will be coming to me."

"Rotten timing." May sighed and turned back to Sophie. "Last chance to change your mind about me accompanying you home."

"You're lovely, but no. One of us, at least, should enjoy this marvelous concert. It's not every day you can hear one of the best orchestras England has to offer play the English Mozart's masterpieces."

Mama appeared in the doorway then, her face anxious as she glanced about. Seeing Sophie, she visibly exhaled and hurried to her side. "Gracious, child, where have you been?" She paused, looking around with a questioning glance. "Where is your beau?"

May offered a sympathetic grimace before slipping away to join her aunt, who was just emerging from the Ballroom. Sophie placed her hand over her mother's elbow and steered her toward the door. "It's a long story, Mama. I'll tell you all about it on the way home, if you please."

Her mother stopped, bringing Sophie to a jarring halt. "It is only intermission, my dear. We still have half the concert left. Come, let us go to the Tea Room and you can tell me all about it over a nice cup of tea."

"Mama, please," Sophie whispered, mindful of the

dozens upon dozens of people loitering about. "I feel quite ill, and I wish to go home *now*."

Over her mother's shoulder, Sophie saw Marianne gliding past, escorted by Lord Bridgemont, the arrogant and condescending heir of the Earl of Marks. Sophie hadn't even known the man was here—not that she would have cared. She was too far below his notice to even warrant his disdain, thankfully.

Mama sent her a stern look. "Oh, don't be so dramatic, Sophie. I'm sure it's nothing a bit of refreshment won't cure." She perked up and waved to someone across the room, her eyes lighting. "Oh, it's Lord Derington. Come along; we simply must greet him."

Sophie felt more desperate than ever to escape. "No, please—"

But it was too late. Mama had already started off, dragging Sophie in her wake. Marianne glanced up as they attempted to wend their way through the growing crowd. Her eyes widened as her gaze met Sophie's, and she quickly tapped on Lord Bridgemont's arm. Something in the way she spoke to the viscount and tipped her head in their direction sent a wave of apprehension straight through Sophie.

Purposely averting her eyes, she sidled up closer to her mother and tried to ignore them as she and Mama pushed through the throng.

"Well, if it isn't Mrs. Wembley and Miss Wembley. What a shock to see you here."

Drat, blast, damn. Sophie straightened and turned in unison with her mother to face the pair. Marianne's face was aglow in a sort of smug gleefulness that instantly had Sophie on edge. "Miss Harmon. Lord Bridgemont," she murmured, dipping in a quick curtsy. "I'm sorry, but we were just on our way—"

"Out of here, I should hope," Marianne replied, her voice sharp and clear.

Mama gasped, taking a step back. "Miss Harmon, I hardly think—"

"*I* hardly think any of us care what you think, Mrs. Wembley. Why, Bridgemont here was just telling me the news from London upon his arrival today, and I distinctly remember a bit of gossip about your daughter."

The people around them hushed, as everyone seemed to collectively lean in to hear whatever delicious on-dit Marianne was about to serve up. Sophie tugged urgently on her mother's arm. "Please, let's go," she hissed, but to no avail. Mama was as good as rooted to the ground, her face a mask of appalled guilt.

Bridgemont clucked his tongue, looking down on them both with a false reluctance as he shook his head. "Such a pity when a child heaps scandal upon her whole family. Running off with a lowly servant—shocking." Each word was clipped and spoken in a nasal tone, carrying over the stunned silence around them.

"No, no," Mama said, looking around to all the scandalized faces around them. "She hasn't run off—she married him! And we'll have another wedding—a proper one—as soon as they return."

Sophie could have melted away in a puddle of mortification. Her mother's defense only made it sound that much worse. Whispers flew through the crowd as the truth spread like a pox.

Marianne shuddered and backed up a step. "An elopement? And how many nights did they share as they made their way to the blacksmith?" she asked, one perfectly arched golden eyebrow lifting in condescension. "What sort of morals have you raised your children with, madam?"

The entire scene was straight out of Sophie's night-mares. She could see May at the edge of the crowd, both of her aunt's hands locked around her arm to keep her from rushing into the crowd to help. Everyone else was a gleeful witness to the Wembley family's downfall. Sophie tugged again, her panic rising. "Mama, *now.*"

A commotion ahead made her look up. Dering was pushing his way through the crowd, using his height and weight to his advantage so those around him had no choice but to make way. "Mrs. Wembley," he fairly boomed, coming to her side. "My carriage is just outside. Might I offer you and Miss Wembley a ride?"

Sophie's relief was so profound, her knees nearly buckled. "Yes, thank you, my lord," she said, yanking sharply on her mother's arm.

"Yes, be on your way," Marianne said, her chin lifting as she looked away. "There are standards in our society, after all. It's a wonder your family has been accepted this long."

"That's enough, Miss Harmon," Dering said, his voice calm but authoritative. He held his arm to Sophie's mother. "Madam?"

Mama looked down at his arm, then clumsily laid her hand upon it. Sophie could feel her shaking, and she was worried that her mother might have a fit of vapors right there in the middle of the Assembly Rooms corridor. Dering started forward and the crowd parted like the Red Sea, turning to stare as the trio passed.

Sophie kept her eyes trained forward, struggling to hold back the tears of humiliation, anger, and hurt. If she could just make it to the doors, everything would be all right. If she could just get into the carriage, she would live. If she could just make it home, things would some-how work out.

When they stepped into the cool evening air, Dering called to a servant and demanded that his carriage be fetched at once. Turning to Sophie, he sighed and shook his head. "That was badly done of Miss Harmon, crying rope like that. Shameful, really."

She swallowed, trying to think past the roar in her ears. She realized that she was shaking nearly as badly as her mother. Drawing a steadying breath, she said, "I cannot thank you enough, my lord."

The door banged open, and May ran out to join them, her cheeks as red as the embroidered silk sash on her dress. "I'm so sorry!" she exclaimed, rushing to Sophie's side. "I only caught the end of it, but my horrible aunt kept me back. Tell me: What can I do for you?"

Sophie looked to her mother, who still seemed dazed. What could May do? Sophie lifted her shoulders in a helpless shrug. "Nothing. Nothing is to be done. We are found out and must quit Bath, just as we knew would happen."

And they *had* known. They had done their best to find a way to fix it, but it was an unfixable situation. With Evan's back turned on them, there was no one that could make this better.

Sucking in a deep, fortifying breath, she looked back and forth between her savior and her friend. "I owe you both a debt of gratitude. Thank you for your kindness."

May stepped forward, her blue eyes flashing. "Don't be ridiculous—you owe us nothing. We are your friends, and no piddling scandal is going to change that."

The carriage rounded the corner and pulled to a stop in front of them. Sophie released her mother long enough to give May a quick, tight hug and Dering a light kiss on the cheek. "The sooner we get home, the better. Thank you again. I don't know what I would have done without you."

Within moments they were wrapped in the oversized opulence of Dering's custom barouche, hurrying toward the townhouse. Exhausted, Sophie drooped back against the velvet squabs. Things would never be the same.

"I thought we'd have a few more days," Mama murmured, her voice a thin thread. Her face was pale, with the exception of two bright pink spots high on the apples of her cheeks.

Sophie shifted and laid her head on her mother's shoulder, feeling truly hopeless for the first time in her life. "I know, Mama. Me, too." Though what good would it have done? Regardless of whether it happened today or next week, the end result would still be the same.

Out of nowhere, her mother sat up abruptly, jarring Sophie in her haste. "Lord Evansleigh! He'll save us, surely. Did he make his intentions known? Is that what he wished to speak about?" Her eyes were overly bright, bordering on wild, as she clung to this one last hope.

Sophie's disappointment washed over her anew, even sharper than it had been when Evan had left her. She shook her head, fighting against the tears that burned at the back of her eyes. "No, Mama. He doesn't want me."

The words echoed through her mind as her mother's last hope collapsed into ash. Mama opened her mouth to speak, but Sophie held up a desperate hand. "No, please. Let us just make it home. Then we may talk."

Thankfully, her mother didn't fight her, and they rode the rest of the way in silence. It gave Sophie the opportunity to try to organize her scattered thoughts—but it also highlighted exactly how upset her mother was. Once they arrived home, they made their way to the drawing room, where Sophie shut the door and led Mama to the sofa.

Her mother's color was better, at least. Her cheeks were still bright pink, but her face wasn't nearly as pale, or her eyes as wild. She actually looked much more self-possessed than Sophie would have expected.

Good—that made one of them.

As Sophie sat down, she couldn't quite shake the feeling of hopelessness. How could she? She had lost both her love and the life she knew all in one evening. Where was she to go from here?

Mama settled onto the chair adjacent to Sophie and laid her hands primly in her lap. "Now then," she said, her voice surprisingly calm as she peered at Sophie with steely eyes. "Tell me exactly what happened."

It was best to get it over with as quickly as possible. Lifting her chin, she said, "I made my feelings known to the earl, and he very plainly turned me away." Such a polite way to say her heart had been ripped in two.

Mama tilted her head, as though puzzling through Sophie's response. "That simply does not make any sense. He seemed plenty interested today when he called. I wonder . . . ," she said, the skin around her eyes wrinkling as she narrowed her gaze. "What matter did he wish to discuss with you this evening?"

Sophie really, really didn't want to say. The last thing she wanted to be was a dreadful scandalmonger like that horrible Marianne. But in this case, she didn't want to lie to her mother, especially since the truth of Julia's marriage would be common knowledge soon enough. Feeling like the worst sort of gossip, Sophie said, "He thought I might know where to find his sister."

Interest flickered in her dark eyes as she leaned forward. "Is she missing?"

Miserably, Sophie shook her head. "She has secretly married their neighbor, the baronet. She did so without Evan's consent or knowledge, and he was understandably upset."

"I see," Mama murmured, sadness chasing across her features. "I can certainly relate. But I still don't understand what could have happened that would cause him to turn away from you in such a short amount of time. Were you insensitive to his predicament?"

Sophie looked down at her hands. It had seemed like such a kindness at the time, sharing how she understood his shock. But sitting here beneath Mama's watchful eye, she oddly felt like a traitor for having shared their shame. Not that it mattered—after the scene tonight, all of Bath would know by morning. Sighing, she met her mother's gaze. "I told him about Penelope."

Mama visibly recoiled. "You did *what*? Sophie, how could you!" She jumped to her feet and began pacing, her expression hovering somewhere between anger and upset. As she paced, Sophie could practically see all the humiliation from the scene at the Assembly Rooms combining with her bitter disappointment and snowballing into fury. "Why couldn't you have secured his promise before all of this happened? You've destroyed your chances. You've destroyed *all* our chances. His status could have easily carried us out of this scandal, were his name aligned with ours."

A flicker of anger ignited in Sophie's belly. Scandal be damned—she wanted him because she *loved* him. The threat of scandal may have been the impetus she had needed to take a risk, but her feelings for the man would have been the same either way.

Crossing her arms, she met her mother's accusing gaze. "I put everything I had into wooing the earl. If I did not succeed, it was not for lack of trying. As for telling him about Penelope, what difference did it make in the end? I'm not sorry for it." She sat forward, trying to make her mother understand. "I said it in order to show him that I knew how he felt, and because I wanted to help lessen the shock of his sister's actions. Who better to ease his pain than someone who had been through nearly the same thing?"

Mama paused in midstep, the anger abruptly draining from her face. "You might actually have a point."

Sophie blinked in surprise. "I do?" She hadn't expected to get through to her mother.

"Yes, you do." Striding back to the sofa, she sat down next to Sophie and grabbed her hands. "Before this all happened, the earl showed quite a lot of interest in you, did he not?"

"Um, well, I suppose," Sophie hedged, not sure how to explain her relationship with him.

"You suppose?" Mama huffed, eyeing her carefully. "Did the earl ever kiss you?"

If she could have said no, she would have, but Sophie's cheeks immediately flamed red-hot, as good as answering the question for her. Knowing there was nothing for it, she nodded.

"Today? On your carriage ride?"

Sophie nodded again. There was really no point in lying about it.

"I see. So his interest remained until he learned the news of his sister." A relieved smile parted her lips. "That is excellent news. There is hope yet, my little magpie."

The growing optimism on her mother's face didn't bode well. Sophie quickly shook her head. "No, Mama. You don't understand. He made it quite clear that he had no intentions of seeing me again. *Ever.* It's hopeless."

Her mother's eyes glinted with hard resolution as she waved off Sophie's words. "Nonsense, child. He was clearly overwrought by the shock of his sister's marriage. He likely needed a bit more time to sort himself out."

Sophie didn't like where this was going. Mama had suffered a shock herself, not even an hour ago. Of course she would be grasping at straws, trying to find a way to fix the dreadful situation they now found themselves in. "You don't understand. He doesn't *want* me." It hurt to say the words, but they were the stark truth.

Her mother sat up straight and tall, her chin lifted in determination. "No daughter of mine will give up this easily. Tomorrow, you shall go to him and be the support he so clearly needs. By then he will have regretted his words, and it is up to you to show your graciousness by looking past his momentary lapse."

"But, Mama, such a thing would be impossibly un-seemly. Without his sister in residence, I can't very well show up on his doorstep."

"First of all, it sounds as though no one knows his sister is gone, and second of all, yes, you certainly can 'show up on his doorstep,' as you so vulgarly put it. He is in his time of need, and clearly propriety is no longer a concern for us here. You have been and will forever be painted with the same broad brush as your sister, in that regard. You might as well use it to your advantage."

Sophie's stomach roiled at the very thought, but there was no mistaking her mother's steely determination. There would be no putting her off. And as pathetic as it sounded, deep down, Sophie wanted to believe her mother was right. Perhaps since he'd now had a little time to adjust to the idea of his sister's marriage, he wouldn't be quite so harsh. It was possible he would regret the way he had handled things today.

Extremely unlikely, but possible.

Taking a shaky breath, Sophie nodded to her mother. "Very well."

"Excellent," Mama replied, clapping her hands together. Turning a sly glance in Sophie's direction, she added, "And Sophie, if he has kissed you once, then there can be no doubt of his interest. I strongly suggest you entice him to kiss you again."

Sophie was so mortified by the thought, she didn't even try to refuse. She simply nodded and came to her feet, wanting more than anything to escape. "Good night, Mama."

Her mother rose as well, nodding. "Good night, magpie. Tomorrow things will turn around. You'll see."

Sophie bobbed her head once before making her getaway. Already her heart was pounding at the very thought of what she would do on the morrow. She had never dreamed to be so bold as to call on a single gentleman, let alone in broad daylight. But with little left to lose, she was about to take the gamble of her life.

Chapter Twenty-three

Evan hadn't slept well. He'd stayed up most of the night, decimating his best bottle of whiskey while contemplating the many things he would say to his sister when she finally showed herself. Of course, he couldn't remember a single one of them this morning. All he had to show for his efforts was a dull, pounding headache and a stiff neck from falling asleep in his chair.

Sitting down to a late breakfast, he ignored the toast he had halfheartedly tossed on his plate and picked up his coffee. Black, bitter, and hot—the perfect antidote to a night spent dipping too deep. After several long sips, he leaned back and sighed.

The breakfast room was distractingly quiet, and the absence of his sister weighed heavily on his heart. He avoided looking at her empty chair, focusing instead on the damp garden beyond the rain-splattered window-panes. At least the weather was cooperating with his foul mood.

The door opened and closed, and Higgins appeared at his elbow. "Pardon me, my lord, but Miss Wembley is here, insisting to speak with you."

Evan jerked around in his chair, sloshing hot coffee

over his fingers. He cursed, shaking the liquid from his hand even as he looked to Higgins. "Miss Wembley is *here*?"

"Yes, my lord. I would have sent her away at once, but she insisted that you would want to see her. I didn't wish to speak out of turn by telling her that Lady Julia was not in residence, and it was therefore highly improper for her to be here."

Evan's mind raced. If Sophie had come here, knowing full well that his sister was not at home, then she must have a damn good reason to do so. Yes, he had been determined to set her aside yesterday, but that was before she risked her reputation by calling on him like this. Tossing his napkin on the table, he came to his feet. "Where is she?"

"Waiting in the foyer," Higgins replied with an indignant little sniff. "I didn't think it wise to leave her outside in the rain, nor did it seem prudent to show her to the drawing room."

Before the butler even finished speaking, Evan strode from the room and bounded down the stairs. When he saw her, he drew up short, surprised at how pale and drawn her features were. Her oversized bonnet cast her face in shadow, and instead of yellow, she wore a dreary dark blue traveling costume.

Swallowing past the rush of tenderness that assailed him, he hurried forward to speak with her. "What is it? Are you not well? Have you had word from my sister?"

She shook her head, setting the damp curls around her face swinging. "No, no, nothing like that. I'm afraid news of my sister's elopement has reached Bath. We are to leave this afternoon."

Despite all of his own turmoil, his heart went out to her. "What happened?"

Her lips thinned as she glanced at the marble tile beneath his feet. "Miss Harmon took great delight in sharing the news during the intermission at the concert last night."

The force of his anger took him by surprise. Damn the jealous chit. He could only imagine how upsetting it must have been for Sophie, right on the heels of their argument. He'd left her hurt and vulnerable, and she'd likely been torn to shreds, if he knew Miss Harmon.

"Damn it all," he said, his voice sounding tortured on her behalf. "You didn't deserve that. Is there anything I can do to help?"

When her eyes flicked up to meet his, the depth of emotion he saw there made him flinch. Hurt and disappointment were in the forefront, but behind it, he could still sense the love she had so bravely admitted to. It made his chest ache so fiercely, it was all he could do not to wrap her in his arms.

"No, I . . . I just thought you should know that we were leaving. And I wanted you to know that I meant what I said about Julia. Try not to judge her too harshly. It's difficult to imagine what you'll do for love until you're faced with the prospect of living without it."

He didn't want to talk about Julia just then. He was still angry enough with her that he didn't trust what he would say. Stepping forward, he started to reach out to Sophie, but thought better of it at the last moment. "No matter what has happened in your family, I believe that you're simply too bright a personality to be kept under a bushel. Someday, a man worthy of your love will come along, and when he does, I shall write you a letter just to say I told you so."

He would also personally investigate the bastard to make sure he was good enough for her. He bit down on the inside of his cheek and tried to regain his control. Just thinking about it made him want to hit something.

Whatever she had been hoping he would say, clearly that had not been it. She looked up at him, her beautiful brown eyes full of both regret and acceptance. Letting out a soft sigh, she reached for his bare hand and lifted it in both of hers. Closing her eyes, she pressed a warm kiss to the tops of his knuckles, then turned his hand and placed another to his palm.

It was the sweetest torture he had ever endured. He stood completely still, unwilling to encourage her, but unable to pull away. Lowering their joined hands, she said, "Please give Julia my love. I shall miss you both greatly."

She turned toward the door, and he stepped forward to open it for her. Everything inside of him screamed for him to slam the door, wrap her in his arms, and make her his own. But too much was riding on his shoulders, especially with Julia's reckless marriage. Clutching the doorknob, he bowed his head as she walked over the threshold and out of his life.

Or so he thought.

She was only a few feet from the open door when her mother came rushing up, her damp coat flapping behind her as her face contorted with outrage. "Sophie Marie Wembley, what have you done?" she cried.

What the hell? Evan bolted outside to stand beside Sophie, who gaped at her mother in openmouthed shock. Putting a hand to her heart, she hurried forward. "Mama, please! Keep your vo—"

"Did he think to take advantage of you in your weakened state?" the woman demanded, rolling right over Sophie's attempt to speak. Color stained her plump cheeks as she pinned her daughter with an accusing glare. "I came the moment I realized you were missing, but clearly I am too late if you were inside his lordship's home. *Alone*," she added, her neck quivering with her dismay.

One of the neighbors' doors opened, and several other curtains were pulled aside. Lady Gorst, who had been stepping from her townhouse two doors down, veered away from her waiting carriage and hurried over, her thin face agog with the unfolding drama. It was just his luck the worst of the busybody neighbors would be witness to it all.

Evan's heart plummeted as he realized where all of this was headed.

Putting up both his hands, he forced a calm into his voice that he didn't feel. "Nothing to worry about, Mrs. Wembley. Miss Wembley merely came to call on my sister, and I informed her that she was not about." It took all of his willpower not to grab the woman and shake the histrionics out of her. For God's sake, it wasn't as though Sophie had spent the night.

But the woman had worked herself up to high dudgeon. She turned to Lady Gorst, her hands to her chest. "How could he have invited my Sophie into his home, knowing full well his sister was not in residence? According to the maid, my sweet, impressionable daughter has been gone for over an *hour*."

The dowager gasped, turning scandalized eyes on Evan. "Lord Evansleigh, how could you? Ruining this child so callously—have you no shame? No honor?"

God's teeth, they were bringing his honor into this? There was only one reason one would mention such a thing, and he refused to allow things to slip down that particular slope. "I've done nothing," he said firmly. Exasperation balled in his chest as he tipped his head toward the house. "For God's sake, Sophie wasn't inside for more than five minutes."

Both women reared back, their movements almost comically synchronized. *"Sophie?"* Mrs. Wembley repeated, tears pooling in her eyes as if by magic. "You, sir, take far too much liberty with my daughter."

Bloody, bloody hell! Evan raked a hand through his hair, trying to recapture some semblance of sanity. "You just called her that. It was a slip of the tongue."

Gathering her affront around her like a cloak, Mrs. Wembley marched closer to him. "Are you willing to swear to me that you have not called my daughter by her Christian name at any other time?"

"Mama, please don't do this," Sophie begged, her voice stained with desperation.

But Mrs. Wembley didn't even acknowledge her as she scowled in Evan's direction. "Answer the question, if you please."

Evan paused to take a breath, attempting to maintain his composure. Nothing would be helped if he lost his temper on the street. "Miss Wembley is a great friend to both my sister and myself. It is possible I have called her by her Christian name a time or two. Such a thing is hardly a capital offense, madam."

The older woman stepped closer still. "It is a slippery slope, my lord. With God as your witness, have you taken any other liberties with my daughter?"

"Of course not," he answered sharply.

"You have not kissed her?"

"Mama," Sophie hissed, grabbing her mother's arm. Mortification and guilt widened her eyes as she attempted to pull the older woman back.

Evan gritted his teeth, determined to stop the impending disaster. He was not a liar, damn it. Still, his very freedom was on the line. "This has gone on quite enough," he said sternly, backing up a step.

The dowager marchioness shuffled forward and thumped her cane on the pavement. "That is no answer, young man. Have you kissed this gel?"

Sophie released her hold and stepped between Evan and his neighbor. "Truly, I was here only a moment. *Nothing happened*."

"Shush, child. I demand to hear the answer from Lord Evansleigh's lips. Have you or have you not kissed Miss Wembley?"

He held his silence, refusing to either answer the question or to lie about it.

Lady Gorst turned her dragon eyes on Sophie. "Has Lord Evansleigh taken liberties with your person? Have a care, gel, and do not dare think of lying to me."

Sophie couldn't believe what was happening. How could Mama have tricked her like this? Panic welled in her chest, stealing her breath. Sophie had *never* wanted to trap Evan into marrying her. She could see the tautness of his jaw, the flinty burn of his eyes. He was trapped, and it was all her fault.

The dowager squinted her eyes, impatiently waiting for Sophie's response. Mama stood before her, a formidable presence. Sophie could so clearly see now what she had missed when Mama suggested she come: Her mother was desperate to save the family's name, and she was not going to allow this chance to go by, no matter what Sophie's wishes were.

If Sophie said no, her mother would know that she defied her. If she said yes, she would effectively trap a man who did not want her into marriage.

"I . . . ," she said, her voice trailing off as she looked for some escape. Neighbors were turning into spectators as more and more faces appeared in windows and doors. She looked back to Evan and saw his eyes boring through her with a fierceness that she felt all the way to the pit of her stomach. She shook her head, unable to be the one to tip the scales in either direction.

Her mother stepped forward, her eyes rounding meaningfully. "Yes or no, Sophie. Honesty is of the utmost importance." There was clear warning in the words. If Sophie did not obey, there would be hell to pay for her decision.

Cool rain drizzled down around them, dampening Sophie's gown and raising gooseflesh on her arms despite her spencer jacket. Looking her mother straight in the eye, she spoke the truth. "Lord Evansleigh has been a perfect gentleman to me. I am honored to call both him and his sister my friends, and wished only to bid them farewell as we return to Appleton."

Her mother's gaze hardened. An angry silence stretched for little more than a heartbeat or two, but to Sophie, it felt interminable. Straightening her spine, Mama stepped back to face the earl. "Look at all of these people," she said, sweeping her arm to encompass the many eyes that were trained on them. "You have irreparably compromised my daughter, my lord. Will you stand there and allow her to suffer the repercussions, or will you do the honorable thing and marry her?"

Almost in a daze, Sophie turned to Evan, light-headed, to learn her fate. His eyes were hooded, impossible to read as he met her gaze. He'd rushed outside without the benefit of a hat, so the rain now dampened his hair and clung to his eyelashes. He made no move to dash the moisture from his face as he silently considered her.

After what seemed like years, he blinked and turned

his attention to her mother. "Perhaps we should adjourn to my study. It would seem that we have much to discuss."

Triumph erupted on Mama's face even as Sophie's heart shuddered to a stop. A second later it roared back to life, leaving her reeling from the sudden rush. There was no mistaking the earl's meaning: He would marry her.

Chapter Twenty-four

The walk to Evan's study felt exactly how he imagined a trip to the gallows would feel. His feet were heavy, but not half so much as his heart. He should have turned his back and walked inside, honor be damned. He should have sent them on their way, knowing full well that this minor, practically manufactured scandal would hardly be worse than that of her sister's elopement.

But he'd seen the look on Sophie's face. He'd seen the heartache, the upset, the anguish at not knowing what to do. And she had done her best to avoid trapping him into this situation once they were confronted outside by her mother. The thought of saddling her with even more shame, ruining her in a way that would follow her for years to come . . . In the end, he simply couldn't do it.

But the question was, would she be any better with him? Stuck in a forced marriage that could never be real, for fear of the consequences he'd spent his whole life avoiding? His jaw hardened as they walked into the study. Turning abruptly, he held up a hand to Mrs. Wembley. "If you would be so kind, I would like to have a moment to speak with Miss Wembley alone."

Her brow wrinkled as she looked up at him with

ready indignation. "I should think not. You've had your time alone with her this morning."

He straightened his back and looked down on her with all the patience he had left—which was exactly none. "Allow me to rephrase. You *will* wait in the drawing room while I speak with Miss Wembley here. Is that understood?"

She faltered, her bravado slipping beneath his commanding tone. "Well," she said, brushing at her sleeve, "I suppose a little time alone together at this stage is to be expected. I shall rejoin you in five minutes."

"You will rejoin us when we send for you."

She lifted her chin but didn't challenge his authority. Evan nodded to Higgins, who quickly led Sophie's mother away, shutting the door behind them. For a moment, neither Sophie nor Evan moved or spoke into the ringing silence around them. Clearing his throat, he gestured to the pair of chairs situated in front of the desk. "Please, let us sit."

Sophie, the most irrepressible soul he had ever met, seemed fragile for perhaps the first time since he had known her. Her features were drawn with worry, her eyes brimming with deep regret and guilt. His heart squeezed with the need to comfort her, but there was too much for them to discuss. This was the rest of their lives; she deserved to know what she was getting into, so that she could make an informed decision.

Sinking into the chair, she tugged at the ribbon of her bonnet and pulled it off. Her dark hair sprang free, spiraling up in a halo of dampened curls. Setting the hat aside, she waited, hands folded, while he sat in the opposite chair.

When he opened his mouth to speak, she broke in, as if unable to stay quiet a moment longer. "Please, let me just say how terribly sorry I am for what has happened. I never dreamed such a thing could have resulted from my silly, stupid desire to say good-bye. I hate it for you, and I promise to do everything in my power to somehow make it up to you. I know it's not what you wanted, but we can make it work, I'm sure of it."

She nodded, but he wasn't sure if she was assuring him or herself. Perhaps both. He sighed, slicking his wet hair back from his face. "Yes, I know. Sometimes things happen that are beyond our control, and it is up to us to figure out how to live with the consequences."

The story of his life, really.

Leaning forward, he set his elbows on his knees and peered at her, trying to find the best way to say what needed to be said. There were two things that he was certain of: Sophie believed herself to be in love with him, and he knew himself to be in love with her.

Painfully, almost desperately so.

So much, in fact, that he could barely stand the thought of sentencing her to a life by his side in a marriage that could never be what she deserved. He wanted to protect her, to keep her from suffering if things went the way he feared they would.

He had to tell her the truth about his past.

He knew it, was resolved to it, but saying the words that hovered on his tongue was still daunting. Meeting her eyes, he said, "Sophie, there is much that you don't know about me. Before we move forward from this moment, before any decisions can possibly be made, there is something I need to share with you. It's something I've never spoken of to another person, other than my sister, and I hope that no matter what we decide today, you will keep what I am about to tell you in strict confidence."

*   *   *

Eyes wide, curiosity burning bright, Sophie dipped her head in a single nod. "Upon my word, Evan; you can trust me with anything." Whatever it was, obviously it was important to him. She may have utterly failed him this morning, but by Jove she would take his secret to the grave.

He nodded and leaned back, idly rubbing his hands together. "I wonder, what do you know of my father?"

Sophie blinked, taken off guard by the unlikely question. "Your father?" What did he have to do with anything? "Only that he died when you were young—fifteen, I think you said? It was a riding accident, if I recall correctly." It would have happened when Sophie was still in the nursery, so it was hardly worth speaking of other than to mark how long Evan had been earl.

Across from her, his shoulders sagged the smallest amount, almost as though he was relieved by her answer. Pressing his lips together, he dipped his head in a nod. "That is correct, in the strictest of terms. But there is much more to the story, I'm afraid." His voice was quiet, serious.

Curling her fingers into her palms to stave off her growing anxiety, she said, "I see. Well, actually I don't see, not at all, but do go on." She bit down on her bottom lip hard, stopping the nervous flow of words.

He looked off toward the window. "My father was very distant when I was growing up. No fond trips to the nursery or doting first riding lessons. When he was in residence, we saw him perhaps once or twice a week. He preferred for children to be out of sight, for the most part."

Sophie nodded, not wanting to interrupt him. It was the kind of upbringing that was all too familiar in the *ton*. While her own father was far from ideal, at least he had interacted with his daughters regularly.

"Most of the time, however, he was either in London or at the small estate we own in Northampton. Truly, if not for his brother's frequent visits when I was young, I doubt I would have known a man's influence at all. But then, when I was fourteen, my father came home one day, and he never left again. He was different, somehow. Obsessive, angry, given to fits of rage and days of melancholy that kept me and my sister walking on eggshells whenever we saw him. My mother let go much of the staff, keeping only the most loyal, and paying them handsomely for their discretion.

"Things grew worse and worse as the months went on, and my mother became fearful and tried to keep us from him. I was old enough to think I could intervene, but—" He stopped, his throat working as he swallowed. Looking over at her, he said, "Suffice it to say, it was a very, very bad time in our lives. In less than five months, he had descended into true madness."

Sophie gasped before she knew what she was about, and quickly put a hand to her mouth. "My apologies. That must have been terrible." It was the understatement of the year, but words could scarcely encompass how he must have felt. Her heart broke for the boy who witnessed such a thing in his father. "What of your uncle? Couldn't he have helped?" Surely someone could have stepped in.

Evan shook his head. "Unfortunately, he had died earlier that year. And with my father's position, it was of the utmost importance that no one learn of his illness. We tried so hard to pull him from the depths of his madness, but nothing seemed to help."

The muscles in his jaw flexed as he drew a deep breath. "In the end, he did die in a riding accident, but it was of his own doing. He stole the horse in the middle of the night, then led the grooms who tried to catch him on a merry chase. He was . . . mostly unclothed, riding bareback through the countryside in the dead of winter.

"He drove his mount directly at the shallow creek that ran along the south end of the property, and when the horse came up short instead of plowing into the icy water, my father was thrown. He hit his head on the rocks and lay submerged until the groom caught up to him several minutes later." He shook his head. "There was nothing to be done."

A cold shiver raced down Sophie's spine at the very thought. Such a horrible way to die. What Evan and his family must have gone through after that, Sophie could only imagine. No wonder he and his sister were so close.

Evan ran a hand over his still-damp hair, cutting sober eyes in her direction. "There is madness in my blood, Sophie." The bleakness in his voice was even more chilling than his story. "It is something that we have managed to keep secret, but it is still there."

Sophie sat back, attempting to grasp the enormity of such a confession. All these years, holding the world at arm's length so no one would learn their secret. If the madness had been discovered, the whole family would have suffered tremendously. The fear that lunacy would be hereditary would have meant a lifetime of scrutiny for him and his sister. The title would have been irreparably tainted. Sophie sat forward, understanding dawning.

"Is that why you were so upset about your sister's marriage?"

His nod was curt. "We made a pact, shortly after Father's death. Neither of us would marry, nor would we have children. If one of us were to fall victim to madness, the other would care for them. No wife or progeny to go through what my family has endured, and no danger of passing the madness on to the next generation."

"But . . . what about an heir?" she asked numbly, unable to believe what he was saying. How could he have been able to cope with such a fate? He and Julia had sentenced themselves for a crime they never committed.

Tipping his chin up, he said, "I have a very capable cousin who will inherit. I see it as my duty to ensure that the title remains unblemished until that time."

It was more than she knew how to take in. He'd been living his life as some sort of pass-through? Living with no real purpose other than protecting the family's secret and preserving the title for another who might be considered untainted? "How dreadful, Evan. You deserve so much more than that."

It was clear her words surprised him. Had he never considered that he was worthy of a normal life, despite what had happened to his father? He shook his head twice, his eyes intense. "No, *you* deserve more. I'm telling you all this because you deserve a choice. Neither option is fair, but they're the only ones you have: Live with the scandal of having damaged your reputation, or live with a shell of a marriage, one that will never be anything more than signatures on a piece of paper."

His forehead creased with lines of strain as he lifted his hands. "Ruined but free, or married and miserable: Which will you choose?"

The stark reality of the situation hit her like a slap in the face. She stared at him, caught in the hopelessness etched in his features. She knew what he was saying: *He* would be miserable if he were married to her. To *anyone*. He'd made his choice, and she and her mother had destroyed his plans. It was a wonder he hadn't slammed the door in both their faces.

Exhaling grimly, she shook her head. "Then it appears we have been brought to Point Non Plus."

Confusion brought his brows together. "Whatever do you mean? There are options—two of them, to be precise."

She shook her head, feeling worse and worse by the moment. "No, there are not. I have a better chance of walking to France than I do of getting my mother to back down. I can tell you with one hundred percent accuracy that nothing I say will persuade her to release you."

His curse was sharp and low. He came to his feet and paced a few steps before turning back to her. "She has no say in the matter. I cannot be forced by her, no matter how she may wish it. What I want to know is, what is *your* decision?"

What, indeed. Both options seemed bleak beyond bearing. To live her life married in name only to a man who desperately didn't want her seemed the worst kind of fate—especially since she loved him so much. Even now, her heart twisted with the pain of it, knowing that he had set his own heart against her so completely.

But . . . at least then she could *try* to make him happy. He might never accept her as a true partner, but what if she could make him laugh, and sing, and live with some semblance of normalcy? What if she could soften the brittleness that bracketed his face when he spoke of his past?

Coming to her feet, she walked over to where he stood. She hated the pain she saw in his eyes, hated the way he held himself so stiffly. Looking into his face, she knew she was fooling herself to think that she could somehow make him love her someday. That by sheer force of will she could make him happy to be wed to her.

No, there was only one way she could make him happy.

Lifting on her toes, she cupped his jaw and kissed him oh so lightly on his lips. He closed his eyes briefly, then met her gaze. Her heart seemed to splinter as she peered into the pale, troubled depths of his eyes. Swallowing, she whispered the words she knew he needed. "I choose freedom."

Freedom for him. Ruination for her.

Chapter Twenty-five

Evan felt as though he'd been dragged behind a runaway horse through a field of rocks, only instead of a bruised and bloodied body, it was his heart that had taken the brunt of the beating.

And that was the *best* outcome the day could have had.

Blowing out a long breath, he pressed the heels of his hands hard against his eyes. He'd been sitting in his study for hours, unable to get the look on Sophie's face when she left out of his head. She'd been wrecked. Heartbroken. And yet, somehow she'd been strong enough to stand unflinching in the face of her mother's fury when Evan decreed that he would not be making an offer.

He reached for the snifter of brandy sitting at his elbow on the desk. At the last second, he dropped his hand. He didn't deserve the escape the liquor promised. Sophie wouldn't have one, so why should he?

For perhaps the hundredth time, he repeated the words he had been saying since she left: *It's for the best.* She had hope of living a happy life, in time, at home in Appleton. The infraction was minor when compared to her sister's scandal. Her family would already be lying low, so in time, it all might just blow over.

If she had chosen to marry him, it would have been a life sentence. In the beginning, they might have found some happiness, but what if he was stricken as his father had been? He would never, in a thousand years, subject anyone to the fate his mother had endured, let alone the woman he loved.

But now, what the hell was he going to do with himself? He was on edge, anxious to do *something*, but what that something was, he couldn't figure out. He wanted to pack up and return home, but another part of him wanted to stay. To be here in case Sophie needed something, anything, before she left. He was fully aware of how ludicrous that thought was, but it was true nonetheless.

"Higgins said I would find you here."

Evan tensed at the sound of his sister's voice. "Julia," he said, unsure whether he was angry, relieved, or irritated to see her. He came to his feet, but didn't move toward where she stood quietly just inside the door, her features calm and collected. Her eyes were brilliant despite the dull day, as if lit from within somehow. She seemed happier than he ever remembered seeing her. Not the brief joy that entertainment or a fun evening brought, but rather a state of being that softened her whole countenance.

In the face of what he had just given up, he was in no mood for her happiness. Did she have no care at all for what she had just done? What Harry might yet have to suffer because of her incredibly selfish and shortsighted decision? "What in God's name were you thinking?"

She pulled off her gloves, much as she had the day she arrived. Hard to believe how much had changed since that day. She met his gaze evenly, one corner of her lip turned up in a light grin. "Well, it's good to know you're still speaking to me, at the very least."

At the very least, indeed. He blew out a breath and shook his head. "I could murder you right now, but I'm afraid I've too much on my mind at the moment to bother with hiding the body."

"If you were to murder me, at least I would die a happy woman, which never would have been the case before."

Scowling, he came around the desk. "Happy? For doing something that not only undermined our pact, but which ultimately could hurt all those you love?" He was veering toward angry, thinking of the chain of events that had unfolded in the last day.

"No," she replied, not at all ruffled, "for doing something that I had fought against for so long, but that I knew my heart so desperately wanted." She walked fully into the study and settled on the chair Sophie had occupied not three hours ago. She patted the adjacent seat and waited until he sighed and came to sit down.

"I told you it was a long story, but let me summarize how this all came about. I've known for years that Harry harbored a sort of puppy love for me, and I was actually quite annoyed by it. He was just a boy, and then just an adolescent, and then just a foolish young man. But when he finished school and came home to take his place as the new baronet, something changed in him."

Her cheeks grew rosy as she twisted the gloves in her hands. "It was no longer puppy love, then. He tried to properly court me, but I wouldn't have it, so he set about trying to wear me down by coming up with a million reasons to visit. It was hard not to be swayed by that kind of persistence."

He knew all about being swayed without wanting to be. Evan rubbed a hand over the back of his neck. "Why did you never say anything to me? Why didn't Mother?"

Lifting her shoulders, Julia sent him a guilty look. "I think deep down I was falling in love with him, and I didn't want to do or say anything that would change the way it made me feel. Until something did change." For the first time since she entered the room, her composure slipped. "One day, when we were walking along the creek, Harry asked me to marry him."

At the mention of the creek, Evan's shoulders tensed. He always avoided going there—the association with his father's death was just too devastating.

"Yes, I know," she said, ducking her head. "It couldn't have been a worse place. I hadn't been thinking about the path we were on until we were there, and then he was on his knee, asking for my hand.

"I froze, panicked, told him I could never marry him, and ran back to the house. He caught up to me, tried to reason with me, told me how he had always loved me and always would, no matter what. The problem was," she said, turning troubled eyes to him, "that I realized then just how much I had come to love him. I knew that I could never have him, so I pushed him away. I came here the very next day."

That explained so much. No wonder she had been so moody and volatile when she arrived. A week ago he couldn't have understood her turmoil, but today, he sympathized only too well. But still, it only made the simmering anger that much more painful. He had tried to walk away. He had tried so damn hard to do the right thing—for him, for his family, *and* for Sophie. Julia had simply tossed all caution and prudency out the window and taken what she wanted.

"So he followed you here, and you suddenly decided to throw up your hands and give in?"

She sat up straight, glaring back at him reproachfully.

"That's not fair, Evan. I *did* fight it. So much so that *you* reprimanded me for being too harsh. Believe it or not, it wasn't until I went to make sure that Sophie was all right that I started to see things differently."

Evan's gaze jerked back to his sister. What did *Sophie* have to do with this?

Lifting her hand to her chest, Julia leaned forward. "Her heart was broken, Evan, and still she didn't regret taking the risk. She helped me see that none of us know what the future holds, and we have to at least try to reach for the things that will make us happy."

After the way he had rebuffed Sophie's advances that night, after the way she must have felt, she truly hadn't regretted it? Evan rubbed his palms over his thighs, trying to rein in his emotions. Everything was crashing down around him, and it all seemed to center on one diminutive brunette.

"Speaking of Miss Wembley," he said, "I'm afraid there is something I must tell you." As briefly and concisely as he could, he explained the events of the morning.

Julia stared back at him, clearly shocked. "My God, Evan. I—I don't know what to say."

"Your condolences would be appropriate. For both me and Miss Wembley. I doubt she is as happy now for her risks as when you spoke with her."

She reared back a little, watching him with thoughtful eyes. "How could you have let her walk away like that? She loves you, and I've seen the way you look at her. I find it impossible to believe you'd rather see her *ruined* than married to the man she loves."

Anger balled in his stomach, low and heavy. "Don't patronize me. You may no longer give a damn about this family, but I sure as hell do. The marriage would have been a sham, harmful to both parties. Sophie is the sweetest person I've ever known. She doesn't deserve to be shackled to a man who may someday turn out to be a monster."

Even saying the words made dread condense in his chest and chill his blood. That was his deepest, darkest fear, the one that made him wake with a start in the middle of the night. What if he turned into his father? Being out of his mind, unable to control his own thoughts and actions—it was the worst possible hell.

"You are not our father," she said quietly, her eyes intense.

He looked down to his hands. "Not yet, anyway. But the possibility remains."

Leaning forward, Julia placed a hand over his forearm. "Neither of us knows what lies ahead. We still don't know if our father's illness is inheritable, just as we don't know if one of us will be struck dead by lightning tomorrow.

"You could be held up by highwaymen on the way home, or fall ill with the plague, or God knows what else. But here is what I do know: I'm ready to start living the life God gave me. I've been given the gift of love, and I won't turn my back on it anymore." She straightened, looking him directly in the eye. "It's my greatest hope that you won't either."

He blinked back at her, at a loss for what to say. Real passion lit her eyes, as though she honestly believed what she said. Didn't she know such a thing was wishful thinking? That she'd been reckless as hell to run off and marry the man she loved? Evan had allowed Sophie to walk away *because* he loved her. It was the noblest thing he could have done.

When he didn't say anything, she sighed and released

his hand. Standing, she shook out her skirts and started for the door.

"Where are you going?" he demanded, turning in his seat.

She smiled at him, an odd mingling of compassion and joy evident in her features. "I've a husband to look after, dear brother."

He came to his feet, pushing back the resentment that threatened to engulf him. She was his only sister, and he loved her, despite wanting to throttle her. "So it would seem. Which begs the question, how is it you were able to marry him so quickly?"

Her cheeks reddened again and she gave a little shake of her head. "Harry went to London to purchase a special license before following me here. He said he wanted to be prepared the very moment I came to my senses."

The clever bastard. If Evan didn't like him so well, he would really hate him right about now. "And you somehow found someone to perform a ceremony at a moment's notice?"

"Indeed," she said, biting back a smile. "Your very favorite vicar, in fact: Mr. Wright."

Bloody clergyman. Evan crossed his arms. "I'll have to remember to thank him," he murmured darkly.

Julia chuckled. "Be nice. I owe him a debt of gratitude."

"I owe him something, all right." Suddenly feeling incredibly tired, he turned to more-pressing matters. "I expect to head back to Ledbury the day after tomorrow. Will you be returning with me?" It felt odd, asking her travel plans. It would take a while to grow used to the idea of her being a married woman.

"Yes, I think so. I'm anxious to check on Mama. I feel terrible for leaving her as I did. I wrote her a long, long letter that I posted yesterday before the wedding, but I'm looking forward to speaking to her in person."

Evan couldn't begin to imagine what his mother would think of this. Both he and his sister had always felt she was too fragile to discuss the events of so long ago, but he felt certain she would have agreed with their pact, had she known. "I wish you would have waited until we could be there with her before telling her. But what's done is done, I suppose. We all must move forward as best we can."

Offering him a sympathetic smile, she closed the distance between them and wrapped her arms around him in a tight embrace. "I love you, brother. Things will work out for us, one way or another."

Evan sighed and patted her on the back. He would have thought she'd stopped believing in fairy tales years ago.

Chapter Twenty-six

"**I** have written your father."

Sophie met her mother's stoic gaze and nodded, too tired to respond. The ride back to the house had been hellacious, as had her mother's furious rant, which had lasted nearly half an hour before she had stormed out of Sophie's bedchamber, slamming the door with a bone-rattling thump.

Sophie had yet to say a word. For two hours, she had sat curled in a ball on her bed, unable to think of what to do next. Pack? Write May and Charity? Plan her bleak future? Nothing had compelled her to move, so she hadn't. She didn't cry, either. She simply sat quietly in solitude, staring at the water-streaked windowpanes and listening to the steady tap of the rain outside.

Now her mother stood tensely in the doorway, her nostrils flared as she looked at Sophie the way one might regard a beggar in the street. "The situation is beyond me, and as such, I have asked him to come. Perhaps he can force the blackguard to show some honor."

There was nothing but accusation in her voice. She was still furious with Evan, yes, but perhaps even more so at Sophie for not helping her ensnare him. Sophie unfurled herself and stood, then wrapped her arm around the bedpost at the foot of the bed. "He won't be cowed," she said quietly. "He knows nothing untoward happened, and he won't allow himself to be unfairly trapped into a marriage."

"Unfairly?" Mama stepped inside the room, her face reddening with affront. "You yourself said that he kissed you. And that's only what you've admitted to," she said, looking Sophie up and down through narrowed eyes. "You'd better hope your father can convince him, because we've no room for a trollop in our home."

Sophie had thought her heart too numb to feel any more pain, but the barb cut deep. Even though she knew her mother was just angry and looking for a way to lash out at her uncooperative daughter, the condemnation weighed like a yoke around Sophie's neck. Still, no matter what her parents said or threatened, she wouldn't be party to her mother's machinations. "What are we to do until Papa arrives?"

Mama's fingers closed over the doorknob. "You shall stay exactly where you are. When your father arrives, I shall leave your fate to him." Nodding decisively, she stepped out of the room and yanked the door shut.

Blowing out a harsh breath, Sophie wilted back onto the corner of the mattress, still holding the bedpost for support. Now, more than ever, she wanted—needed—her friends. She needed someone to understand, and to support her decision. But she had no illusions that Mama would allow any visits. Until Papa arrived, she was as good as stuck.

As for after he arrived? Sophie shuddered at the thought. It was time to start thinking of what she could do to earn her keep somewhere. She'd be a terrible governess, but perhaps she could be a music tutor. She snorted miserably and lay back on the mattress. Yes, because there were so many aspiring young oboe players out there desperate for a moderately capable teacher. Well, there had to be *something* she could do. Perhaps Charity or even Julia could help her find a position somewhere.

Thinking of the earl's sister brought to mind their last conversation. Now that things had come to this, could she still say that she was happy to have taken the risk? Sophie closed her eyes, remembering the earl's private outdoor serenade, their shared kisses, the passion he had evoked in her, and the moments of breathless anticipation at seeing him again. They had been the best moments of her life, and no one could take that from her. Yes, if she had known the future, she would have given them up to spare the earl the pain she had caused him, but for herself? She swallowed past her suddenly tight throat.

It was impossible to regret even a moment of the time she had spent with the man she loved.

"There's talk, you know."

Evan set down his fork and flicked a glance across the table to his sister. "And this is a surprise to you?"

It had been two days since the incident with Sophie, and he had steadfastly refused to see any of the half dozen or so callers who were suddenly interested in visiting him. He had no doubt that word of their dramatic scene had spread through Bath, particularly with the indignant dowager marchioness no doubt spreading tales. He had neither confirmed nor denied offering for Sophie, and he doubted her mother had spoken, either.

It was nobody's damn business, and he had no intention of indulging anyone's curiosity. If and when Mrs.

Wembley chose to speak on the matter was up to her. As for him, well, they would be departing for Ledbury after breakfast, so as far as he was concerned, the topic was closed.

Julia shared a glance with Harry, who wisely returned his attention to his plate. The baronet was still on thin ice, as far as Evan was concerned, and should consider himself lucky to even be invited into the house, let alone to dinner.

Shaking her head, Julia turned the full weight of her gaze back on Evan. "I've barely gone anywhere, yet the moment I leave the house, some gossipmonger or another pounces, wanting to know exactly what happened."

Again, no surprise in that. He grunted noncommittally, reaching for his wineglass. Of course there would be talk. There was *always* talk. Without gossip, the bloody *ton* would probably wither and die like a fish left in the sun. Wasn't that why he had walked such a fine line all these years? Engaging just enough not to raise eyebrows, but not so much as to cause someone to look closer?

Narrowing her eyes, Julia dabbed her mouth with her napkin and tossed it over her plate. "I'm not sure you understand just how much Sophie is being disparaged. Whether she had succeeded in securing your hand or not, the gossip is vicious in either direction. If she succeeded, then she did so through trickery and entrapment, and if she didn't, then she is a ruined social climber who couldn't secure your hand even through the basest of means."

His jaw hardened, but he refused to be drawn in. What did she suggest he do about it, anyhow? Take out an advertisement in the paper explaining the truth?

"In fact," she said, doggedly continuing, "yesterday when Harry and I were walking, some cocksure young lord whose name I cannot even recall came right up to us and confessed that he hoped you had managed to avoid the grasping hands of 'that fortune-hunting Miss Wembley.'"

Fury speared through Evan, swift and white-hot. His hand clenched around the stem of his goblet so hard it was a wonder the thing didn't shatter. "If you'll kindly recall the gentleman's name, I will happily correct his misconception." With his fists, he thought darkly.

"Would you?" she retorted, crossing her arms. "Because you seem perfectly content to allow the world to think the worst of Sophie. After what happened with her sister, the general consensus is that she and her mother were attempting to force you into marrying her in a desperate bid to redeem the family name."

He could easily believe such a thing of her mother, but Sophie? He slammed his wineglass to the table, rattling the place settings and sloshing liquid over his fingers. "What utter nonsense," he growled, glaring at his sister. "Sophie was completely innocent in this all. If anything, *I'm* the bastard here. Wasn't I the one who supposedly compromised her?"

It was maddening that anyone could blame another without a whit of knowledge about the situation. If they could have only seen the way Sophie had stood quietly beside him as he informed her mother that under no circumstance would he be forced to marry anyone. He had given her an impossible choice, and she had chosen as well as she could. As much as it pained him, he knew it was the *right* choice. He had felt better, knowing that she would be free of him and his family's insidious secret.

Julia held up her hands. "I know who the bastard is," she said, not even flinching at the word. "But as far as society is concerned, a desperate, shamed young woman attempted to force your hand, and deserves to be put in her place."

God's teeth, was his sister *trying* to spark his fury? His gut burned with the injustice of Sophie's predicament. Yes, he'd known she'd be ruined, but this was not the way he had imagined it. He had assumed she'd be rebuffed for a while, turned away by the sticklers of societal morals. It had only been a few moments alone, after all. He had even thought her sister's elopement might help deflect the blow, since her family was already in the midst of judgment.

But instead, they had taken her family's shame and magnified it, branding Sophie some sort of scheming harlot. Damn it all, what was wrong with the world? Why were they so bloody gleeful at tearing down their peers? Why couldn't they be content to leave well enough alone on things that had absolutely nothing to do with them?

It was wrong. So damn wrong. His arms ached with the need to find Sophie and pull her into his embrace, to somehow offer comfort in this impossible situation. He hated knowing that she was being so unfairly judged, especially when there was nothing he could do to make it better. Shaking the drops from his hand, he abruptly stood, his chair screeching against the wooden floor.

Julia started, her dark gold eyebrows rising up her forehead. "Where are you going?"

Taking a deep breath, he set his fingertips on the table and met his sister's curious gaze. "Home. The sooner we leave, the sooner the scandal will die." At least he damn well hoped it would. It was the only thing he could think of to deflect the scrutiny. "You and Harry may take your time, but I'm going now."

Let the carriages and luggage come after him. He wanted—needed—the freedom and speed that could be had only on horseback. "Higgins!" he called, moving away from the table. The servant quickly materialized, his brows raised in question. "Have Wolfgang saddled at once. I'm riding ahead to Leighton Hall."

The sound of the doorknob turning roused Sophie from her thoughts. She'd been sitting by the window for hours, contemplating the days and weeks ahead. It was near sundown now, and she'd yet to come to any definitive conclusions. She watched, mildly curious, as the door swung in. To her immense surprise, May slipped silently inside. She quickly closed the door behind her and gave an exaggerated exhale.

Sophie immediately popped to her feet, so grateful for the sight of a friendly face that she very nearly started weeping. "May!" she exclaimed, rushing toward her.

"Shh," she replied, but eagerly swallowed Sophie up in a tight embrace. "We don't want your mother to know that I'm here." Her voice was low and quiet as she led Sophie over to the settee she had just vacated.

"But how did you get here?" she asked, dutifully keeping her voice to a whisper. "Mama decreed no visitors until Papa arrives."

Giving her a mischievous little grin, May raised her shoulders. "I told you I have my ways."

For the first time in days, a hint of a smile lifted Sophie's lips. "If you tell me you broke in through a window, I may well have to call the watch."

"Do please give me a little credit. I didn't break any windows, but I may or may not have bribed Lynette. She is a peach, that one. She'll come and get me when it's safe to leave." Sighing greatly, May tilted her head, her eyes brimming with sympathy. "Now, my darling girl, do please tell me everything. I want to know what I can do to help."

"Just being here is more help than you could possibly imagine." Already Sophie felt a thousand times better, for no other reason than to have somebody on her side— both literally and figuratively. "What do you know already?"

For the first time, May looked hesitant. She plucked at her jade skirts, smoothing out the wrinkles. "I'm afraid there isn't much to go on, so the gossips are filling in their own blanks. All I know is that you were discovered at the earl's residence, without the benefit of either a chaperone or his sister's presence. There was a confrontation, and the earl ushered you and your mother inside to talk over . . . well, I'm assuming marriage. After that," she said, lifting her shoulders, "no one knows anything."

Sophie's heart sank. It sounded very much like she and Evan were on many a tongue. What surprised her was that he obviously had yet to say anything about the outcome of that meeting. She would have thought he'd be anxious to set the record straight. "It sounds like I am quite the fodder for gossip. Is it very bad?"

May's face said it all. Then compassion softened her gaze as she clasped Sophie's hand in both of hers. "The good thing about gossip is that there is always more to take its place as time goes on. As soon as it is known whether or not you are betrothed, I imagine it will be only so long before they move on to bigger and better things."

That was a resounding *yes*. Sophie took a deep, calming breath, trying to overcome the flurry of nervous energy that pinged around inside her like ricocheting buckshot. She had never been the sort to seek out attention. She loved to be a part of things, but not the one everyone looked to. Even when she played her oboe, she felt safer with others playing around her. Now, not only were she and her family the talk of the town, but she had dragged Evan into it with her.

Turning miserable eyes on May, Sophie sighed. "We are not betrothed."

May gasped, rearing back in outrage. "He's left you to the wolves?" she hissed, her voice a furious whisper. "The scurrilous, toad-spotted weasel!"

"No, please," Sophie begged, shaking her head, "don't blame him. My mother tricked us both, and I couldn't bear for him to pay the consequences. Mama doesn't know it, but I released him from his offer."

That certainly caught May's attention. "You . . . released him? The man you are madly in love with offered to marry you, and you said no?"

Though she was clearly trying to keep a straight face, Sophie could see the incredulousness in her friend's expression. It was the way most people would react, if Sophie were to guess. Leaning back against the cushions, she lifted her lips in a sad smile. "Yes, I love him. So much so that I could never allow him to be miserable on my account. I know you don't understand, but I simply couldn't be the reason for his unhappiness."

For a few seconds, May just sat there, looking as though she'd just seen a mermaid. Then her lips curled into a rueful smile as she shook her head. "That may very well be the most disgustingly honorable thing I have ever heard."

"Yes, quite," Sophie said, giving a helpless little shrug.

"So what will you do?"

Ah, the very question Sophie had been contemplating for so long. "First, I must wait until my father arrives, which will most likely be tomorrow. I'm sure much more unpleasantness will ensue, and after that, if I am lucky, they will tote me back to Appleton, where I will do my best to lie low until the storm of scandal around both me and my sister blows over."

Looking down to her hands, she nibbled on her lip for a moment. "I may at some point need assistance looking for a position of some sort. I hope you and Charity will keep an eye out for possibilities."

"Yes, of course. I only wish I weren't quite so new to England. I feel as though I'm still adrift in this little country, especially with my aunt's iron control. My only saving grace is her rigid sleep schedule. Thanks to that, I'm able to sneak out in the mornings for my time in the park and dash off at night to visit my imprisoned, oboe-playing friends." She winked, her perfect teeth flashing in a fleeting smile.

"I'm so honored to be a part of your illicit routine," Sophie said, sincerely meaning it despite her light tone.

"I only wish there was more that I could do to help you."

Sophie knew all about feeling helpless. Here she sat, waiting for her father as one waits for an executioner. No wonder Mama wanted him here. Since Evan hadn't spread the news of their parted ways, Mama must still believe Papa had a chance of changing the earl's mind. Poor Evan would be dragged right back into things all over again. Her family seemed to be a plague to his peace.

Sitting up suddenly, she squeezed May's hand. "There is. I think you are right about things calming down faster once the suspense is gone. Can you serve as my herald, and let the world know that I am not to be married? Please, please don't share the details behind it—that's immensely private and I would hate for my mother to actually have to kill me should she hear of it. Just please let it be known that Evan and I are not betrothed, and my family will be returning home very soon. *Alone*."

The sooner this mess was over, the better.

May lifted a delicate brow, turning slightly as though attempting to read her. "Are you absolutely certain that is what you want?"

Sophie nodded emphatically, ignoring the desolation that crept up her chest to steal her breath. "Yes, absolutely." Once her father arrived and they realized that pursuing Evan was a lost cause, they could return to Appleton all the more quickly.

Sighing, May bobbed her head. "Then I shall do it. I've never been a gossip, but now sounds like an exceedingly good time to start."

A scratch at the door was followed by Lynette poking her head in. "Are you ready, miss?"

Sophie looked to her friend, tearing up at the thought of losing her. After today, there was no telling if they would ever see each other again. They both stood, and Sophie pulled May into a quick but fierce hug. "Thank you for everything. I'm immensely glad your father forced you to come stay with your dreadful aunt in the middle of this 'soggy country,' as you so affectionately refer to it."

May's laugh was quiet, but her eyes glistened with unshed tears. "I'll never admit it to him, but I am immensely glad as well. You and Charity are the sort of friends one keeps forever, so stop looking at me as though you must memorize my every feature. Some way or another, I promise you, we shall see each other again."

Sniffing and resolutely blinking back the tears, May smiled. "Now then, I expect you to write. A lot, in fact. No one as loquacious as you has any excuse not to inundate me with letters. And I promise to reciprocate."

One more quick hug, and she was gone. Sophie stood in the middle of her room, acclimating to the silence once more. Her new normal.

Sucking in a long breath, she willed her tears to stay at bay. She couldn't take all the waiting anymore. She needed to *do* something. Scraping the curls back from her face, she marched over to the armoire and pulled open the doors.

It was time to pack for home.

Chapter Twenty-seven

The sight of the home Sophie had left behind not two months prior caused an unexpected hitch in her breath as their carriage turned onto the drive. The same old trees lined the narrow lane, casting moving shadows along the pebbled path. The fields beyond were just as green as when she'd left, the cows still munching contentedly in the distance. The house itself was completely unchanged, looking more stately than anything owned by her family had a right to.

And yet, everything had changed.

This was no longer to be her childhood home; it would likely be her forever home. She couldn't help but remember all the times she had daydreamed about what her home would look like once she was settled with a husband. She had imagined everything from grand estate homes to modest cottages, never really caring what the outside looked like, so long as the inside would be filled with love and laughter. She had never once, in all those years, imagined that her future would reside here.

Across from her, her father sat with his arms tightly crossed over his rounded belly, his frown amplified by his whisker-covered jowls. Neither he nor her mother had spoken a single unnecessary word to her since they'd all departed Bath at the crack of dawn the day before. Papa had been furious to discover upon his arrival in Bath that Evan was gone. Not only did he not have the satisfaction of confronting the "scoundrel," but the added cost of coming unnecessarily had rankled him. Sophie knew enough to hold her tongue about the whole mess.

The horses slowed to a stop, and Sophie eagerly disembarked first. The sooner she was gone from her parents' forced company, the better. The smell of roses and grass welcomed her home. Sighing, she made her way inside, nodding to the maid who opened the door at their arrival. The house was dark and warm as Sophie made her way upstairs. Each step brought her closer to the room that she had shared with Sarah, but that would now be hers alone for the foreseeable future.

Alone. The key word when it came to anything regarding her future. Sighing heavily, she pushed the door open, only to come up short. Her sister Penelope sat at Sophie's writing table, a quill frozen in her hand as she glanced up from the desk in surprise. "Sophie!" she exclaimed, dropping the quill and jumping to her feet. "You're home sooner than expected."

Sophie stood rooted in place, so shocked at the sight of her sister that she couldn't speak. All of the emotions she had suppressed during the day and a half trapped in the carriage with her parents came rushing back to her all at once. She desperately tried to hold back the hurt, the anger, and the sadness as she stared at Penelope. Penelope, who had robbed Sophie of the chance for love. Penelope, who looked as fresh and bright as a daisy, her cheeks glowing and her eyes alight. Penelope, who had been able to grasp onto that which she had wanted, even at the expense of those who loved her.

"What are you doing in my room?" Sophie finally asked when the tightness in her throat had eased enough to speak. Yes, she had forgiven her sister, in theory. But being faced with her when Sophie's nerves were still so raw, her heart still shattered, was like rubbing salt in fresh wounds.

Shifting her weight from one foot to the other, Penelope gestured to the table. "Writing you a letter. I . . . I didn't expect to see you." She was unsure, her eyes as nervous as a cornered rabbit.

Despite Sophie's vow to be kind, she could feel the tightening of her jaw, the stiffening of her spine, the heat of anger flushing her cheeks. Her eyes filled with tears as she shook her head. "How could you, Pen? How could you damn us all with your impetuous actions?"

But even as she said the words, she moved forward. The old floorboards creaked beneath her weight as she approached her sister, whose own eyes were filling with tears. She opened her mouth to speak, but Sophie didn't let her. Instead, she swallowed her in an embrace, holding her tight enough to make her arms ache. So many emotions swirled within her, it was impossible to separate the good from the bad. Sniffling, she pulled back and looked into Penelope's distressed eyes. "I love you, even though I hate what your actions have brought about for this family. Please, please tell me why you chose to elope."

The relief in her sister's eyes was only second to the regret. "Oh, Sophie, I'm so sorry. I love him so much, so very, very much, and when Papa forbade us to be together, I couldn't handle it. I was stupid to do it, I see that now, but at the time, all I knew was that I would die if I couldn't be with him." She put her hands over her heart, brimming with earnestness.

Sophie pressed her eyes closed briefly. It was a feeling

she understood completely. Penelope lowered her hands and slipped them over Sophie's forearm. "I should have waited until you were here. I should have tried to wear Papa down. I was just so mad at him, and then so very happy when Luke asked me to run away to get married, and it seemed so perfectly romantic at the time." She shook her head, causing the tears to cascade down her smooth cheeks. She looked so terribly young, hardly more than a girl, really. "Please forgive me, Phie."

Exactly what she had urged Evan to do for his sister. Sophie swallowed thickly, setting aside her fears for what the future would hold. Placing her hand over Penelope's knuckles, she said, "I can no sooner hold your love against you than I could condemn my own. You're not the only one who has made questionable decisions in the name of love. The consequences are simply harder to swallow."

Penelope's relieved, watery smile was quickly eclipsed by tears. Sophie wrapped her little sister up in her arms, comforting her even as she knew her own heart would never be whole again. After a moment, a sound at the door made her glance that way. Her youngest sister, Pippa, stood in the doorway, uncertainty puckering her brow. Pulling away from Penelope, Sophie came to her feet and held out her arms.

But Pippa hesitated, her resentful gaze darting to Penelope. "What is *she* doing here?"

Empathy welled in Sophie's heart for both her sisters. Going to the doorway, she wrapped an arm around Pippa and guided her into the room, shutting the door behind them. "Well," she said calmly, rubbing her hand over her sibling's arm, "Pen was asking for forgiveness, and I was granting it."

Jerking away, Pippa backed up a few steps. She looked hurt and betrayed, but most of all upset. "Why would you ever forgive her? She's ruined us all! She's snatched both of our dreams away, and she has the gall to walk in here like she's still a member of the family."

A week ago, Sophie had felt the exact same way. So her heart went out to Pippa. She was young, and all her hopes for balls and parties and shared moments with handsome gentlemen had just been dashed upon the rocks. Sighing, Sophie nodded. "She made a bad decision, and she admits it. But her motivation was not a spiteful one. She did what she thought she must in order to be with the man she loved."

If the tables were turned, and Evan had begged her to go to Gretna Green, would she have been able to refuse? It was impossible to say.

Pippa's dark eyes darted to where Penelope sat slump-shouldered on the bed. "Congratulations, you've married the man you loved at the expense of the two of us ever having the same chance."

"Oh, Pippa," Sophie said, shaking her head sadly. "There's still hope for you and me. Love is stronger than any scandal, I assure you. If you find your match, love will always find a way."

"Like it did for you? I know why Papa went after you, and I don't see a wedding ring on your finger."

Sophie gasped at the fresh pain that broke through her carefully erected dam. Drawing a long, steadying breath, she stepped toward her youngest sister and reached for her hands. "What happened in Bath has nothing to do with Penelope." It had nothing to do with her sisters, and everything to do with giving the man she loved what he wanted: freedom. But she couldn't share that now. "Sweetheart, I know we've been put in a terrible position, and I'm sorry for that. But don't let someone else's mistake guide the choices you make in life."

If Sophie had allowed that to happen, she'd be betrothed by now, and they would have both been worse off for it.

Pippa bit her bottom lip, sending an uncertain look to Penelope. "It's difficult not to when all of one's choices have been taken away."

Shaking her head, Sophie said, "You have the choice to live honorably. You have the choice to find joy in life. You have the choice to forgive those who beg for your mercy. You have a choice in all of these things, and through living well, I believe good things will happen for you. For us *both*."

Penelope rose then and came to stand beside them. Meeting her younger sister's pained eyes, she said, "I love you, Pippa, and I am so terribly sorry to have hurt you in this way. I hope that you can find it in yourself to forgive me someday. Please."

Pressing her lips together, Pippa's gaze flitted back and forth between them. Compassion and anger warred in her expressive features, before finally she made a small sound of distress and fled the room. Penelope sagged with disappointment, her whole countenance crumbling. "She's never going to forgive me."

"Give her time," Sophie said softly, offering a small smile. "It's a lot for her to take in, and she needs time to come to terms with the thought of not having a Season like she expected."

"And you don't?"

It was a loaded question. Sophie pursed her lips for a moment before commenting. "I've accepted the fact that my future will not be what I originally expected. But I will survive, as will Pippa." She was surprised to realize that it was the truth. Even though at one point she would have given anything to be the Countess of Evansleigh, she knew that she'd made the right decision in walking away from him. In that, Penelope's choice had little bearing on Sophie's life. After all, she couldn't imagine ever wanting to marry anyone else.

She had loved someone—still loved, in fact—and though her heart still ached fiercely at the loss, she was better for having experienced that love.

Evan's mother had once been beautiful. Tall for a woman, she had the regal bearing of royalty despite her family's low ranking. Long neck and limbs, high cheekbones, beautiful hazel eyes—she had all the makings of a diamond of the first water. When Evan was very young, he had thought she must be the most beautiful woman in the country.

After Evan's father died, or even in the year before, she had started to lose that aura of beauty that surrounded her. Her eyes had dulled, her skin paled, and even her hair lost its luster. She'd turned into a shadow of the woman he remembered, as fragile as a fine crystal vase.

Now, as he greeted her in her private salon at Leighton Hall, he was struck again by just how delicate she was. She sat quietly composed on the sofa, idly running a slender, fine-veined hand over the curving arm of the sofa while reading a book. She had already retired for the evening when he'd arrived a little after eight last night, and she had yet to come down by the time Julia and Harry had shown up this morning. Now it was half past eleven, and her maid had finally announced that she was ready to receive visitors.

He paused in the doorway, not wishing to startle her with his presence. Gently, he cleared his throat, catching her attention. She looked up, blinked, then smiled in that ethereal way of hers. "My dear John. How good to see you." Her voice, high and quiet, had always reminded him of a soft wind blowing through chimes.

Julia came in behind him, pausing at his elbow. Mother shifted her gossamer smile to her daughter. "And Julia. How much I've missed hearing you play."

Walking over to where she sat, Evan kissed his mother's cool cheek before taking a seat on the closest chair. "I am most anxious to hear how you have fared in our absence. Is all well?" It was a relief to see her calm and collected.

She blinked at him as though he'd asked if she liked cake. "Of course. The discomfort of being alone was well worth the sacrifice. My only daughter has married a most beloved friend of the family, and I could not be more pleased."

"So you are not cross with me for marrying by special license?" Julia asked, coming to sit beside her. She spoke with the same soothing, low-pitched tone she had always employed with their mother. It was similar to the one Evan adopted around her. They had spent so much of their lives trying not to upset the tentative peace that had emerged following her deep fit of the blue devils that had lasted for months following their father's death.

"I've waited so long for the day you would find your happiness. I am delighted that you did not delay." Her smile dimmed as she looked to her folded hands. "Such a precious gift, to marry the man you love."

Evan and Julia shared a wide-eyed glance over the top of their mother's head. She'd never once let on that she had any wish for either of them to marry. And in all his life, Evan couldn't once remember her speaking of love.

He sank down into the chair facing the sofa, trying to make heads or tails of her response. "Are you saying that you *wanted* Julia to marry Harry?"

"Of course. Why else would I have told him where she had gone? He told me then his intentions but, well, I hadn't much hope for Julia's acceptance."

"But . . ." Evan struggled to make sense of what she was saying. She was the one who had suffered the most at the hands of Evan's father. Even before things had gone so terribly wrong, she had always been tense and unhappy when he returned home. The lines around her mouth would harden when he was there, never lifting in the easy smiles that she shared with them when he was gone. He had never considered that she had any love for the man at all. "That is to say, I wouldn't have thought you in favor of marriage."

For a moment she sat quietly, her fingers going to the cross she always wore at her neck. "I am in favor of love. Never of forced marriages, but always of love." Her fingers rubbed their familiar path, back and forth over the well-worn gold.

Julia's gaze flickered to Evan's, her brow reflecting the same confusion as she placed a hand on her mother's knee. "I'm so very glad to hear that. But I wonder: Do you not worry if I have children?"

Evan sent his sister a scathing glare. This was not a topic he wished to bring up—not now or ever. They had spent years insulating their mother from the stress of their father's death. He sure as hell didn't want to bring up the topic of his madness now.

But his mother surprised him. Instead of becoming agitated, she looked confused. "Whatever for? Yes, childbearing is a dangerous business, but you are of hearty stock, I am sure." She patted Julia's hand as though reassuring her.

"But do you not worry that I may pass on . . . less savory parts of my heritage?" His sister persisted, earning another warning look from Evan.

"Julia, this is not the time—"

But their mother lifted a hand, stopping him at once. "Julia, my dear, what do you mean?"

His sister's gaze flicked to Evan for a moment. He recognized the expression in her eyes; it was the same way she had looked at him when she'd tried so hard to persuade him to try for love. Glancing back to her mother, Julia licked her lips before continuing to speak. "Because of Father's illness, Mama. Evan and I decided years ago that we wouldn't marry or have children for fear of passing the madness on, or even succumbing to it ourselves."

Their mother's already pale skin whitened, and a hand went to her mouth. Damn it all, Julia had gone too far. He came to his feet, scowling mightily at his sister as he stepped forward to place a comforting hand on his mother's shoulder.

"You don't need to answer her, Mother," he said, working to keep his fury at Julia from tainting his voice. "In fact, I hope you'll forget that she ever said it. Perhaps now would be a good time for Julia to play for you. I know how much you enjoy her harp."

She looked up at him, her mossy green eyes stricken. Evan might well murder his sister yet. He offered his hand, but instead of taking it, his mother put her fingers to her heart. "John, is this true?"

"Truly, Mother, don't think on it at all. Julia spoke out of turn and—"

"Is it true?" The words were stark, an echo of pain he had hoped never to hear from her again.

He bit hard on the inside of his cheek, at a loss for what to say. He didn't wish to lie to her, but he would not purposely cause her any more pain by bringing up memories of the darkest time in her life. "It was simply a measure to ensure that none of us or those we loved would ever have to go through something like that again."

Closing her eyes briefly, she exhaled, her slender frame sagging. Turning to look at Julia, she said softly, "Why didn't you ever tell me?"

Julia shook her head, tears shimmering in her eyes. Perhaps she saw now how much pain she had caused. "We didn't wish to further upset you. It was an easy enough decision at the time, when neither of us knew what it was like to love or be loved."

"It wasn't just the easy decision," Evan cut in. "It was the *right* one. And it still is, no matter how much you attempt to justify your actions."

He scrubbed a hand over his jaw, trying to rein in his temper. Sophie came unbidden to his mind, making his breath catch in his throat. He'd put her through hell because it was the right decision. The pain now was to protect her from a much greater pain later.

The tentative serenity that his mother had lived with for so long seemed to dissolve before his eyes. Sorrow and pain filled the void, and something terribly akin to guilt. "All of these years, you have lived in fear of being like him?"

Julia nodded, tears rolling down her cheeks. It was impossible to tell if they were from regret at having upset their mother, or relief for finally having the truth out between them after so many years. Either way, he could do little more than grit his teeth, wishing like hell she would have dropped the whole matter when she had the chance.

Their mother's fingers found the cross again, rubbing hard between her thumb and forefinger. "This is all my fault. If I hadn't tried to protect you, I would have set you free."

Evan sank back down into his chair, staring at his mother's bowed head. What on earth was that supposed to mean? Across from him, Julia brushed away the tears and looked to their mother. "Mama?" she whispered, prompting her to go on.

"I was in love, once." The words were quiet but unmistakable. Mother glanced up then, meeting Evan's eyes. "So much so, I could hardly breathe with the force of it. James knew it when he offered for me. It was his way of showing his superiority to his younger brother. My father eagerly approved the match, uncaring of my wishes to marry Matthew instead."

Evan stared at his mother, rapt. He could easily picture his father's younger brother, who was a very frequent visitor. He had died only months before Father had come back to Ledbury to stay. Unease gathered in Evan's gut, the way one feels when ominous clouds appear on the horizon. She had been in love with Uncle Matthew?

"So you married against your wishes?" Julia breathed, sympathy wrinkling her brow.

Tears rolled down Mother's cheeks, furthering Evan's unease. "Yes. James always showed signs of darkness, though nothing like . . . in the end." She hesitated briefly, then pushed on. "I had no choice but to accept his hand. As soon as we married, he took pleasure in tossing me aside. He spent all his time in London, winning and losing great sums at the tables, enjoying his many . . . lady-birds, frequenting all manner of ill-reputed establishments."

Evan was aware of his father's pastimes, but he'd never imagined that the darkness within him had always been there. "So you are saying he had always been somewhat off?"

She nodded. "He had great swings of moods. Some days he was full of excitement and verve, and others he was empty of all that life had to offer. Even so, he could still seem normal when he wished. It was almost easy for him to fool those he ran with in London. It wasn't until after Matthew's death that he succumbed so fully to the disease."

Evan rubbed a hand over the back of his neck. He hadn't considered the timing of things before. "I don't think I ever put that together before."

Shaking her head, Julia sat back against the cushions of the sofa. "I don't understand. If Papa married you to spite his brother, why was he so affected by his death?"

"Because," Mother whispered, her voice barely audible, "in my devastation following Matthew's passing, we argued bitterly." She seemed lost for a moment, her eyes unfocused as if she looked into the past. "It was then that he discovered that Matthew was the true father of my children."

Chapter Twenty-eight

Evan sat reeling, his blood roaring in his ears. Disbelief, anguish, as well as an enormous sense of relief, and a dozen other emotions clogged his throat and twisted his gut. Uncle Matthew was their father? He gaped at her, shaking his head. "Why didn't you tell us?" They were the only words he could manage to speak.

His mother brought the cross to her lips and kissed it before meeting his eyes again. "I never wanted you to doubt your rightfulness to the earldom or to think yourselves inferior for the circumstances of your birth. And there was also the shame for what I had done. Matthew and I never stopped loving each other, but that didn't make it right."

She looked between Evan and Julia, tears heavy in her eyes. "It was my fault that James lost hold of his sanity. You children suffered so much from those months, I just wanted everything to be better for you. After he died, I had thought you moved on. That you'd healed from the pain he caused us."

She didn't mention her own overwhelming grief, but

Evan remembered it all too well. What he'd never guessed, never even imagined, was the possibility that she would have felt guilt for some of the pain they had suffered. How could he not have known?

Raking both hands through his hair, Evan struggled to come to grips with what she was saying. Her words brought a surge of hope, and he grasped them like a lifeline. "Are you absolutely certain that we could not be his?" His heart felt as though it teetered on the edge of a precipice.

For the first time, color tinged her paper-white cheeks. "I am. James believed that both of you were born early." She pressed her lips together, unwilling to say more.

"Good God," Julia breathed, her hands going to her throat. "He truly wasn't our father?"

Mother nodded, sadness weighing down the corners of her mouth. "If I had known your fears, I would have told you so long ago." Her voice was growing hoarse. He couldn't remember his mother talking as much in the last five years.

"Evan, do you know what this means?" Julia said, hope glittering in her eyes like diamonds.

He didn't answer her right away. He was too busy examining the revelation from every possible direction. Matthew and James were still brothers, so the possibility of madness in the bloodlines still remained, but to know the old earl had always shown a tendency for his illness was tremendously freeing. If Evan were destined to succumb to insanity, wouldn't it have made itself known by now?

Swallowing, he looked back and forth between his mother and sister. It wasn't impossible that his children might inherit the tendencies, but it was significantly less alarming. He'd been prepared to pass the title to his father's cousin, had he not?

Profound relief washed through him, a desperately needed rainstorm after decades of drought. Then he closed his eyes against the sudden thundering of his heart. Could he truly be free to have her? To love her, to marry her, to live the rest of his life basking in her sunshine? Blinking, he looked to his sister. "Sophie."

Wiping away tears, she smiled and nodded. "Yes . . . Sophie."

She turned to their mother and gathered her hands in her own. "You've given us a great gift today, Mama. Please know that you've caused only joy by telling us. Now, I think Evan has a lot to think about."

Their mother's hazel eyes flitted to Evan's, uncertainty in their depths. He stood and offered her his hand. When he'd helped her to her feet, he leaned forward and placed a gentle kiss on each of her cheeks. "Thank you, my dear mother. You've set me free at last."

After returning to his chambers, Evan paced back and forth, a million thoughts running through his head. He felt like a condemned man who had just received a pardon. His life was his again. It was a feeling he had never known as an adult. Nothing would dictate what he did with it other than his own wishes.

God, he had to see Sophie. As soon as possible, he had to go to her, to beg her forgiveness for the pain he had caused her and her family. Would she still have him?

Of course, it wasn't just about what she thought anymore. From what Julia had said, her reputation had been well and truly ruined. Even if he married her, people would still say that she'd somehow trapped him into doing so. It wasn't fair to her.

No, he needed to come up with a way to show the world that she was his choice. That he loved her, and desperately wanted her to be his wife.

He continued pacing, mulling over all the ways he could try to accomplish such a thing. It had to be much more than him simply telling people he loved her. It had to be something that would spread just as quickly as the negative gossip had, something that no one could deny or misconstrue.

In a flash of insight, an idea came to him. He went straight to the library, grabbed the book he needed, and quickly flipped to the page he remembered. With the idea solidifying in his mind, he couldn't help but exhale a nervous breath.

With what he had planned, no one could possibly doubt the way he felt about Sophie—most especially not her.

"You've a letter, Sophie."

Glancing up from her book—or more accurately, from her woolgathering—Sophie inwardly cringed at the sight of her mother standing in the doorway, her mouth pinched in a disapproving grimace. Things had been strained since their return, despite Sophie's attempts to bridge the chasm that had opened between them in Bath. Both her parents were tense and worried, which was making life nearly unbearable.

Tossing the book aside, she stood and stepped toward her mother. "I'm sorry—I know postage is a cost we can ill afford right now. I'll respond and ask them not to write again this month."

"See that you do. Your friend Miss Bradford clearly doesn't understand the wastefulness of a two-page letter." Handing over the missive, Mama turned on her heel and marched out of the room, obviously unwilling to speak to her any longer than necessary.

Sighing, Sophie watched her mother go. She never would have imagined that she might miss her mother's meddling ways, but it was certainly preferable to the cold shoulder. Returning to her sunny spot on the sofa, Sophie unfolded the note, which was covered in May's chicken scratch handwriting. The second sheet of paper was tightly folded and sealed with a gummed wafer. Odd—the stationery was of a heavier stock than the outside piece.

Curious, Sophie skimmed through the note. Her friend spoke of how much she missed Sophie, and how the festival had lost its allure without her. She went on for a few paragraphs about a recent outing with Charity and Lord Cadgwith. At the end, her final sentence elicited a sharp gasp from Sophie:

Now, hopefully my ramblings have been sufficient to mask the true purpose of this letter. Open the accompanying note. Don't forget to write me back—I am dying to know what this is all about.

With her heart in her throat, Sophie turned her attention to the little square. She drew a breath, popped the seal, and made quick work of unfolding it. The handwriting was unfamiliar—perfectly correct, but without any unnecessary swoops or curls. Her mouth went dry as she realized that the words weren't in English.

Godiam la pace,
Trionfi amore:

Ora ogni core
Giubilerà.

With her heart pounding wildly in her chest, she flipped the paper back and forth, desperately searching for something more — an explanation, a signature, or even a word of English — but there was nothing else. There were only the nine tantalizing words, written in a language that she couldn't understand, but that spoke volumes to her.

Evan.

Her hand went to her lips without conscious thought as hope cruelly sprang forth with enough force to rob her of her breath. Why would he send this? Was she still in his thoughts? Did he lie awake at night, staring into the darkness and thinking of her as she did of him? Did he remember the feel of their bodies pressed close, or of their lips and tongues sliding together?

She read the words again, imagining him whispering them to her. Especially the one word she did recognize: *amore*. Love.

Lowering the paper, she leaned back against the cushions, her eyes closed as she turned the word over and over in her mind. *Love.* Even after all that had happened, she still loved him so much it hurt — a physical pain that cut sharper than glass when she thought about the loss of him in her life. Was it possible he felt the same way?

Soon, she'd write May a letter, demanding to know how on earth she had gotten the letter in the first place. Sophie wanted to know if her friend had seen him, or spoken with him as Sophie herself had dreamed of doing again every day since they had parted.

But not now.

In this moment, she would hold on to his words, along

with the flicker of optimism it brought to her heart. She didn't know what the foreign words translated to, why he had written them, or what he had meant by them. But what she did know made all the difference:

Evan was thinking of her, and for now, that was enough.

Chapter Twenty-nine

Beautiful, sweet, wonderful music surrounded her. It slipped in and out of her dreams, seeming so real that she stirred in her sleep, wanting to somehow pull it closer. It was soft and light, floating like a feather on the summer breeze. Slowly, Sophie came to wakefulness, confusion already knitting her brow as her eyes blinked open.

Music?

It was muted and soft—angelic, even—but she would have sworn it was real. Where on earth was it coming from? She sat up in bed, squinting in the soft early-morning light. No, it was most definitely not a dream. She started to lift the covers, but the sound of a voice, sweet and pure, froze her movement. Her heart nearly shattered with the force of her shock as she realized exactly what was happening.

Throwing the blankets aside, she raced to the window, tears blurring her vision, and threw up the sash. Her hands flew to her mouth as she took in the sight on the ground below her window.

There in the tentative light of the dawning day, Evan stood not twenty feet away. His arms were lifted toward her as he sang, accompanied by nothing more than the tender strains of a lone harp. Sweet, talented, unbearably handsome Evan. Sophie's hands dropped to her heart as the tears overflowed and streamed down her cheeks. The letter had come only the day before—how was it possible that he was here now? How had he even found her, tucked away in the country as they were?

It was then that she realized who the harpist was: Julia! A delighted laugh bubbled up from deep within her.

Below, Evan's voice rose, pure and glorious, heralding the first blush of dawn as he serenaded her with . . . *The Barber of Seville*! She recognized the song from the opera she had seen only two months earlier.

He was serenading her, just as Count Almaviva had his beloved Rosina.

"Sorgi, mia dolce speme, vieni, bell'idol mio." The words flowed forth like warm chocolate, the sweetest she had ever heard. She shivered at the beauty of his voice, at the loveliness of the foreign words, and most of all, at the man she adored, professing his love in the most spectacular way she could ever imagine.

Her door squeaked open and Pippa hurried into the room, her bare feet slapping against the wooden floor in her haste. "What is going on? Do you *know* that man?" she asked, her voice utterly incredulous.

Sophie moved aside to make room for her at the window, her heart overflowing with the sort of joy she'd thought never to feel again. "I do. He's the Earl of Evansleigh," she replied, not even trying to temper her smile. "The man I love."

Pippa sucked in a surprised gasp, then turned back to the window with widened eyes. "But I thought . . . the elopement, the scandal . . . wasn't he scared away?"

Evan kept singing all the while, his voice rising higher

and louder as the aria carried on toward the final crescendo. *Oh istante d'amore*—Love! That one Sophie knew. She bit her bottom lip, hardly able to contain the happiness that seemed to fill her beyond what she had ever thought possible.

"Oh dolce contento! Soave momento che eguale non ha!"

His voice rose to the heavens as he carried the final note, his vibrato warm and full of tender passion. Tears filled her eyes as the song ended with a flourish. She suddenly couldn't bear to be separated from him for even one more second. Grabbing her wrapper, she stepped into her slippers and dashed for the stairs. Her sister was right behind her, neither one of them bothering to quiet the pounding of their feet on the treads.

When she emerged into the cool morning air, Evan was waiting for her, his beautiful clear eyes untroubled for the first time since she'd really come to know him. She slowed, soaking in the incredible sight of him and savoring the delicious anticipation that coursed through her like a drug.

His hands went to his sides, and a flicker of nervousness crossed his features. "Did you receive my note?"

Amore. She nodded, biting her lip against the giddy smile that threatened.

He stepped forward, coming close enough that she could have touched him, were she to reach out. "Do you know what it said?"

She swallowed and shook her head, not caring in the least that their sisters were standing together, watching them with wide smiles.

One more step closer. Less than an inch separated them now, and she caught the tantalizing hint of his shaving soap, a scent she had thought never to smell again. "'Let us enjoy the peace. Let love triumph,'" he whispered, the words almost a caress against her skin. "'Now every heart will rejoice.' I wanted you to know that something was about to change. You deserved to hear it from me in person, but I didn't want you to go a minute longer than you had to without knowing that I was thinking about you. That I was coming for you. That I would be there for you. Now and always."

The door pushed open again, and her parents appeared in their nightclothes, demanding to know what was going on. Pippa quickly shushed them, but Sophie ignored them completely. Thankfully, so did Evan. Slipping his hands into hers, he laced their fingers together tightly and said, "Sophie Wembley, only you could make my heart sing with love. I've denied it for too long, and I find that I can no more walk away from you than I can cease to breathe. Please, put me out of my misery, and say that you will be my wife."

It was as though the whole world stopped in that moment. Sophie looked up at this man whom she loved, the man who had broken her heart, but now sought to mend it in the most amazing way possible. The man whom she had loved for so long, who haunted her dreams and filled her thoughts.

"Well, don't keep him waiting," Pippa said, making Sophie grin back at her. Her sister's brown eyes were bright with excitement and, even better, hope. It was the first time Sophie had seen hope in her sister's eyes since she'd arrived, despite all of Sophie's assurances that everything would work out.

Lifting her eyes to Evan once more, Sophie nodded, over and over again until she could finally speak past the lump in her throat. "Yes. Yes!" she said again, louder this time. She didn't care what anyone said of them, or what anyone would think. She loved Evan with every piece of her soul.

Grinning broadly, he wrapped his arms around her and lifted her from her feet, swinging her around in a joyous circle. A small cheer went up from their family, making her laugh out loud. It was the single best moment of her entire life, completely wiping away all the hurt and pain of the last week. Whatever they had gone through, it had all been worth it for this one perfect moment.

When he set her back down, she had only a moment to catch her breath before his lips captured hers in a quick kiss right there in front of everyone. "Forgive me," he whispered with a wink when he pulled away, "but I hope never to deny myself the pleasure of your company again."

She hoped that meant many, many more stolen kisses from the earl she adored. Biting back a wide grin, she wrapped her arms around his waist. "I wouldn't have it any other way."

"People are looking at us."

"Yes, I know." Evan smiled and nodded toward the gawking neighbor in the next box. The woman's eyes widened before she snapped up her fan and looked back toward the stage.

"And that doesn't bother you?" Sophie whispered, her fingers squeezing his tightly.

He lifted their joined hands and placed a kiss on her knuckles. "Not in the least. The whole point of coming here was to show the world how we feel about each other. I don't want one iota of doubt to remain in anyone's mind that I chose you, and vice versa."

"And here I thought it was because you wished to see your favorite opera."

Grinning unapologetically, he shrugged one shoulder. "That, too. But I am much more keen to show off my betrothed."

He loved the blush that tinged her cheeks. It had been his idea to return to Bath for the remainder of the festival. He wanted to make a statement that no one could misinterpret: Sophie and Evan were indeed betrothed, and they were both *very* happy at the turn of events.

Julia leaned forward from her seat beside Sophie and lifted an eyebrow. "If you two don't stop, I may be forced to separate you."

"I'd like to see you try," he challenged, purposely tugging Sophie that much closer to him.

It hadn't been difficult to convince Julia and Harry to serve as their chaperones—though Evan still chafed at the fact that his younger sister and her still younger husband were fit to fill the role. Still, they were as lenient keepers as he could ever hope for.

Sophie grinned, not resisting his efforts at all. "Hush, now, you two. The opera is starting, and you know how much I adore Rossini." She gave him a private little wink, full of all sorts of promises. He would always be grateful to Rossini for giving him the perfect song with which to win his betrothed's hand.

As the lamps were turned back and the room grew quiet, Evan savored the contentment that filled his heart. He'd spent so many years denying himself the things he truly wanted in life—the only things that really mattered. Without Sophie, he never would have broken free of the chains of his past. He intended to spend the rest of his life showing her just how much he appreciated her. Right now she was the woman he loved, but soon, and for the rest of their lives, she would always be the countess he adored.

Epilogue

"This is terribly unseemly, my lord."

"Excellent," Evan replied, grinning wickedly at Sophie. "I find I rather like being unseemly."

Sophie pressed her lips together, but couldn't hold back a smile to save her life. Especially considering the fact that she was sitting rather firmly in her betrothed's lap. "Thank goodness," she said, slipping her arms around his neck. "I feel *exactly* the same way."

Around them, the lanterns reflected against the labyrinth's tall hedge, enveloping them in warm, beautiful colors. It was gorgeous, but not nearly as much as the love in his eyes as he chuckled. "Good, because if you think this is unseemly . . ."

He leaned forward and captured her mouth, tightening his arms around her as he kissed her within an inch of her life. She shivered with the pleasure of being so thoroughly kissed while wrapped in his arms. Desire spread through her like tinder catching fire, warming her from the inside out. She moaned and tilted her head, fitting their lips together that much more perfectly.

Her heart had never been so light and free, nor her mind so wonderfully at peace.

She still could hardly even believe how things had changed in such a short time. First, to awaken to Evan's glorious proposal, then to learn of his tremendous news about his true father, and then to see the joy on the faces of all those she loved: Mama and Papa, May and Charity, and even Julia. Evan had proudly escorted her to event after event, introducing her as his betrothed to everyone they saw.

She sighed happily against his lips.

Ending the kiss, he pulled back and lifted an eyebrow. "What was that sigh about?"

Toying with the silky strands of his unbound hair, she smiled. "I was just thinking that I love being your betrothed."

"Do you?" he said, then kissed her once more before guiding her to her feet and standing beside her. "Because I find that I don't, really."

She stepped back, startled. "You don't? Surely you must be teasing me."

He shook his head. "I assure you, I am one hundred percent serious. I loathe it, actually."

Why would he say such a thing? One minute, he was kissing her senseless, and the next . . . "Are you saying you don't wish to be engaged any longer?"

"That is *exactly* what I'm saying. Which is why I took the liberty of procuring this." Reaching into his jacket, he pulled out a rolled piece of paper, tied with a slender yellow ribbon.

Cautiously, Sophie plucked it from his outstretched hand. He couldn't possibly be breaking their agreement. No, she was sure he wouldn't. She glanced back up at him. Yes, she was positive he was watching her with tenderness. Drawing a breath, she pulled off the ribbon and unrolled the paper. Her eyes skimmed over the words until she realized what she was holding. Gasping, her gaze shot back up to his.

"A special license?" she said, giddiness bubbling up from her core. "You got a special license?"

His smile was sweet and wide as he nodded. Stepping forward, he cupped either side of her face with his hands. "Sophie Marie Wembley, will"—he paused and kissed her right cheek—"you"—then her left—"marry"—her forehead—"me"—the tip of her nose—"right now?"

Her eyes widened as she gaped at him. "Now? As in *right* now? But there's no one here to—"

He cut her off with a swift kiss to her lips, making her giggle. "Please just answer the question, Sophie Hood."

Still laughing, she nodded, tears filling her eyes. "Yes! Please—the sooner the better!"

Evan released her face and wrapped her in a huge hug, lifting her feet from the ground. "I was hoping you'd say yes," he said, his eyes dancing in the lantern light. Putting his fingers to his lips, he whistled, sharp and shrill.

Winking at her, he tipped his chin toward the path they had come down only minutes ago. Sophie turned and watched, and moments later she laughed in delight as Mama, Papa, and Pippa emerged from the maze, followed by Julia, Sir Harry, and Lady Evansleigh, Charity and Lord Cadgwith, May, and finally, a broadly grinning Mr. Wright.

Turning to Evan, she squeezed his hand, unable to believe he had organized this. Through the hedge, the sound of music drifted on the night air, making the moment absolutely perfect. "Is that an orchestra just for us?" she whispered.

"But, of course, my love. Where would we be without our family, friends, music, and most of all, each other?"

As the people they loved gathered around them and

the vicar opened his small prayer book, Sophie let the tears of joy fall freely down her cheeks. She had risked everything she had—her reputation, her dreams, and her heart—and in return, she had received everything she ever wanted in life.

Don't miss the next sensual romance in the
Prelude to a Kiss series by Erin Knightley,

The Duke Can Go to the Devil

Coming from Signet Eclipse in July 2015!

To most, Mei-li Bradford's aunt was known simply as Lady Stanwix, second wife and widow of the old earl. To a very select few, she was referred to as Victoria. To the servants, she was called something not entirely fit to repeat. But to May, her father's sister—with whom she'd be living until Papa returned from his current voyage—was more often than not the Warden.

An entirely fitting title, given how often she required May to stay buried in the suffocating opulence of the grand house the older woman had called home for the past two decades. The rooms were large, but that didn't make the place any less confining. Especially since, thanks to her aunt's uninspired sense of design, the place was as dark and dreary as a mausoleum.

Fortunately, May was nothing if not resourceful.

And while she prudently avoided clashing with her aunt whenever possible—she had made a promise to her father to behave in his absence, after all—she was not above exploiting the Warden's weaknesses.

Which was precisely why May had been sneaking out every morning for the past three months. She had a routine to keep, and after a lifetime of tropical living, she refused to do her morning exercises within the olive- and brown-walled confines of the lifeless old house. Although, to be fair, it was hardly *sneaking* when one walked straight out the front door. If her aunt chose to keep to a rigid routine that consisted of being awoken at nine o'clock sharp every morning—and not one minute before—then that was her prerogative. Just as it was May's to rise before dawn and start her day.

Smiling, she breathed in the cool morning air as she pulled the door closed behind herself, more grateful than ever for the quiet solitude of the city this early in the morning. Unlike many of the cities May had visited in her life, Bath had a certain laziness to it at this time of the day. This was a city that came alive in the evening, with the monied glow of hundreds of beeswax candles lighting the rented homes and public gathering places, which were overflowing come sundown.

Walking along the deserted streets in the timid predawn glow, one would never suspect that thousands upon thousands of visitors filled every available inn and townhouse—nearly all of whom had flocked to Bath for the first annual Summer Serenade in Somerset music festival.

The festival, along with the new friends it had brought her, was the only thing making this forced visit bearable. *Until last night.* Her jaw tightened at the memory of the disastrous evening she had endured, thanks to the combined efforts of the Warden and one self-entitled, pompous visitor in particular. As quickly as the thought had popped into her mind, she mentally shoved it away again.

Coming to the park by the river today wasn't about her aunt or, more specifically, defying her aunt. Nor was it about the encounter last night, as infuriating as it had been. Coming here today was about *her*. It was about doing what she had done every morning for years, whether she was in the Far East, the East Indies, the open ocean, or right here in Bath.

And she'd be damned if she'd let her aunt's dictates or last night's confrontation spoil it for her.

Arriving at the park at last, May slipped out of her shoes and stepped onto the soft, dewy grass. *Bliss.* Next she shed her dull gray pelisse, letting the ugly fabric fall in a heap on the damp ground. The coat had been the first thing Aunt Victoria had commissioned for her upon May's arrival this past spring. It had seemed a nice enough gesture, until she realized it was the Warden's attempt to cover May's bright and exotic wardrobe.

Sighing happily, she stretched her hands over her head, reveling in the loss of the restrictive garment. God bless the English and their propensity to sleep in. Not only did she actually have a moment to herself this time of morning, but there was no one around to dissolve in a fit of vapors over the thin silken tunic and pants she wore.

The whisper of the fabric was nearly lost in the muted flow of the River Avon as she walked toward the clearing beside the river, limbering up her body as she went. Rolled shoulders, windmilled arms, a few neck stretches— just enough to get the blood flowing for her routine. The light was particularly lovely this morning, all pinks and purples with the blushing promise of a new day. In this light, the green of the trees and grass and shrubs and, well, *everything* in this bloody country, wasn't quite so obnoxious. Truly, it was as though the king had ordained exactly one shade of green for every plant, leaf, and blade of grass in the country, and the flora, being good little English subjects, had obliged.

She caught herself sliding down the familiar path of negativity, and firmly banished the thoughts from her mind. She was here to find peace. To be centered for the day, to start off on the best possible foot.

Breathing in a long, slow lungful of the fresh morning air, she cleared her mind of all the clutter it had accumulated over the past twenty-four hours. And there was a *lot* of clutter, thanks to yesterday's debacle. Getting her body into position, she closed her eyes, imagined her favorite place on earth, and began her routine.

Each movement was slow and controlled, as she glided effortlessly from one position to the next. She took slow, measured breaths and focused on the feel of the air as her hands swished through it, on the gentle sound of the river flowing against its banks, and on the soft, spongy grass beneath her feet as she slid from one step to the next.

Yes, the routine that she'd learned from Suyin, her friend and lady's maid, was technically a form of martial arts, but it could more accurately be described as meditation in motion. The movements were so familiar, it was as though her limbs moved themselves, following the age-old rhythm that she'd learned years ago. The sleeves of her tunic slid along her skin like cool water, pooling at her elbows before slipping their way back to her wrists. Again and again the silk caressed her skin, a sort of silent lullaby.

As the minutes ticked by, the knotted muscles of her upper back loosened, and her body became more and more relaxed. The tension caused by the day before melted like candle wax. Her mind settled as well, letting go of all the negativity that had plagued her since yesterday.

Just as she reached the perfect place of quiet clarity, the sound of a cleared throat startled her from her peace, wrenching her back to the present. She straightened abruptly and swung around, her heart pounding. She saw the interloper at once, standing only a dozen feet away with arms crossed and lips raised in a slight sneer that she was beginning to think was the only expression he was capable of. His strong, aristocratic jaw was tipped up in a look of superiority as his decidedly disgusted whiskey brown eyes raked her over from the top of her head to the bottom of her bare feet. May silently cursed.

In four different languages.

The Duke of Radcliffe, it would seem, was not as easily forgotten as originally hoped.

ALSO AVAILABLE FROM

ERIN KNIGHTLEY

THE BARON NEXT DOOR

A Prelude to a Kiss Novel

After an exhausting Season, Bath's first annual music festival offers Charity the perfect escape. Between her newly formed trio and her music-loving grandmother, Charity is free to play the pianoforte to her heart's content. That is, until their insufferably rude, though undeniably handsome, neighbor tells her to keep the "infernal racket" to a minimum.

Hugh Danby, Baron Cadgwith, may think he's put an end to the noise, but he has no idea what he's begun. Though the waters of Bath provide relief from the suffering of his war injuries, he finds his new neighbor bothersome, vexing, and…inexplicably enchanting. Before long, Hugh suspects that even if his body heals, it's his heart that might end up broken.

Available wherever books are sold or at
penguin.com

ALSO AVAILABLE FROM

Erin Knightley

MORE THAN A STRANGER

A Sealed with a Kiss Novel

When his family abandoned him at Eton,
Benedict Hastings found an ally in his best friend's sister,
Evelyn, with whom he began a heartfelt correspondence.
Years later, Benedict has seen his share of betrayal, but
when treachery hits close to home, he turns to his old
friend for safe haven, and finds Evelyn is no longer the
demure young girl he remembered—but a woman who
sets his heart racing...

**"This sweet treat of a romance will entrance
you with its delicious humor, dollop of suspense,
and delectable characters."**
—*New York Times* bestselling author Sabrina Jeffries

Also available in the series:
A Taste for Scandal
Miss Mistletoe (an e-novella)
Flirting with Fortune

Available wherever books are sold or at
penguin.com

S0424